Struggles in a Boston Marriage

Ellen M. Levy

(Author of *Romance at Stonegate*)

The characters in this book are fictional.
The places, weather, newsworthy events, ("Billy Sunday Blizzard,"
suffrage parades, etc.), and times (for train schedules, Shabbos
candle lighting, etc.) are historically accurate.

Boston Marriage Press • Dedham MA
Printed in the United States of America

ISBN: 9798646092718

Dedication

This book is dedicated to everyone who believes in Deborah and Miriam, as I do.

TABLE OF CONTENTS

TABLE OF CONTENTS (CONTINUED)

Preface

Ɒeborah Levine and Miriam Cohen were caught in the intrigue of first love in *Romance at Stonegate*. The girls faced rejection, isolation, and anguish in a world prejudiced against intimate relationships between females. In *Struggles in a Boston Marriage*, they fight the Jewish and cultural mores that continue to challenge them. Their commitment to one another helps them to deal with adversity, but does not solve the rift developing between them.

Now, in 1913, they are overwhelmed with adult responsibilities: a business, a child with special needs, and illness all around them. Their "honeymoon" is over.

Currently the couple own and operate a Yiddish printing and publishing business with Miriam's sister, Hannah, and Hannah's new husband, William. William, who worked at this shop under the tutelage of Miriam's recently deceased father, has taught them the skills necessary to run this growing business. But, due to the huge increase in the Jewish population in Boston, they are overwhelmed by the massive demands on them. They need help.

The baby they took in, Sylvia, whom you met in the first book, generates both pleasure and concern. She would currently be diagnosed with Down Syndrome, yet in their era she is considered a Mongoloid idiot. They work hard to support her development, while feeling pressure to institutionalize her, the most common outcome for children like her.

Their troubles continue. The couple face medical problems in Mother, Bubbie, and Hannah, as well as with their own daughter. During this time period, there was little information shared with families, and they were often uncertain about treatment options.

During the years 1913 to 1915, changes in the culture affect the girls greatly. The suffrage movement was robust, with the first eleven states passing the right for women to vote. Although Deborah and Miriam are unable to volunteer for this cause as they had before, they are deeply affected by progress in this movement. Through their friends from Barnard College, Susan and Helen, they keep up to date with each positive action leading toward the vote for women.

Of great significance during this time was the underlying tension regarding the impending world war, which Europe entered in 1914. Though the United States did not enter the conflict until 1917, there were ramifications and unrest for several characters, as many young men felt responsible to fight for their country.

Also, the Settlement House movement was a backdrop for the girls' lives. This country's second such organization was Henry Street Settlement House, where Miriam volunteered in *Romance*. Now they are fortunate to be in Boston, where the third settlement house, Denison House, attracts both girls. This woman-led organization was at the forefront of not only programing for immigrants and the poor, but also the formation of one of this country's first lesbian communities. You will learn about their connections and temptations.

The stressors facing Deborah and Miriam are significant, rattling their steadfast love affair. Though you will be saddened by their relationship challenges, remember they are only twenty and twenty-one in 1913, young to cope with the strains they face. They gather a loving support system, though possibly not soon enough to save them from destroying their connection with one another.

Spoiler alert: Deborah and Miriam continue. The third book in the series is in its final edits. It takes the girls through 1916, prior to the United States' involvement in the Great War. The fourth book, which takes them through wartime and the 1918 Flu Pandemic, is filled with fascinating history of the era.

Acknowledgements

As with my previous book, I have relied on the assistance of others to create this story. I am especially grateful to those who read the book in order to give me feedback. My wife, Pauline Albrecht, read an early version and my sister, Nancy Levy, let me read her the entire manuscript; both offered me valuable insight into inconsistencies. Phyllis Guilliano, as with my other book, offered me many valuable suggestions, both in content and writing style as she read the book over and over. I read the book out loud to Jody Boehmer, who guided me to remain consistent with the times; to Peggy Finnegan who found a few significant inconsistencies; and to Julie Greenbaum, a fine editor with fabulous suggestions. With their feedback, the book is greatly improved.

After I received significant feedback from my editor, I realized that I was no longer a compliant author who would follow every suggestion offered. Although I agreed with most suggestions, I found I was unwilling to blindly follow the path she was setting for me. Rather than acquiesce or dismiss her wisdom, I enlisted three readers to assist me in deciding whether my stubborn adherence to my ideas was unwise. After receiving feedback from Harriet Miller, Judith Sullivan, and Sara Fleming, I persisted in two of the three arenas where I was readying myself for a fight. In the end, my editor agreed with the direction I took.

With the final manuscript completed, I submitted my photographs to my talented layout designer, Sara Yager. She worked her magic with faded photographs from the early 1910s and internet pictures that were sometimes inaccurate to the times.

The photographs were again a challenge. Whenever possible, the scenes you view are the exact places mentioned in the book. I went on location and took as many of the photos as possible. Thanks to the collection of pictures taken in the early 1900s by a talented photographer, Hugh Mangum, I was able to find portraits of new characters. I am pleased to credit "Hugh Mangum Photographs, David M. Rubenstein Rare Book & Manuscript Library, Duke University" for providing the photographs of Chava, Deborah, Elizabeth, Marilyn and Julie, Mildred, Rachel, Rivkah, and Sadie.

The final copy edit was done by Elizabeth Andersen, a capable addition to my editing team.

Most importantly, I again relied on my mentor, Fay Jacobs, for her scrupulous review of my book. She shared her wisdom, guiding me with both the story and the prose. Without her, this book would have been a challenge to read.

Family Tree

(Age in 1913)

LEVINE

MANHATTAN; GREAT BARRINGTON, MASSACHUSETTS

Mr. Levine
(43)

Mrs. Levine
(41)

Deborah
(21)

Milton
(17)

Anna
(14)

45 West Street, Great Barrington, Mass.

410 Riverside Drive, New York City

The Levines are a warm, loving family with an affluent New York City life. They are excited with their new country home, where they can be closer to nature and can get away from the hectic pace of the city.

Family Tree
(Age in 1913)

COHEN
BOSTON, MASSACHUSETTS

Bubbie
(71)

Mr. Cohen
(died July 22, 1912)

Mrs. Cohen
(42)

Miriam
(20)

*22 Homestead Street
Roxbury, Mass.*

William Goldman
(28)

Hannah Cohen Goldman
(24)

Soon after immigrating to the United States, the Cohens moved to Roxbury, Mass.
Mr. Cohen's successful Yiddish publishing company on Boston's Newspaper Row
allowed them to purchase a single-family home near their temple. Mr. Cohen's
mother, Bubbie, moved in with them after her husband, Zadie, died.

Family Tree
(Age in 1913)

GOLD
MANHATTAN; GREAT BARRINGTON, MASSACHUSETTS

Mr. Gold (49)   Mrs. Gold (38)

Ruth Gold Bernstein (21)   David (18)   Beth (16)

Michael Bernstein (22)   *94 West Street, Great Barrington, MA*

The Gold's are a successful, cosmopolitan New York family. They have a great interest in accumulating anything that will showcase their material wealth, such as high fashion, a particular passion of both their daughters.

Family Tree
(Age in 1913)

BERKOWITZ

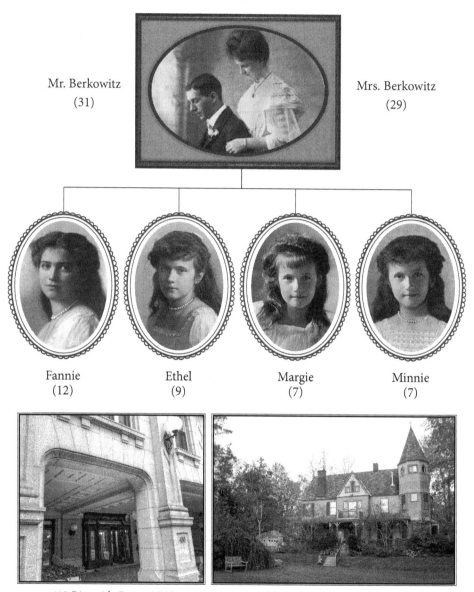

Mr. Berkowitz
(31)

Mrs. Berkowitz
(29)

Fannie
(12)

Ethel
(9)

Margie
(7)

Minnie
(7)

410 Riverside Drive, NYC

11 Old Stockbridge Road, Lenox, MA

This young family moved into the same building as the Levines in New York City, and they quickly became close friends. The Levines were quickly drawn to the sweet parents and their four adorable daughters. The Berkowitzes later purchased a large cottage in Lenox, MA.

Other Characters

(Age in 1913)

Chava (22)
Deborah's new friend

Leah (11)
Neighborhood girl in wheelchair

Marjorie (20)
Miriam's best friend from childhood

Micah (21)
Marjorie's boyfriend

Sadie (20)
*Miriam's friend, volunteer
at Denison House*

Marilyn and Julie (23, 24)
New friends

Susan and Helen, (22, 22)
Students from Barnard College

Girls from Denison House

(Age in 1913)

Elizabeth (14)
Daughter of Suffragette

Mildred (9)
Girl on Orphan Train

Rachel (15)
Jewish girl at Denison House,
Rivkah's sister

Rivkah (11)
Jewish girl at Denison House,
Rachel's sister

Yuan (16)
Chinese girl at Denison House

DEBORAH LEVINE   MIRIAM COHEN

SYLVIA

CHAPTER ONE

In Boston

Early July, 1913

"Deborah! Come quick! She's not breathing!"

Tripping over the shoes she'd just taken off, Deborah scurried to fifteen-month-old Sylvia's room. By the time she reached the bedroom she heard the baby's wails. "You scared me so! And you woke Sylvia and frightened her!"

"I'm sorry," Miriam gasped. "When I came to check on her before I got ready for bed, she was lying absolutely still and didn't move when I touched her. She always squirms when I rub her back."

"Please calm down," Deborah said loudly. "You took years off my life."

Then they heard the worried voice of Miriam's mother, Mrs. Cohen, from the bottom of the staircase. "Is everything all right? I heard Miriam scream."

"Everything is fine, Mother. I just had a scare." Miriam called as loudly as she could between her pounding heartbeats.

"Good night."

Deborah peered at Miriam's pursed expression and spoke harshly. "I hope our daughter doesn't take after you. You frighten so easily."

"You would have been panicked too if you thought our baby was dead!"

"But she was just sleeping soundly. I can tell the difference," Deborah said angrily, biting her lips so she wouldn't say more.

"I'm truly sorry, but ever since the doctor told us she's a Mongoloid I've been worried."

"Her medical problems are no reason for you to be so unsettled. I get frustrated when you react so strongly." Deborah took in a deep gulp of air and let it out dramatically.

Miriam sighed audibly. "I wish I could tell you I'll change, but I can't promise."

Deborah left the baby's room while Miriam rocked Sylvia back to sleep. Within ten minutes Miriam sheepishly entered their bedroom. She looked around the simple yet comfortable room, with the same blue-flowered spreads that had been on the beds since she first showed Deborah her bedroom, three years earlier. This room usually comforted her.

"You can come in. I won't yell at you anymore," Deborah said.

Miriam sat on the bed next to Deborah and took several deep breaths. "I'm sorry I upset you."

"Apology accepted."

"Most of the time, I think our life together is amazing and we're so lucky, and then something like this happens to shatter our equilibrium. I'm not as strong as you. I get rattled easily and then I mess things up." She began to cry.

Deborah reached out to her. "Come here. I'm sorry I yelled at you. I know you were scared, and I was too harsh."

"I, I didn't mean to worry you, but I was afraid something awful had happened to Sylvia." She sniffed as she tried to control her tears.

Deborah sighed and her shoulders relaxed. "We do have a wonderful life together. I have the girl of my dreams sleeping next to me every night, an adorable baby close by, a thriving business, and my writing is being published. Life at Homestead Street, Roxbury, is good. What else could I ask for?"

"For goodness to continue," said Miriam with a sincere smile, which quickly shifted to a frown. "I can't help but also think of the trauma we've faced since meeting one another, with my father rejecting me, then quickly getting sick and dying. It happened so fast.""

"That was a horrible time. There was so little I could do to comfort you. But we must look to the future."

"I'll always be grateful to you for the way you cared for me," Miriam said.

"I'm glad you feel that way although I felt quite helpless. And I was really sorry that you and your father never resolved things before he passed away."

With a lump in her throat, Miriam said, "I wish we could have fixed things, but I doubt that would have happened even if he had lived a long time. He was such a firm believer in Jewish laws that there was little possibility he could ever accept us, two women, together."

"I know, Miriam, and I fear there will be more troubles ahead for us. I still worry we'll face judgment because we're together, and what if someday Ruth regrets giving us her child and causes us problems?"

"Stop! You're sounding like more of a worrier than me!"

"For good reason. We're living a life that isn't acceptable in most people's eyes. And I'm also fearful about this brewing war, which everyone says is inevitable."

"Oh, Deborah. Let's be grateful for what we have and think positive thoughts before we go to sleep. Remember that good things have happened, too. It pleases me so much that my sister, Hannah, has found love."

Deborah grinned. "Yes, Hannah and William are a well-suited pair, both quite awkward, yet bright and sweet."

"They certainly are." Miriam thought for a moment before softly commenting. "If all my dreams were to come true, we'd be respected for our loving relationship."

"That's a wonderful dream, my love. But you know we need to keep the nature of our connection a secret. From everyone."

"My mother and your mother know, and they still love us," Miriam said with her glistening eyes, looking directly into Deborah's. "I want us to focus on wishes for our future."

Deborah thought for a moment. "My dream is one I think we share. It is for our love to remain strong forever."

"Don't you trust we'll always love one another?"

"I know I'm not the easiest person to live with. Maybe you'll tire of me."

"Deborah Levine, I love you the way you are and I'd never tire of you. You always keep life interesting."

"Interesting it shall remain." Deborah took a deep breath. "But I continue to be anxious, afraid we'll be caught, and afraid our wonderful life together will fall apart."

"You said I was the anxious one, but I think it's you. Mine was a momentary frantic, yet yours just goes on and on."

"I know of a way you can relax me," Deborah said with a wink and a caress of Miriam's face.

Miriam turned toward Deborah and kissed her warm, moist lips that were filled with promises. They loved each other with insistence that night. Their lovemaking was less frequent these days with the challenges of taking care of the baby, the printing business, and household responsibilities. But tonight, they caressed each other with alternating passion and tender love. When they'd fulfilled each other's desires, they fell asleep entwined.

The next morning they sat enjoying the taste of the bubbling cheese omelet Miriam's grandmother, Bubbie, had prepared for breakfast. Miriam turned to her mother, who was holding Sylvia on her lap, and said, "Last night Deborah and I discussed all our good fortunes. Many of them are due to you."

Mrs. Cohen smiled.

"Mother, you offered us a place to live, a business, love for our child, and most importantly, acceptance. I know it has not been easy and I hope I remember to say 'thank you' often enough."

"You don't need to thank me. You are my daughter and I would do anything for you."

Deborah joined in. "Well, you have done just as much for me and I'm not your daughter, so I'm the one who should be offering the thanks."

"You are like a daughter to me. I'm grateful to you for making my Miriam happy and to both of you for bringing little Sylvia into our lives." Then, with a full smile, Mrs. Cohen added, "We certainly are a rosy bunch!"

Miriam, always the most cheerful family member, looked around at their warm and inviting home. With the dark furniture well-worn from years of use, it remained comfortable. The wallpaper, though a bit faded, still charmed. Miriam's memory of a happy childhood in this house with her now-married sister and her late and much-missed father made her a bit melancholy.

Just then everyone sniffed the air as Bubbie entered the room with a warm *babka*, right from the oven. Everyone's eyes bulged as she put the coffeecake on the table. Though already full, they each consumed a piece, as no one could resist this lovely treat. Even Sylvia had a bite.

"I happy you like it. *A dank*, tank you," Bubbie said in her typical broken English speckled with Yiddish.

The next day brought joy. In the mail was a note from Deborah's Barnard College mentor, Grace Hubbard, who was about to publish a book. It was to include Deborah's essay, "Parents of Young Women," which she'd written as a tribute to her mother.

"You're a famous author!" Miriam said with glee.

"I doubt I'll be famous, but I'm thrilled my work will be in print. Professor Hubbard requested more of my articles, but I'm not sure which one to send her."

"You could send her a few and let her choose. Do you have any idea where she wants to send your next stories? The magazine she chooses may help you to decide."

"I'll gather a few articles and ask her. I'm inspired to write about parenting. There are certainly lots of women's magazines that would welcome this topic."

"Would you write about parenting a child like Sylvia?"

"Yes, since that's the only parenting I know."

"I look forward to reading your perspective."

Deborah hunched over the desk for the next few evenings after Sylvia was asleep, taking this new task to heart. Miriam waited patiently, knowing Deborah would eventually hand her the paper for review. She waited until Deborah climbed into bed each night to soothe the lines etched across her forehead and to calm her fingers, cramped from firmly gripping her pen. Once she relaxed, Deborah encouraged the caress of her more private areas, and Miriam was pleased to oblige.

❧❧❧

After three nights and many drafts, Deborah said, "Here it is, my article, 'Parenting a Special Child.' Are you ready to read it?"

"Ready? I've been waiting for days!"

"As usual, I'd like your critique of my writing, not just your accolades. Can you do that?"

"I've gotten brave over time, but I'm not always certain you like my new-found self-assurance," Miriam said.

"Yes, I do, my dear. It's been an adjustment to see my sweet innocent turn into a bold young woman with strong opinions."

With a twinkle in her eye, Miriam said, "Not as strong as yours."

"You're right. Now take some time to read my ramblings and give me some suggestions how to make it better."

Grace A. Hubbard

PARENTING A SPECIAL CHILD

Parenting is all at once sweet, terrifying, satisfying, frightening, and the greatest experience a woman can have. When caring for a child with special problems, it is also overwhelming.

Mothers expect their babies to be dependent for all their needs, yet they are ready to relinquish control when the time comes for the baby to take its own path. Dealing with a child who will never grow normally requires a different manner of thinking. Independence, the goal of most children, may be impossible for my baby. She may always need me to be her logic, her decision-maker, her guide.

I feel powerful at moments, experiencing enthusiasm and courage. It is a blessing to be her mother. I cherish her small victories. I can often be patient, the quality I believe is of greatest importance when parenting her.

But there are many dark hours, when I am challenged, exhausted, or disappointed. I feel intimidated by my lack of knowledge of how to guide her, and isolated, knowing others cannot relate to her needs. At times I am wracked with guilt for not giving her more, while at other times resentful of the endless hours she requires. I compare her to other children, envious of their accomplishments and the small wonders she may never achieve.

The pendulum swings on a daily basis. I have learned to be more realistic about her abilities and my capacity to provide adequately for her. I am learning to trust my instincts on this journey of discovery and to celebrate her successes. I forgive my mistakes, for she will never know them. I provide her with love, the quintessential gift for her growth.

Tears flowed from Miriam's eyes as she read Deborah's words. She hoped a heartfelt embrace said enough.

Miriam's Diary, July 7, 1913

I'm touched by Deborah's honesty about being a parent. She doesn't talk of regret, though she's filled with apprehension. Her concerns about Sylvia's needs are similar to those I've never articulated. But I'm too caught up in this topic to have a critical eye toward her writing.

My hopes for the future are mostly regarding Sylvia; I dream our little girl has a full, healthy life. I also hope for well-being for my Bubbie and my mother, who both seem old these days. Additionally, I dream we'll find friends who understand us. My friend Marjorie and my sister Hannah are the only two who know about our situation and I don't dare to tell anyone else. Here I am, at 20-years-old with few people I can count as true friends. Despite having a loving relationship, I feel a bit lonely.

Deborah's Journal, July 7, 1913

Why is it that Miriam can't give me constructive ideas about my writing, even when I ask for them? I knew she'd have lots of feelings about the topic of parenting a child with medical problems, yet I clearly asked for her opinion about my composition, not just the content. It frustrates me when she's sweet when I need her to be strong and to stand up to me. I want this, even if I'm being difficult.

My worries are so much more than those I listed for Miriam. What if my own father never truly accepts us? I haven't seen him since he dismissed me from his life after learning the true nature of our friendship. He sent me the lovely note saying he still loves me, yet that's the only time I've heard from him since his rejection.

I also have concerns regarding the publishing shop. It has been overwhelming since we took it over, following Miriam's father's heart attack and death. There must be a way for it to be less consuming. With the influx of Jews to Boston, following the Prussian ouster of the Jews, there is an increasing need for Yiddish publishing. I want the business to grow, but given how hard we're already working, that seems impossible. It's helpful to have Miriam's friend, Marjorie, working with us, but her assistance isn't enough.

And I have more thoughts about my desire to develop friendships with girls who are like me. I'm lonely here in Boston, since this is Miriam's hometown, not mine. I miss my girlfriends back in New York yet they might never understand us. I want to have real friends, like Susan and Helen. When I met them at Barnard College, I knew right away I was comfortable with them but I haven't met anyone else like us or to my liking since moving to Boston. I wonder how I'll ever find any new friends since all I do is work and care for Sylvia. My world is very small.

Everything overwhelms me these days.

Bubbie

Bubbie's stove

CHAPTER TWO

Bubbie's Decline

Mid-July, 1913

An hour after she finished cleaning up from dinner, Miriam smelled something burning and rushed into the kitchen. "Bubbie! Bubbie! What happened? Are you all right?"

"I burn cookies," Bubbie said with a dazed glance at Miriam as she tried to get up from the floor.

"Deborah. Deborah. Come quick! Bubbie has fallen!"

"I be fine."

"You're not fine, Bubbie. You're on the floor. What happened?"

"I burn cookies."

"I don't care about the cookies. I just care about you."

Deborah raced into the kitchen in time to help Miriam lift Bubbie onto a chair. Frantically she asked, "Are you hurt?"

"No. Cookies burn."

Rescuing the cookies from the oven was paramount in Bubbie's mind, and until they got the smoking sweets out of the oven, they'd never find out if she was indeed all right.

"I be fine," Bubbie repeated, brushing off invisible crumbs from her apron as she sat up straight, as if nothing had happened.

After examining Bubbie carefully, Deborah and Miriam deemed her unhurt, despite the fall. But they couldn't get an explanation.

After helping her scrape the poppy seed cookies off the baking pan, Miriam said, "There's no need to bake another batch of *munn* cookies this evening. We've enough to last another day."

Bubbie acquiesced, but refused assistance to her bedroom, just a few steps off the kitchen.

As Deborah and Miriam opened the door between the kitchen and the dining room, the burnt aroma escaped.

"I smell fire!" Miriam's sister, Hannah, called. She rushed in from where she'd been sitting on the porch with William after dinner. Simultaneously,

Mrs. Cohen, who was upstairs getting Sylvia ready for bed, yelled, "Is something burning?"

The girls calmed everyone down, explaining the burned cookies, but not telling them about Bubbie's fall.

After giving Sylvia final kisses goodnight, Miriam walked into the bedroom and said, "Bubbie is really frail. What do you think happened this evening?"

As they began to fold the laundry, which Bubbie had piled at the bottom of the stairs so she wouldn't have to go up, Deborah said, "I don't think we'll ever know. She doesn't seem to remember."

After a moment's thought, Deborah said, "71 is old! Lots of my girlfriends in New York lost their grandparents at ages younger than that. Given the number of funerals Bubbie has been to since I moved here, I'd guess many of her friends have died."

"You can't really count the number of funerals to determine which of her friends are gone. She's always going to funerals. I asked her one day why she was gone for so long, and she told me she got to her friend's funeral so early she was in time for the previous service. So she went to that one too! She had no idea who died, but she figured another person praying for the departed would be a good thing! She seems to be drawn to funerals."

Deborah smiled. "That sounds like something Bubbie would do. But I'm worried about her."

"So am I," Miriam confessed, handing one end of a sheet to Deborah so they could fold it together. "Losing her husband and her son was stressful enough, and now taking care of Sylvia is wearing her out."

"No. I think Sylvia is one of the joys that keeps her going. But I do agree the days are long for someone her age."

"Maybe my mother should provide some of the childcare for part of each day. She'd have a wonderful time with Sylvia."

"Do you really think Bubbie would give up any of her hours with the baby?" Deborah asked. "And when would your mother have time?"

"Mother certainly is busy with household chores while we're at work."

Deborah put down the folded sheet and picked up another. "And since your father died, she's taken over paying all the bills."

"And she makes lunch for us on workdays."

"I guess we answered our own question. If she were to take care of Sylvia, she'd have to give up her temple Sisterhood meetings, the one thing she does for herself," Deborah said, shaking her head.

"I wonder who else could take the baby for a while each day so Bubbie could rest."

"I have an idea," Miriam blurted. "What about our neighbors? Leah, the little girl I visit, the one in the wheelchair, would love having Sylvia around. Because she doesn't walk, she can't come to us, but she'd welcome company. What if Sylvia were to visit with them for an hour each afternoon?"

"This is a good idea, but how would Sylvia get there? If Bubbie were to walk her there, it would defeat the rest we're trying to get for her."

"True, it won't work. I'll try to think of other ways we can help Bubbie."

"I have another idea," Deborah said. "I know Bubbie loves to go to temple but she's not been joining us regularly on Shabbos. I think it's because the walk is too hard. What if we get someone to drive her?"

"But no one Jewish will drive a car on Shabbos. Let me think … how about the delivery man who picks up papers at the shop each week? He isn't Jewish, and I bet he'd like to earn a few extra pennies to provide her a ride. He could tell Bubbie he had to pick up his daughter at just the time when temple gets out. That might be a good reason for his offer."

"Miriam. That's a fib! I can't believe you would be party to suggesting something like that," Deborah said, not too harshly.

"Maybe we should just ask Bubbie what would ease her stress."

Deborah shook her head. "You know she'll say she's just fine."

"I know she will."

Deborah let out a puff of air. "Maybe there's something wrong with her that made her fall. I've never known Bubbie to go to a doctor. We should make her an appointment."

"No! Bubbie hates doctors. My father was in the hospital when he died, so now she's even more leery. She blames the doctors for not saving him."

"He was just too sick …."

Miriam, sighed. "I know, but Bubbie will never believe that."

"I think we should tell her we're concerned."

"I think we should watch her, but she wouldn't appreciate knowing we're anxious about her health."

"So, we'll do nothing but remain worried," Deborah said with another sigh as she folded the last of the laundry.

Crank start advertisement

Crank start diagram

CHAPTER THREE

Driving

Early August, 1913

"I'm thinking about learning to drive," Miriam announced.

"Doing what?" Mrs. Cohen asked in a high-pitched tone. She dropped the silverware she was holding with a clang.

This caught Miriam's attention, but she kept her voice calm. "Father's car has been sitting in the driveway since his death, except when William uses it. Since they live just a few blocks away from us, we all rely on William to drive us everywhere, which is unfair. I think it makes sense for one of us to learn to drive," Miriam said. "I could take Bubbie to temple and to funerals, her favorite activities."

"But you cannot drive on Shabbos, Miriam," her mother said.

"I'm certain G-d would understand if I were doing this so Bubbie could go to services."

"But what will the neighbors and our friends say?"

"It will give them one more reason to talk about us. I think they should look on it as a *mitzvah*, a good deed, to get Bubbie to *shul*."

Mother shook her head. "But to get the car started you would need to work the crank start, which takes a man's strength."

"I am strong."

"And who will teach you this new skill? I certainly can't teach you."

"I'm certain William would," Miriam said confidently.

When Miriam told Deborah about their conversation, Deborah felt pleased with Miriam's new independent streak and bravery.

"I bet you're doing this in order to transport Bubbie."

"You're so smart," Miriam said, smiling.

On Sunday, Hannah and William came to the Cohen's house, each with a mission. Hannah had very little experience cooking since Bubbie never allowed anyone in the kitchen, but Bubbie told her it was important she learn.

"You need feed you husband," Bubbie said. "I teach you."

"I want to learn how to make your special recipes for *tsimmes*, and sweet and sour cabbage rolls."

"No, too hard. I teach you roast chicken."

Bubbie took the chicken from the brine where it had been soaking and shook it over the sink. She handed the *kosher* bird to Hannah, whose nose wrinkled as she held it at an arm's length. Bubbie handed her the kitchen tweezers and told her to pluck the feathers.

Hannah carefully, delicately plucked a feather or two until Bubbie said, "No. Like this," grabbing the chicken firmly, holding it against her apron, and vigorously plucking each feather. Hannah attempted this messy activity with little enthusiasm, so it took her a long time to ready the bird for the oven.

Miriam also asked to learn cooking, feeling some urgency to learn the recipes while Bubbie was still capable of teaching them. But it would need to be another time, because that day she was to spend with William, learning to drive.

Miriam was quite nervous, partially from the task she was about to undertake but also about spending so much uninterrupted time with William. He wasn't much of a conversationalist.

William silently drove them to a quiet neighborhood and turned off the ignition. He began with the basics. "This is a 1910 Ford Model T, one of the first cars that people like us could afford. It is made of high-quality steel, so it is durable. It is also versatile, easy to maintain, and very practical."

Miriam smiled. "I remember how excited my father was when he got this car. I think he could actually have afforded a fancier car, but he was always so frugal."

William, not noticing Miriam's wistful look, said, "First, I need to teach you how to work the crank start."

"I'm ready," Miriam said, standing up to her full height of five feet, two inches and following him to the front of the vehicle.

"I will do it the first time; then it is your turn," William said. "The most important thing is to have the key off. When the engine is cold is the only time to use your right hand to crank. Otherwise, use your left hand, in case it backfires. It could break your arm if it snapped back."

Miriam looked wide-eyed and nervous.

After demonstrating a complex series of maneuvers, William directed Miriam to change places with him and sit in the driver's seat. She obediently gathered her long skirt and indelicately climbed in.

William blurted out a series of instructions all at once. "Push the crank in. Pull out the choke lever and prime the engine to get fuel into the cylinders. Then turn the key on. Set the throttle and the choke. Parking brake on. Lever in. Push the lever quickly to the right. And it starts."

"William! There are too many things to remember," Miriam said, panicking.

William repeated the first half of the instructions, one step at a time. Miriam tried to follow the confusing sequence of actions, and after three failed attempts she started to giggle.

William looked at her with amazement, not understanding what was so funny. Ignoring her laughter, William insisted with continued seriousness, "You need to keep trying. You will get it." He explained the second half of the instructions, even though she hadn't perfected the first half.

Miriam giggled again, and when William saw no humor in the situation, she burst into wild merriment. Even though he still didn't understand that her giggles were a release of tension, he too started to laugh in the face of her infectious laughter. The two of them had a grand chuckle, laughing until tears streamed down Miriam's face.

"I don't know what's so funny," Miriam said as she gained control of herself.

"Neither do I," William said, glad there wasn't a joke he missed.

After they both stopped giggling, Miriam tried again and finally got the car started.

"I did it!" Miriam exclaimed, but William made her shut it off.

"Try again."

Though she was already exhausted, William went on with his explanation. He pointed to the three pedals on the floor and explained, "The right pedal is the brake, the middle is reverse, and on the left is the clutch. The accelerator is this hand-controlled device to the right of the steering wheel."

"Slow down, William. What's a clutch?"

"I will show you, rather than explain."

William demonstrated a series of awkward moves to get the car in gear. Miriam tried, but she stalled it every time.

"This is much more complicated than I thought it would be."

"You will learn. But I almost forgot to explain the brake. You will need to know how to stop once you get it going."

Miriam, overwhelmed by so many instructions, gladly relinquished the driver's seat to William. He explained the multistep process of putting the car in neutral, then applying the brake, showing her several times. He assumed she had retained the information. She had not.

As William headed down the side streets, he commented, "It is easy to drive." It seemed anything but easy to Miriam.

Once William's instructions ended and he drove through the neighborhood, William became surprisingly talkative. Miriam wondered if this was to keep her calm, but nevertheless she was pleased with this opportunity to get to know him better.

"I want to thank you for everything you have done for Hannah and me. You got us through the wedding ceremony. Rarely has anyone been so kind to me." William spoke with little inflection in his voice, as most people would have when sharing something so emotional.

"Certainly I'd help out my sister and her husband. But what do you mean? Most people weren't kind to you?"

William's voice got quiet. "I always got teased. First by my brother, then the other students in school. Even my parents made fun of me because I never fit in and I never knew what to say."

"I'm so sorry to hear this, William."

"Your father was the first person to accept me the way I am. He took me into the shop and respected me for my abilities. Having this job made me feel good. And then I was fortunate enough to meet Hannah, and she has made me so happy. She is bright and caring and thoughtful and sensitive. I never thought I would find anyone to love me."

Miriam smiled at her awkward brother-in-law, happy that he shared these emotional details. "You're both lovely people, and you deserve all the goodness of marriage. I only wish my father could have seen the happiness you have found together."

"Thank you for saying that."

And with that, William pulled over, turned off the ignition, and stepped from the vehicle. It was time for Miriam's first drive. Miriam came around the car and climbed into the driver's seat, with William as passenger.

Miriam silently went through her checklist of actions and heard the Ford come to life.

"I did it! And on my first try!"

With trepidation she headed down the street. "The car is wobbling from side to side."

"You must control the steering wheel."

Soon she caught on. As they pulled up to her house, she came to an abrupt stop, jolting them both.

William ignored the rough end of their ride and said, "Good job. Can I take you again next Sunday?"

Miriam was pleased she'd done well enough that he'd try again. Might she actually like driving?

❧❧❧

Following a second lesson, William encouraged Miriam begin to take the car out on her own as needed. She went downtown by subway, filled out some paperwork, and got her driver's license.

Back home she explained. "Getting my license was a very simple process. There was no test of my driving. I guess they had confidence in me." Miriam waved the license, and Deborah, who was rocking the baby, looked up. "Can I take you for a ride?

Mother and Bubbie both refused to ride with her, but Deborah had no such qualms. Their first ride together, just a few blocks, was uneventful so Deborah came back to the house, recommending Miriam's driving.

After another week and several more short jaunts, Mrs. Cohen dared to climb into the car for her first ride chauffeured by Miriam. "Very nice," Mother said when they returned home, though she quickly got out of the vehicle. Bubbie still refused to ride with her.

One day later in the month Miriam took the car to work to help with a delivery. William packed the automobile with the completed project and sent Miriam off on her own. An hour later when Miriam had not returned, Deborah began to worry. "The errand shouldn't have taken that long."

When more time passed, everyone grew concerned. Deborah speculated out loud. "Did she run out of gas? Did the car break down?"

Marjorie continued the list of concerns, "Did she get lost? Was she in an accident?"

When no one had an answer, Deborah announced, "I'm going to find her."

"But where will you go?" Marjorie asked. "The delivery was to be in the South End, not far from the office, but too far to walk."

"If I take the subway to Copley Square, I can walk from there."

William interrupted. "No, it would be better if I drive. Where do you think I could borrow a car?"

"I'm certain you can borrow our neighbor's car. Leah's father is a doctor who works at Boston City Hospital. It won't take us long to walk to Harrison Avenue to get it," Deborah said.

"Marjorie and Hannah, please watch the shop while we're gone," William said. "It might take us a while to find Miriam."

Deborah and William were gone for a very long time. Marjorie and Hannah became very anxious but there was nothing they could do. While waiting, Hannah said, "If we had a telephone, we would have gotten a call by now. Maybe it is time to get one for the shop."

Without it, all they could do was wait.

What was happening just a short distance away was a different scenario than any of them had guessed. William and Deborah pulled up to the delivery site to find a huge commotion. Miriam was lying on the ground in a most unbecoming position with police and bystanders all around. Just as they got there, a black Model T Ford with the word "ambulance" written in large, bold letters screeched to the curb.

Deborah and William pushed their way through the small crowd, making it to Miriam just as the ambulance drivers reached her. "We're her family," Deborah announced, but the medical workers asked them to step aside so they could check their patient.

Deborah and William could overhear Miriam's explanation. Crying softly, she said, "I was just pulling away after the delivery when a small child ran into the street, directly into my path. I was certain I was going to hit him."

As Miriam's crying became louder, Deborah wanted to comfort her, but the ambulance workers wouldn't let her near. Finally, after Miriam couldn't get control of herself, they let Deborah close enough to hold her hand. Miriam's crying slowed enough for her to continue.

"Luckily, the child heard his mother screaming and stopped. I was able to swerve, so I missed him." Miriam said, breaking down again as she remembered how close she'd come to hurting or even killing the child.

A passerby explained that Miriam got out of the car and immediately fainted right on the street where she was now lying, which was why they had called for the ambulance.

The medical team found Miriam physically unhurt, but because she'd fainted they decided to transport her to the hospital.

Deborah and William followed the ambulance to Boston City Hospital but weren't able to be with Miriam in the examination room. Once the doctors sedated her, they were assured Miriam was fine and resting comfortably.

Back at the shop, all work halted as no one could concentrate while waiting for Deborah and William. Just as they were about to close, William returned.

"Where is my sister?" Hannah called out as he walked in the door.

"She is better. The doctors are checking her over."

"Oh my G-d. She was hurt. She was in an accident. I knew it."

"She will be all right," said William.

Hannah insisted. "Tell me what happened. What is wrong with her? Can I go see her?"

"I hope we'll go to the hospital together to pick her up. She should be released soon."

"But you haven't told me what happened, William."

"Give him a chance," Marjorie exclaimed.

Hannah finally calmed enough for William to explain everything he knew.

"But if no one was hurt, how did she end up at the hospital?" Hannah asked.

William continued. "Well, she fainted. That's all."

Hannah interrupted, "Can we go see her?" So they all piled into the car and headed to Boston City Hospital to pick Miriam up.

The patient, still groggy, was discharged. But she strongly announced, "I'll never drive again."

One evening after life returned to normal, as they were folding napkins, Deborah said to Mother, "I think it's time to get a telephone for the shop."

Mrs. Cohen reacted strongly, putting down her task and saying, "Why would you want to spend so much money on a telephone? I do not understand. Just because everyone had to wait a few extra minutes until you knew Miriam was all right does not justify the cost."

"It certainly would have helped in that situation, but more importantly, we need it at the printing shop. As business continues to grow, we need to take orders and answer questions by telephone."

"That is ridiculous," snorted Mrs. Cohen. "Maybe I should not have turned this business over to the four of you!"

"No, Mother. It's not ridiculous," said Miriam, who had just walked in. "I just read an article in *The Boston Globe* which says almost six million people in the United States have telephones. We need to keep up with progress."

Mrs. Cohen huffed, "Next thing I know, you will be wanting to get a car for the business."

Miriam smiled. "We've been talking about just that. There have been many times we have had more than one rush order at the same time. Luckily, thus far the deliveries were in the same direction so we managed, but if we take on more projects, we might need a delivery vehicle. If we got a second car, William could use it when it wasn't needed for work."

"You two are going to spend all the money before we make it. It will cut down on the profits."

"No, it won't," Deborah and Miriam said simultaneously, smiling at each other.

"I can see I'm outnumbered. I guess I need to let you figure it out since you are now the owners of this business. If you spend too much, then you'll be the ones to suffer." She turned her attention back to the pile of unfolded napkins.

"I'll make certain we don't spend foolishly. My intention is for this business to grow so it can support us all comfortably." Deborah turned to Miriam, who nodded in agreement.

"Then we shall have a phone," Mrs. Cohen said, not unhappily. "I will get it for you, Deborah, for your birthday next week. Would that be a good birthday present?"

"Oh, yes! Thank you, Mother."

"But let's talk more before you purchase another vehicle. That is an even larger expense."

"I appreciate your trust in us, Mother."

The next week they got telephones for both the shop and their home.

CHAPTER FOUR

Sylvia's Medical Crisis

Mid-August, 1913

𝄓eborah, realizing it was now up to her to learn to drive, took to the activity with more ease than Miriam.

"I'm pleased with William as my instructor," she said to Miriam. "Though he didn't talk as openly as he did with you."

"Maybe it's because I'm Hannah's sister."

"I think it's also your gentle personality, so different from my brash manner. Your way is more in keeping with his shyness."

In a few weeks, Deborah got her driver's license, and for her first independent journey she drove to the doctor with Miriam and Sylvia.

"I'm happy," Miriam said, "that we found a doctor with experience with Mongoloids."

"Me too. But I hope he doesn't call Sylvia a 'Mongoloid idiot' like the doctor in Great Barrington. I can't bring myself to call her an idiot. It's so hurtful."

They arrived at the Back Bay office, hopeful this doctor would provide them with guidance to help Sylvia advance. Yet the appointment was upsetting. The doctor spent minimal time with Sylvia and had no good news at all.

During their conversation, Miriam asked the doctor, "What can we do to help her outgrow her problems?"

"You should place her in a special school where they can train her."

"NO!" said Miriam loudly.

"Well, if you're going to care for her at home, be aware she may be prone to more medical problems than other children. And, I must tell you, she has a heart condition, which is very common in children like her."

"Is it serious?" asked Deborah.

"It doesn't seem to be. But I assume you know these children don't live to full maturity."

Both girls blanched and stared at each other. They had never heard this before. And they hardly heard anything else he said, except for his recommendation of a heart medication for their child. They walked out with a prescription for the heart medicine to be brought to the pharmacy.

"What are we going to do?" a worried Miriam asked, walking to the car.

"I have no idea if we should give her the medicine," Deborah responded with equal angst. "I'm pleased he didn't call her an idiot, but I wish I knew more about Mongoloid children. He really had no good news for us. Maybe I'll go to the library to find some articles to help me."

"Oh, Deborah. I'm not sure if the library is the right place to turn when facing a medical decision. I don't know where to turn. I could ask my mother, who certainly knows something about heart conditions, but I don't want to worry her. Life for her has been difficult since Father died, and bringing up the topic of heart conditions would just rattle her. And she's so in love with our little girl that discussing Sylvia's medical problems would certainly upset her."

"Could we go to the Experimental School for Feeble-Minded Children in Waltham? They deal with children like Sylvia," Deborah asked.

"I don't know, Deborah. I'm afraid they'd want to take Sylvia away from us and put her into their school. I don't want her in an institution!"

"Me either. But I also don't like the idea of putting Sylvia on heart medicine for the rest of her life."

"The doctor wants to give her the same medication they gave my father for his heart condition," Miriam said. "The medicine made him feel sick, and I don't want that for Sylvia."

"Neither do I," Deborah said, shaking her head. "Is there a doctor at your temple we could talk to?"

"We could ask Leah's father. And I'm certain he knows about children's special health problems because of his own daughter's circumstances—and after all, he's a doctor. When I visit Leah tomorrow, I'll approach him for advice. I'd trust a neighbor, especially one who knows us and knows Sylvia a little bit."

On a warm summer evening a few days later, Deborah and Miriam took a walk around their neighborhood, enjoying several flower beds in full bloom. Along the way Miriam talked about her visit with Leah's father.

"Now I really don't know what to do. Leah's father suggested we subject Sylvia to a strange test, the string galvanometer, which will test the rhythm of her heart. It sounded cruel, making her put her hands and feet in buckets of salted water. He explained he'd attach something called electrodes to her chest to evaluate her heart's electrical activity. It frightened me."

"I don't think we should do it. Nor do I think we should give Sylvia medicine. If our daughter has a heart problem, I hope she can live with it without consequences. The doctor said it wasn't a serious condition. This testing and treatment might make her uncomfortable, and what I want is for her to be secure and happy," Deborah said, her cheeks wrinkled with stress. She pointed to an especially pretty garden lined with rose bushes, and for a moment their thoughts were focused on beautiful flowers.

But soon, Miriam spoke. "I feel so alone in this, Deborah. We have each other but we don't know any other ill children, except Leah, and her problems are quite different from Sylvia's. There are so many ways we're alone, especially because we haven't had any time to develop friendships together."

"I know how important it is for us to find friends, but all our focus has turned to Sylvia and the print shop. I wonder how we'll ever do anything different than we do now since we have such busy lives."

Miriam thought a moment. "We shouldn't complain. So many worse things could be happening. My friend Ruth had to give up her child—luckily for us!— Leah is facing life in a wheelchair, and all those young families I worked with as a volunteer at the settlement house in New York live extremely difficult lives."

"And also frightening to me," Deborah said with sadness, "is the war that's approaching. I fear my brother Milton and many of his peers will volunteer for what everyone sees as an inevitable war."

"Marjorie's boyfriend Micah is already determined to go to war. What will happen if William is called to serve his country? How will we ever manage the business without him?"

The Experimental School for Feeble-Minded Children

"Miriam. Right now, we need to focus on Sylvia's needs. We can worry about everything else at another time."

But fret is what both of them did, for Milton, for Micah, for Sylvia, for Mother, for Bubbie, for themselves. To settle her mind, Deborah put her thoughts to paper in a letter to Mrs. Berkowitz, who'd always supported them, especially when Miriam's father rejected her.

August 19, 1913

Mrs. B.,

    I'm writing regarding Sylvia. As you know, writing soothes me, and you always have such wise opinions.

    The doctor prescribed heart medicine and tests, which we're leery about. I suggested to Miriam that we bring her to the Experimental School for Feeble-Minded Children for their advice. Miriam has refused, fearful they'll want to institutionalize her. Everyone tells us institutions will provide her with better care but, in my heart, I don't believe that. What are your thoughts?

Love,
Deborah

P.S. We'll be coming to Great Barrington to visit my family for the Labor Day weekend as a belated celebration for my birthday and I'm hoping to visit with you.

August 24, 1913

My Dear Deborah;

    I'm sorry we won't get to see you, as we'll be heading back to New York City before the holiday weekend to get the children ready for school. I hope your birthday was a pleasant one.

    I feel honored you reached out to me for advice, but I fear I've little to offer. I don't know much about children like Sylvia, having been blessed with four healthy girls. But I think you and Miriam are being very wise, looking at all the options and weighing the effects on your baby. I, too, would have refused both the medications and the tests.

    I don't think I would have refused the trip to the Experimental School. I hope they could not take your child from you against your will.

You two are strong, and I know you would weigh the advice you receive, as you have done with every other suggestion. I know of nowhere else for you to turn. The school may have the best advice to offer.

Please keep me abreast of your decisions and your concerns.

With Love,
Mrs. B.

✿

"Do you think William, Hannah, and Marjorie can handle the shop while we're in the Berkshires?" Deborah asked as they sat in the parlor one evening. "I'm worried we'll fall further behind."

"We really need this vacation. I'm sure it will be all right," Miriam said, not entirely sure she was correct.

"I really want to talk with my mother about Sylvia, since I'm certain she'll have opinions about medicine and treatments."

"I'm glad you'll have that opportunity."

Just before the weekend visit Mrs. Levine, Deborah's mother, sent a note. "Not only are the Berkowitzes gone from the area, but your father has caught a cold and must remain in New York instead of joining us."

Deborah was most upset about her father's absence. She'd been looking forward to seeing him for the first time since he rejected her. She thought about that terrible day when he had found the romantic Valentine's Day card she sent Miriam. She'd been aching to see him since, especially after he sent her the telegram saying he still loved her. Other than that, there had been no communication and it made Deborah uneasy.

"I'm sorry our reunion will be delayed," she said to Miriam with a deep sigh. All evening she thought about her father's absence and wondered if he was avoiding her.

August 29, 1913

Dear Mrs. B.,

I'm writing to you from the train to Great Barrington. Both Miriam and Sylvia are napping. I find it hard to sleep during the daytime. I've been watching the pretty countryside, glad that there are no signs of the leaves turning yet. I'm not ready for summer to end, though I love the colorful fall trees.

*I'm so appreciative of your response to my concerns. I received your
letter yesterday and shared it with Miriam. After we talked she told me
she'd rethink the idea of approaching the institution for advice. We've
made a pact to keep Sylvia at home, no matter what their suggestions are.*

*Thank you for the part you played in making this happen. And yes,
thank you for your birthday card and birthday wishes. I'm sorry we won't
see you this weekend. Hugs to the girls. Safe travels back to New York.*

Love,
Deborah

Deborah and Miriam were excited to get to Great Barrington, as it was
their only summer visit. They had a wonderful time with Mrs. Levine, who
as usual was insightful. She agreed with Mrs. B. about the girls approaching
the Experimental School for some advice, though she would have been more
open to giving Sylvia the heart medications. Deborah remained firm about
avoiding the pills.

The family celebrated Deborah's birthday during her visit. Miriam's gift
for Deborah was tickets for the Boston Symphony Orchestra for the first performance of the thirty-third season, which wouldn't happen until Saturday
night, October 11. The famous conductor, Karl Muck, was serving his second
tenure. Deborah had always admired him and several times had mentioned
her desire to see him. The program included works by Beethoven, Brahms,
Liszt, and Wagner, which Miriam was certain would please Deborah. The rest
of Deborah's gifts were clothing. Her mother and father provided Deborah with
new outfits to replace those she had soiled while working, and her siblings
gifted accessories to match.

Deborah and Miriam were charmed, as usual, by Deborah's siblings, Milton
and Anna. Deborah was glad both had found friends. Milton at 17 had not
yet found a girl to occupy his attention, but he spent his days skipping stones
in the Green River and playing ball games with others his age. Some days he
seemed still to be a young boy, and other days she saw hints of his imminent
adulthood. Anna had a gaggle of silly 14-year-old girls with whom to spend
her days. She usually had a smile on her face, though she occasionally faced
typical adolescent turmoil in which small concerns seemed monumental.

In the evenings, the whole family sat in the parlor talking and playing
games. Miriam noticed that Deborah's mood was lighter when she was with
her family. She wasn't prone to complaining as she might at home.

CHAPTER FIVE

Sylvia is Special

Early September, 1913

"We've not been to the Museum of Fine Arts since we moved to Boston as a family. I'm excited to return to one of our favorite places," Miriam said.

"Thank you for suggesting this. And I'm glad to bring Sylvia. It's never too soon to expose her to art."

Their seventeen-month-old was usually quiet, but as soon as they got inside the spacious building, she began to fuss. She made loud noises and rocked her carriage from side to side, bothering people nearby.

"She's being stubborn. She wants you to pick her up. You always do whatever she wants, so go ahead and carry her around with you," Deborah said with her lips pursed, ready to continue with a string of complaints.

Miriam interrupted Deborah's tirade, whispering, "Please be quiet, Deborah, so others don't hear us quarreling. Sylvia is just letting us know her needs." She looked down rather than at the small number of people who had turned to look at their family.

Sylvia

"You and Bubbie are always giving in to Sylvia's demands. It's not good for her to get her way all the time."

"But it's important for her to express herself. Because she doesn't have language yet, she needs to find ways to tell us what she wants."

"So you give in to anything she asks for?"

This was a familiar argument. They continued to disagree and argue until Deborah huffed and walked away. She wandered into the next gallery, wondering what to do about this latest disagreement.

Miriam took her time before entering the next exhibit, needing a chance to calm down and think. As she walked into the next room, she came face-to-face with Deborah, who was obviously waiting for her. "I'm sorry," Deborah said. "I didn't mean to argue with you."

"You disagree with me a lot these days." Miriam moved close to Deborah so no one would overhear. "I want to have discussions with you about what's best for Sylvia, but it always turns into an argument."

"You always think you know what's best," Deborah said.

"Well, I do," Miriam said with a glint in her eye and a smile on her face. She knew Deborah would likely give in when she took a cute way out of the argument.

"You do, half of the time," Deborah conceded with raised eyebrows and a slight grin. The disagreement was over.

Pierre-Auguste Renoir's "Children on the Seashore" at Museum of Fine Arts

Sylvia had fallen asleep while they were bickering, and her disruptions abated. With both Sylvia and Deborah being cooperative, the trio enjoyed the rest of their day at the museum. They headed first to the Impressionists, since these were Miriam's favorites. They spent time viewing the Renoir painting that Miriam most admired. Deborah cuddled up as close as she dared and whispered into Miriam's ear that she'd purchase a reproduction of this piece and have it framed as a gift. Miriam would have squealed had they been in a less refined setting.

At Deborah's suggestion they walked through several rooms of antique furniture and visited the collection of Paul Revere silver bowls. Miriam loved the period furniture and feigned interest in the same bowl that she'd viewed on practically every visit to this museum. They both left satisfied.

Later, upstairs, Deborah brought up the afternoon argument. They discussed everything calmly, agreeing they both wanted what was best for Sylvia.

After a great deal of uncertainty by both of them, Miriam said, "We need to do what's best for Sylvia." She took a deep breath and said, "I'll agree to go to The Experimental School. It might be the only place to find some answers."

"Thank you, sweetie, for your willingness to go. I'm as frightened as you are that they'll encourage us to commit our baby to this institution, yet we have nowhere else to turn."

"Let's go before the winter sets in to make traveling easier. Actually, we should go before the *Sukkos* holiday. It's October 15th this year."

Miriam's Diary, September 17, 1913

I don't know why Deborah is so disagreeable these days. She argues with me often, as she did today. Then she gets sweet and confuses me. I'm trying very hard to stand strong for the things I believe, rather than remaining quiet as I used to do. She says that's what she wants from me, but almost every time my opinion differs from hers, she fights with me. I try to quiet her at these times, but I don't want to go back to being compliant.

I'm glad that we both agreed to go to that school, even though both of us are afraid. Maybe it's fear that makes her argumentative. I'll try to pay attention to what upsets her. I'm glad we agreed to a moratorium on discussions about what's most advantageous for Sylvia until we get some expert advice.

The trip to the Experimental School in Waltham was difficult, despite it being a lovely fall day. Sylvia was bundled in Miriam's embrace the whole way as Deborah drove over bumpy roads.

"Fourteen miles is the farthest I've ever driven," Deborah said wearily after driving for over an hour.

"The sky is filled with dark clouds from smokestacks, so I think we've reached the town of Waltham, which is full of industries," Miriam said.

"It's about time we arrived."

Miriam pointed to their left, at the large sign: The Experimental School for Feeble-Minded Children. "There it is! My, I'd no idea what to expect. It's huge!"

They pulled into a campus of over seventy buildings. Anxious and wearing a stern expression, Deborah parked the car and headed toward a huge brick building with four tall pillars topped by a clock tower, assuming it was the main office.

"What's taking you so long?" she asked Miriam.

"I had to gather all Sylvia's things," Miriam said, not surprised Deborah was a bit on edge now that they'd reached their destination.

Neither girl spoke and Sylvia made no sounds as they entered the cavernous entry hall. Deborah pointed to a photograph of Walter E. Fernald, the superintendent of the school, on the wall in front of them. The plaque under his picture called the institution by its previous name, The Experimental School for Teaching and Training Idiotic Children.

After reading the inscription Deborah said, "This school claims to be the oldest institution to serve … idiots. Oh, I hate that word." Then she read from the plaque, "The school takes a scientifically focused approach to treatment of the feeble-minded."

"It's encouraging that they see themselves as progressive in the treatment of children. Maybe they can offer us some worthwhile advice."

"I hope so," Deborah responded hesitantly. "But I do wish they'd use gentler words than 'idiot' and 'feeble-minded.'"

Miriam found another picture of interest. "This plaque says the school was started in 1848 by Samuel Gridley Howe. He was the husband of Julia Ward Howe, who wrote the 'Battle Hymn of the Republic.'"

"And," Deborah said, "I'm pretty sure she was a suffragist."

They both hummed the first line of the well-known song.

With their moods slightly elevated, they went through a set of doors, where they found an office and told the gray-haired woman at the desk they were seeking advice about how to care for their little girl.

She said harshly, "Wait here while I see if there is anyone available to talk with you. Usually people have appointments."

As the woman walked off with a determined gait, Deborah said, "I knew we should have written a letter before just showing up. This is a long way to come if no one can speak with us."

"You're probably correct. I just thought they'd be more willing to see us if we were here."

After they sat in silence for five minutes, the stern woman returned, telling them to follow her. She walked silently down the long sterile white corridor, up the stairs to the second floor, and into a room through a huge wooden door with a small window. On the doorplate they found they were about to meet Dr. Howard Kingsley.

"Come sit down," said the white-haired thin man of about fifty years of age, with a dark tailored suit and flat expression. "I assume you're here to inquire about admission for this little girl."

"NO!" said Deborah and Miriam at the same time, both standing tall.

"I see. Then what are you here for?"

"We've come to get advice about caring for Sylvia," said Miriam. "We plan to keep her at home with us, and we'd like to know what we can do to make her life better."

"Please sit down. Most young children who are Mongoloid idiots, like your girl, are placed in schools like ours."

Deborah and Miriam looked shocked. How did this doctor know she was a Mongoloid without examining her? They had not told the dour receptionist about the diagnosis.

"We know that," Deborah said very quietly. "But we're not placing her here or anywhere else!"

The doctor looked a bit confused when they both spoke up about her care. "So which of you is the mother? And where is the father? Is he in agreement with keeping her at home?"

Both girls got an uneasy feeling. Would they need to explain their circumstances?

Deborah spoke up, trying to turn the conversation around. "We're sharing responsibility for this child, who was born to friends who couldn't take care of her. We want what's best for her and we'd like advice about what to do. Can you offer us some help?"

Deborah's ploy to distract Dr. Kingsley worked. He continued, "We don't yet have an outpatient clinic, though the State Board of Insanity has been talking with us about creating just such a program. Maybe we will have one in another year."

"We can't wait that long," Deborah said with alarm.

"You don't need to wait. I'm glad to examine the baby right now."

"Thank you so much," Miriam said sweetly. "We'd appreciate some suggestions. We want to do anything possible to make her life healthy and happy."

Suddenly they saw a smile cross the doctor's face, and the awkward interview took a turn. He led them into a different building, into an examination room with a strong antiseptic smell. He reached for Sylvia.

"We want to go with her," Miriam said sharply.

Dr. Kingsley explained he needed to evaluate her without them, and Miriam said, "You must promise us you won't conduct any tests, which would be uncomfortable for her."

After the doctor agreed, he led the girls into a dreary office down the hall to sit while they worried what was happening to their child.

Deborah looked around at the bleak white, unadorned walls and said, "This is a hospital, not a home. I'm glad Sylvia will never have to live here." Miriam nodded. Had they seen the roach-infested, drab buildings where the residents slept, they'd have felt this even more vehemently.

After almost an hour, they heard the door open.

"Here's my girl," Miriam said, reaching for Sylvia as the doctor walked through the doorway. Sylvia didn't show any signs of distress, but clung happily to her mother.

Dr. Kingsley invited them into his office and motioned toward the stiff, functional chairs across from his large desk. Instead of telling them what he learned, he said, "Tell me about Sylvia's mother and her birth."

When they mentioned Ruth's fall from the horse, causing her broken leg during her early pregnancy, Dr. Kingsley's eyes opened wide. "Tell me all the details you know about the accident and the mother's recovery."

They wondered if he thought this event was connected to Sylvia's problems. Maybe he thought the fall had damaged the baby she was carrying. Eventually, Deborah and Miriam, exhausted from this line of questioning, each let out a sigh.

Dr. Kingsley stopped his interrogation and commented, "I examined your daughter thoroughly and she was very cooperative."

"She always is," said Miriam proudly, relieved with the change of topic.

Dr. Kingsley went on. "She is definitely a Mongoloid idiot. I could tell from her facial features and I confirmed this by finding the simian crease across her palms, proof of my diagnosis."

Before Deborah and Miriam could ask questions, Dr. Kinsley continued. "If Sylvia were a little older, I would give her the Binet test for intelligence, but for now, it's not important. We can just assume she'll be limited in all abilities throughout her life."

"Is there anything we can do to cure her of this illness?" asked Miriam, hoping for good news.

"No, my dear. There is no cure. But I can prescribe some pluriglandular extracts and preparations that contain vitamins, which might have some positive effects on both her physical and mental condition."

"Will there be any ways these extracts could harm Sylvia or make her uncomfortable?" Deborah asked.

"No, I assure you they're safe, and we just might see some positive results. Some doctors from London a few years back discovered some active stimulants, which they named hormones. They can help to coordinate the activity of some of her organs. No harm can be done if we use them."

"Then we'll try them," Miriam said, pleased he said "we," as if he were to be part of Sylvia's treatment.

He went on. "I noted some atypical heart sounds, which is very common in Mongoloid idiots. Had they been severe, she wouldn't have lived this long. I'm glad to report that, although abnormal, she doesn't seem at risk of serious heart complications in the near future."

Deborah sighed with relief. "That's the best news we could have heard. We'd been told of her heart condition before, and we were encouraged to give her medicine for the rest of her life."

Both girls grinned when Dr. Kingsley said, "Medication is not necessary." Based on this comment alone, they were beginning to like him.

They went on with a discussion of Sylvia's care. Many of Deborah and Miriam's concerns were typical of new parents, rather than related to her disorder, though the kind doctor answered them patiently. They also asked questions relevant to her slow development: her limited understanding of language, her awkward gait, and her inability to follow simple instructions that other children her age seemed to grasp. After a long conversation, he walked them back to the main office, where he instructed the stern woman at the desk to set up another appointment with them.

Deborah and Miriam both said, "Thank you." He grabbed Miriam's hand in a lovely gesture of connection.

After he left, Deborah whispered, "I don't think we should set a date to come back until after we've talked with one another."

"Fine, though I think we've found an ally in the care of our daughter."

The ride home was easier, mostly because they weren't worried, as they'd been on the way there. They drove through the town of Waltham, which Deborah, true to her nature, had researched at the Boston Public Library.

"I learned that Waltham was significant in the American Industrial Revolution, housing multiple textile mills. They harnessed the power of the Charles River to create a network of canals."

"I don't understand how canals would improve the mills," said Miriam.

"The water was channeled through water wheels to create power that helped to mechanize the factories. Also, the canals provided easy transportation for materials needed and helped them distribute the finished product."

"I see. You are so smart."

"Not smart, just curious. Research at the library has provided me with a larger view of the world."

"Can I bore you with one other interesting fact about Waltham?" asked Deborah.

"I don't find this boring at all. Please tell."

"Waltham has been called "Watch City" since the Waltham Watch Company opened in 1854. It was the first company to ever make watches on an assembly line."

"My father had a Waltham Watch. Let's see if we can find the building."

It wasn't difficult to find since it was located just outside the center of Waltham on the Charles River, along with many other thriving factories. Miriam got out of the car, handing a sleeping Sylvia to Deborah while she went up to the front door to read the plaque placed at eye-height.

"Did you know the Waltham Watch company won the gold medal at the Philadelphia Centennial Exposition in 1876?"

"No, I didn't. See, now you're the smart one."

During the rest of their trip, they avoided talking of Dr. Kingsley's findings, instead noting the scenery, which they'd barely seen on the way to Waltham.

When they arrived home, Mother asked, "How was your visit with the doctor?"

"He said Sylvia was healthy and suggested some vitamins to help with her growth," said Miriam.

This was enough information to satisfy Mrs. Cohen.

Once in their bedroom that evening, Deborah said, "I'm very pleased we went. I felt Dr. Kingsley was more familiar with our daughter's condition than anyone else we've asked for advice."

Miriam reluctantly agreed. "You're right. I shouldn't have resisted your suggestion we go to this school. I was just afraid…."

"Enough. No apologies needed. We just need to look ahead to the possibility the extracts and vitamins will make a difference in her growth."

Miriam looked Deborah in the eye and said, "I hope they're good for her."

Pleased with Dr. Kingsley's suggestions, the women relaxed and showed their joy by caressing one another. Soft touches led to more intimacy, and before they knew it they were caught up in a frenzy of loving play, falling asleep soundly in each other's arms.

Soon after their visit, Deborah went to the Boston Public Library to get more information about Mongoloids and to find out about the simian crease Dr. Kingsley had mentioned. When she got home, she shared what she'd learned.

"I read about the studies of Dr. John Langdon Down and his two physician sons, Reginald and Percival, who were the first to study Mongoloidism. The books said the simian crease is always evident in Mongoloids and often found in primates. Some people claim this crease shows this disorder might be (she read from her notes) 'a reversal to primitive humankind.'"

"That's terrible."

"And Dr. Kingsley was careful not to discuss eugenics with us, which I also read about."

"What is that?" asked Miriam.

Deborah read, "… an increasingly popular belief that the world would benefit from the reduction of feeble-minded and mentally deficient individuals."

"How awful!"

"I can't believe people really feel that way," Deborah said.

Both girls glanced at their sweet, sleeping child and reflected on the disturbing information Deborah had uncovered.

Dr. Kingsley

CHAPTER SIX

Making Babies

Late September, 1913

"Now that I'm driving, everyone seems to need me. First, your mother requested I do errands for her, and now your sister Hannah has asked for a ride to the doctor," said Deborah on their way home from the shop.

"What's wrong with Hannah? She never sees the doctor unless she's really sick, and then he usually makes a house call," said Miriam.

"I've no idea. I'm just the chauffeur. I don't ask questions."

"She and William want us to stop at their house after dinner tonight, so I'll ask her about it then. Will you keep William occupied so I can talk with her alone?"

"And how am I supposed to do that? It's not so easy to occupy him for more than one minute and, also he follows Hannah around, rarely leaving her side," Deborah said, shaking her head.

When they reached home, they sat quietly in the car for a few minutes until Deborah blurted out, "I've got it! I'll ask him about the car. That should keep him busy for a short while."

After dinner, when the dishes were done, Miriam and Deborah put Sylvia to bed, then took the short trip to Hannah and William's house, leaving Mother and Bubbie to listen for Sylvia.

Soon after they arrived, Hannah brought out a plate of *mandel brot* she'd made, clearly proud of her first baking attempt.

"It looks just like Bubbie's," said Miriam, though as soon as she tasted it she realized the similarities ended with the look. It was overcooked and too sweet.

After she managed to eat two pieces, Miriam asked Hannah for some private time. Hannah looked to William, wanting him to join them.

Deborah immediately piped up. "William, would you look at the car with me? I'm having difficulty with the crank lately and I'd appreciate your expertise."

William nodded and followed her outside as the sisters sat down in the kitchen.

"Deborah tells me you asked for a ride to the doctor. What's wrong?"

Hannah hesitated. "I'm worried. I know William and I have been married for just three months but there is no baby on the way yet. Do you think I am too old to carry a child? We want so badly to have one but I am concerned it is not going to happen," Hannah said to her sister with atypical emotion.

"I'm sure you're not too old to have a baby. Twenty-four is not old! There are lots of women older than you who bear children. And I've heard it often takes a while to get pregnant."

Miriam glanced at the lovely apartment Hannah and William had created. The newlyweds both had simple tastes, but they'd gotten some lovely, decorative items for their wedding, including a cut-glass pitcher and a crystal vase. There was also a porcelain bowl similar to those Hannah and Mother admired at the museum. Both families had supplied used furniture, and the couple had splurged on a lovely new bedroom set made of rich mahogany. The artwork on the walls, clearly chosen by Hannah since they were prints of some of her favorite pieces from the Museum of Fine Arts, added charm.

Hannah took a deep breath, then said, "Can I talk with you openly?"

"Certainly."

"I am worried we are not doing something right. I do not know anything about marital relations except what you told me before our wedding."

Cut glass pitcher and crystal vase

"I'm not the best person to ask since I've never had the kind of marital relations that produce babies."

"But you might know more than I do. I have never talked to anyone about what it takes to make a baby. Mother never discussed anything with me, and I am afraid we are doing it wrong." Hannah blushed.

Miriam thought for a moment, wondering whether she knew enough about the process to help her sister. She took a deep breath. "You'd better tell me a bit, and I'll see if I can help you."

"It is awkward to talk about, but I'll try."

"So, tell me what you do to get pregnant."

"We have marital relations quite often. We found we both like it."

"I'm not surprised!" Miriam said with a nervous giggle.

"But what am I to do with the, um, stuff that gets all over our sheets? I don't know what to do with it. Do I rub it down there?"

Miriam's eyes widened, and she wondered how to tell Hannah exactly what she should do.

"Do I eat it?" Hannah asked.

"No, Hannah. I read in books, I, um, understand that it needs to get inside you, but not through your mouth."

"How else would it get inside?" Hannah asked with great curiosity.

Miriam realized the importance of her next words and the incredible awkwardness of this whole conversation. "Oh my. I'm not an expert on this. We don't, um … but from what I've read, or know, I think it goes in through your …" Miriam motioned down below, "… through your women's area, the part that feels good when it's touched."

Hannah looked at Miriam, baffled. "How does it get in?

Miriam stopped again, carefully continuing, "I think the man's part goes into the woman's part." Miriam looked at Hannah, hoping her words were enough to make her sister understand.

"The man part goes inside me?" Hannah repeated, sounding confused.

"Yes. Then the, the um …what comes out goes to the right spot in your body. At least I think it does."

"Oh, Miriam, we try to catch it in a handkerchief so it won't make a mess." Hannah looked directly into Miriam's eyes, then asked, "Will it hurt? William's, William's um, part gets really big. There is no room for it in my little place."

"Oh, Hannah, it's supposed to feel good, I think. But I really don't know. And I've never seen one. I mean, I don't know what it's like to put anything inside other than a finger. Oh my. I'm really not comfortable talking about this."

"But this will help me to get pregnant?"

"And maybe to have more enjoyment. Women seem to like it. Well, I assume they would, or they wouldn't keep having babies."

"Do they do it just to have babies?"

By this time, Miriam wanted to disappear, but she knew how important it was.

"No, I don't think it's just to make children. I do it because I like it, it feels wonderful, and it's not to have babies. Oh, that's just too much to say. How about if I go to the library to see if I can get you a book to help explain, better than I can, what you need to do? Can we please stop talking about this now? I can't think of anything else to say. And this whole conversation is making me nervous."

"I'd much rather talk with you than the doctor about this. I'll see if I can try your suggestion and hope it works."

With great relief Miriam patted her sister on the back, sighed deeply, and quickly left the room.

Later, Miriam told Deborah that Hannah was fine and planned to cancel the doctor's appointment.

"She's just anxious about becoming a mother someday," Miriam said, hoping the news would be enough to end the conversation.

The next day, Miriam went to the library, feeling greatly embarrassed to ask for books on marital relations. She assumed the librarian, who blushed bright red, thought this information was for her. She let the librarian think anything she wanted.

Armed with a couple of books which she placed in the small satchel she brought to the library for that purpose, she headed home. Knowing that no one could see what scandalous books she was carrying did not make her anxiety any less. Miriam sweated the whole way.

When she headed to Hannah's the next day with the package in her arms, she worried Mother or Bubbie would ask what she'd wrapped. She wanted to keep the discussion between the two of them.She could not wait for this episode to end.

Hannah greeted Miriam with a huge smile and Miriam wondered what was on her mind. Hannah blurted out, "We did it."

"You did what?" Miriam asked innocently, focused on her upcoming lesson.

"We figured out how to fit William's thing into me."

Oh my, thought Miriam, not knowing what to say except "Good for you." Oh how she hoped this was the end of the discussion. But Hannah continued.

"As you suggested, it felt really good. It was a whole new feeling, having him inside me."

Miriam blushed, hoping Hannah didn't feel compelled to explain in any greater detail.

"But there was one thing that concerned us."

Miriam steeled herself and asked, "Was it the blood on your sheet?"

"Yes. That was exactly it. We thought he was so big that he tore me inside. It didn't hurt, but I bled."

"He sort of did tear you, but it was normal. For the first time. Was there a great deal of blood?"

"No."

"Then it was as expected," Miriam said, hoping again that this was the last of the instructions she had to impart.

"I hope that soon I'll be pregnant. Maybe it will be in the next couple weeks, by the time of the High Holidays. I am certainly going to have fun trying!"

Miriam smiled in happiness and a measure of relief. She was glad her sister was enjoying somewhat similar intimacy as she and Deborah shared, but prayed that this embarrassing educational lesson was finally over. Handing the books to Hannah, she said, "I don't think you'll need these now, but when you have read them, please return them to the library."

It was Hannah's turn to be eyed by the blushing librarian.

Ruth

Swan Boat

Boston Public Garden

CHAPTER SEVEN

Yom Kippur Forgiveness
Early October, 1913

The month began with the holiday of *Rosh Hashana*, the Jewish New Year. Miriam knew the High Holidays would be different without her father as he always led the ritual service. This year there would be a huge gap at the head of the table.

William, the obvious successor, wasn't a capable leader. He knew the prayers and had a passable voice for chanting, but he'd be uncomfortable in this role, much as he was on Shabbos each week.

During a conversation about the holidays, Mrs. Cohen said, "Maybe Uncle Abraham could lead the services this year."

"Or Marjorie's boyfriend, Micah," suggested Miriam. In the end, it was decided Miriam would conduct the prayers, something making her both proud and nervous. Could she live up to her father's standards?

The very next day, it became obvious to Miriam that there would be more changes for this holiday than being the service leader. She arrived in the kitchen to find Bubbie seated, breathing heavily, staring at the frying pans on the wall. Although Bubbie said she was fine, Miriam was increasingly aware she was struggling to complete her regular activities.

Miriam gathered Deborah, Mother, and Hannah for a meeting. "We need to discuss ways to lessen the burden on Bubbie. She typically spends a full week preparing the food, and I don't think she has the energy for it this year."

"What tasks would she give up?" Mrs. Cohen asked. "I doubt Bubbie has the energy to make her own *gefilte fish*, or to grind her own horseradish with vinegar and minced beets."

"What about the *tsimmes*? I've seen her spend an entire day cooking the brisket, then adding the carrots, sweet potatoes, prunes and honey," Miriam said.

"Don't forget the grated white potato she adds to thicken it," offered Mrs. Cohen. "But I doubt she'd let us have a holiday meal without those special dishes, and she wouldn't believe anyone else could make them."

Hannah added, "And I don't want to have a *Rosh Hashana*h meal without her fabulous honey cake."

"Can't we do without it one year?" Miriam asked in frustration.

"All right," said Hannah sheepishly, though they decided it needed to be included with Bubbie's list of tasks she'd be unable to give up.

"We've just described enough dishes to keep her busy the whole week," Mrs. Cohen said.

"What if we take over everything else? I'm happy to participate in any way I can," Deborah said.

"That might work," Miriam agreed. "Let's make a list of everything we need to do and divide it between the rest of us."

In the end, Deborah and Miriam agreed to make the vegetables, *kugel* (potato pudding), and the brisket. Mrs. Cohen took on the labor-intensive task of making the soup with *matzoh balls*, something usually reserved for Passover, but a tradition in their family for both holidays.

Hannah, always in charge of setting the holiday table with their best linens and china, agreed to arrange the customary plate of apples and honey, to get the special round *challah* with raisins from the bakery, and to pick up the ceremonial wine. They hoped this would make the holidays less of a burden on their beloved Bubbie.

Miriam talked with Bubbie about this plan, explaining that they all wanted to learn how to make the holiday foods. At first Bubbie resisted, but eventually agreed to follow their suggestions and to let Miriam help with all the traditional dishes "so she could learn how to prepare them." In the end, Bubbie instructed Miriam, who did a great deal of the work, while Bubbie supervised.

When the holiday actually arrived, there were more challenges. Bubbie didn't go to services the first evening, *erev Rosh Hashanah*, saying she needed to prepare the meal. This was the first time she ever missed a holiday service, and they all figured it was because the walk to shul was tiring. After walking to temple the next morning, it was clear that Bubbie was exhausted.

As they sat in their seats, Deborah turned to Bubbie and said quietly, "I'll get the car to pick you up after services end, Bubbie."

"I no hear you."

Deborah repeated her statement loudly enough for Bubbie and everyone sitting near them to hear.

"I no ride on holiday."

"You need to get home to prepare the dinner."

Exhausted, Bubbie let that explanation take hold and quietly nodded. Deborah left services quite early, bringing the car to pick her up. When they got to the house, Bubbie went to her room to rest before beginning the food preparation.

Miriam arrived with Sylvia a short while later to start last minute dishes. She put Sylvia on the floor with a rag doll to play with. Everything was already heating in the oven before Bubbie woke from her nap. Together, the women set out the plates of *gefilte fish*, garnishing them with bits of carrot and celery from the brine it had simmered in. When everyone arrived, the kitchen was a flurry of activity, with everyone doing the work while Bubbie looked on in amazement.

The morning of the second day of the holiday Deborah said to Miriam, "I'm going to give Bubbie rides both ways today and again on *Yom Kippur* next week. I'll drop her off and pick her up one block from the *shul*, so she doesn't have to admit to anyone she can no longer manage the walk—or that she accepted a ride on the holiday."

"I doubt she'll go with you."

But Bubbie accepted the rides both ways. And she was even more exhausted on *Yom Kippur* a week later, even though they all helped her prepare the huge evening meal they ate in preparation for the whole next day.

The *Kol Nidre* service, on the first night of *Yom Kippur*, was unusually long since the holiday began on Friday night, requiring all the Shabbos prayers to be added to the holiday prayers. A few times Miriam nudged Deborah, pointing out Bubbie was nodding off.

After a meaningful service, Bubbie and Miriam, with Sylvia bundled against the cool fall air, walked to the car, which Deborah had stopped at the next corner. Sylvia fell immediately asleep once in the car. Once home, Bubbie headed directly to her room.

Seated in the parlor, Miriam said to Deborah, "I was thinking of the rabbi's speech of forgiveness at *Yom Kippur* the year I believed I'd be absolved and accepted for my choice of loving a girl. I was so very naive."

"Yes," Deborah said. "Even though there was no forgiveness for us, we're fortunate that both of our families and most of our friends have been surprisingly accepting. I think it's because you're so sweet."

"I believe it was in their hearts to be tolerant. At least I hope so."

Miriam continued. "I've been thinking of the *Yom Kippur* tradition during this holiday for individuals to repent for sins, offering *teshuva*. We ask forgiveness from G-d, but it is also common practice to ask for forgiveness and to repent with anyone we offended during the past year. Deborah, I've been thinking about poor Ruth. I wronged her by assuming she was incapable of parenting Sylvia. May we invite her here to talk with her about that? Since Hannah's wedding, I've been writing her letters, but she rarely responds to anything I write about."

Deborah said nothing, sad that Miriam still didn't see this as part of Ruth's self-absorption.

"Or maybe," Miriam said, "she could be withholding because we took over the care of her child."

"She might, but I'm worried about you inviting her to Boston."

"Why are you concerned?"

"She's difficult to be with."

"I'm certain you can tolerate her for a few days. This is important to me, Deborah. And maybe, now that she's married to Michael, she's changed."

"All right," Deborah said without enthusiasm, "but only because you want this to happen."

On October 11, Deborah and Miriam dressed in their finest clothes, ready for the Boston Symphony Orchestra concert Miriam had purchased for Deborah's birthday. Unaccustomed to going out for the evening, they'd both taken afternoon naps, hoping they could stay awake for the entire performance and that Sylvia would stay asleep and not wake Mother or Bubbie.

In an unusual splurge, the concertgoers called the Taxi Motor Cab Company of Boston for a ride to Symphony Hall, arriving with their tickets clutched firmly in Miriam's gloved hands.

"I've only been here a couple of times," Miriam said, "but I always find it breathtaking."

Deborah, though used to New York's Carnegie Hall, was equally entranced by this lovely venue. She stared at the sculptures positioned around the room and the ornate furnishings. Both girls watched the people all around them in awe, gawking at the exaggerated headpieces on many of the ladies. Miriam pointed to the program note clearly forbidding hats that obstructed the views of other patrons, and she waited to see if the ladies with large, feathered hats would oblige.

As the musicians filed onto the stage, Miriam saw that many of the women around her quietly removed their hat pins, then their hats, and placed them on their laps. She assumed they'd return the hats to their heads in time for intermission, so no one would see their flattened coiffures!

As soon as Karl Muck climbed onto the podium, their attention was riveted to the stage. Throughout the stellar performance, neither Miriam or Deborah closed their eyes for a second, afraid they'd be easily lulled to sleep by the beautiful music.

At intermission, they silently followed the throngs of women to the Ladies' Parlor, marveling at the costumes and hoping not to be caught with lingering gazes on the most extraordinary outfits and beautiful women.

Later, taking the taxi back to Roxbury, they realized they'd forgotten all their woes for a few hours. Back home, relaxed and joyful, they fell into each other's arms with tenderness. Deborah teased Miriam's hair out of its ornate twist and gently caressed her entire body. It had been a wonderful delayed birthday celebration.

Just before Ruth's arrival, Deborah and Miriam moved Sylvia and most of her belongings into their room to provide a private space for Ruth.

Miriam said, "It's wonderful to have Sylvia so close by, even if the room is crowded. As for Ruth, even though she gave up parenting willingly, I wonder how she will react to seeing Sylvia."

With raised eyebrows, Deborah said, "I doubt she cares. In all this time, Ruth hasn't asked any questions about Sylvia or shown any interest at all."

In letters, Miriam warned Ruth that they needed to work at the shop during her visit and wouldn't be free to have a social week as was Ruth's style. They received this terse note in return:

October 13, 1913

Dear Miriam,

I'm pleased to accept your invitation to come to Boston. It's fine with me if you conduct your regular activities while I'm visiting. I'm used to being alone, since Michael rarely has time for me either.

Fondly,
Ruth

As she disembarked from the train at South Station, Ruth said, "Thank you for picking me up, Deborah. I had no idea you could drive. You have many skills I know nothing about." She turned to Miriam. "I wish you could help me find something I'm good at. I don't seem to have any worthwhile talents."

"I'm certain there are many things you do well. For one, you have a wonderful ability to bring people together," Miriam said sweetly.

"If you can figure out how that could benefit me, then maybe I won't be so lonely."

Deborah had parked the car near the station, figuring the three of them could manage the luggage. But Ruth walked ahead, leaving it all for them to carry. Deborah was about to make a comment, asking Ruth to help out, when Ruth said, "You girls are so strong and capable. I'm weak. All I can manage is my hat box."

Deborah steamed, but said nothing.

They rode through Boston with Miriam pointing out all the sites, just as her mother did when Deborah first arrived in the city. It was hard to know if Ruth was interested in what she was seeing as she said nothing at all. This was a glaring contrast to Deborah's enthusiasm during her first visit.

"How nice to see you again, Ruth," said Mrs. Cohen, who had met Ruth at Hannah and William's wedding. "I am glad you have come to visit. The first activity in this house is always to eat some of Bubbie's *munn* cookies."

"I don't want any, thank you," Ruth said. "I'm trying to get my girlish figure back."

"Probably better not to have any then, since I never saw anyone stop after eating just one," Miriam said.

Deborah went upstairs to get Sylvia and brought her into the parlor.

Looking straight into her little girl's eyes, Miriam tried to make this meeting easy by saying, "Sylvia. This is Ruth." Miriam looked at Ruth to see her reaction to her own child.

Ruth said nothing, not even the general patter most people would exhibit when a baby enters the room. Deborah, standing behind Ruth, shrugged and lifted her eyebrows, finding the situation truly unbelievable.

When Deborah left the room, Miriam asked Ruth directly about her reaction, "How is it for you, seeing Sylvia again?"

"Fine." Ruth immediately changed the subject, asking, "Can you show me where to put my things?"

Miriam, unsure how to encourage any more conversation, invited Deborah back into the parlor. Quickly, Deborah realized she was being summoned to carry the luggage, which took her three trips upstairs with the heavy suitcases. Ruth didn't even carry her own hat box and never even said, "Thank you." By this time, Deborah was annoyed and wondering why she had ever agreed to this visit.

After Miriam settled Ruth into her room, Miriam assumed Deborah would say something about Ruth's lack of reaction to Sylvia. But instead she said, "I overheard Ruth refusing Bubbie's cookies. I was so glad Bubbie wasn't present. How insulting! And she never asked about Bubbie's welfare or suggested we thank her for preparing the snack. I'm already annoyed with her and she's been here under an hour."

"Calm down, Deborah. Please don't get upset. I'm certain she had other things on her mind. She's had a long trip, and it can't be easy seeing us as Sylvia's parents. I'm certain her silence is not from unconcern, but from hurt and awkwardness."

"I don't think so. Ruth asks nothing about our lives or interests but instead talks about her clothing and her things. You're always making excuses for her."

"Give her a chance," Miriam said softly.

"I don't want to make things uncomfortable for you. I'll stay away and let you spend time with her."

"That would be awkward as well. I don't want you hiding. I'm certain you can tolerate her for one week."

Deborah took in a deep breath, letting it out slowly, resisting the urge to comment further.

As the two of them took a walk the next evening, Deborah said, "Miriam, Ruth's presence here is disturbing me. I was glad she didn't want to talk with us about Sylvia. She's been like this ever since I met her. Look at what happened yesterday when you tried to discuss Sylvia's condition. When you explained how we were providing vitamins to help her development, Ruth was totally disinterested and talked about the vitamins that she takes to improve her complexion. This is not normal."

"I keep hoping she'll become more concerned," Miriam answered, sadly, pulling her shawl around her in the cool evening air.

"I'm sure you see this as a pattern. She has never been any different."

"Yes, just this morning, fulfilling my *Yom Kippur* pledge, I tried to ask her for forgiveness. It isn't required for her to accept my apology or to forgive me, but she interrupted me with a story about a new dress she'd seen in a shop window. She didn't take my request seriously. I'm not even sure she understood why I felt the need to seek forgiveness."

"But that's the reason you invited her to Boston."

"Yes it was. But she wasn't interested in listening and didn't seem to hear what I said."

"I'm not surprised. Ruth just talks about what's of interest to her. I haven't heard her ask a single question about your life. This is the same way she behaved when pregnant. You've been tolerating this behavior for a long time—far too long. It has to stop."

"You're right. I don't understand why I keep making excuses for her."

"Or why you keep trying. She isn't really a friend to you. You don't need someone in your life like her. You have many wonderful friends who really care about you."

"But she's the person who gave us our child. She'll always be in our lives, for that reason alone."

"Will she? Not if she doesn't care. And if she does not care, why would we continue with the relationship?"

When they got home, they entered the house quietly, hoping Ruth wouldn't even notice they'd returned.

The next day, Miriam said to Ruth, "I'm really pleased with the progress Sylvia is making doing daily exercises. She gets better at them every day."

Ruth turned to Miriam. "You know, exercises can't really help her learn new things. She'll never be normal." Ruth added, factually, but coldly, "She'll always be an idiot."

Miriam was dumbstruck by Ruth's chilling response and glad Deborah had not overheard the exchange.

And before she could think of a response, Ruth said, "I've tried exercising, but it never works to make me thinner. No matter what I do I seem to keep this extra weight around my middle."

Ruth carried on with details about her exercising plan, never bringing the conversation back to Sylvia. She accepted another full day of hospitality with no interest on her part about anything to do with them or their daughter.

That night, after putting Sylvia to bed, Deborah and Miriam retired early also so they wouldn't have to spend another evening with Ruth. Miriam took a deep breath. "Ruth upset me today, making disparaging comments about Sylvia."

"What did she say?"

"That Sylvia will never be normal. She'll never learn new things."

Deborah snapped, "That's it. I'm done with her. It's one thing to omit saying nice things, but I won't tolerate her saying something negative about our child."

The next day, Miriam and Deborah sat in the parlor with Sylvia, offering her toy after toy to play with. Sylvia's attention was very short, so it took the whole bucket of toys to occupy her for an hour. But Sylvia was delighted when they played with each of the same toys a second time. Ruth came downstairs just as Miriam offered Sylvia a cookie, which she ate quickly. Miriam then bounced her happy daughter on her lap.

"You shouldn't do that," said Ruth sternly.

"Do what?" Miriam asked, startled.

"Bounce her right after she's eaten."

"She just had one cookie. She'll be fine."

"No. You're never supposed to be active with a child right after eating."

Deborah could not hold her tongue. "Ruth. We know what we're doing. We wouldn't bounce her immediately after a whole meal, but she's fine after just one cookie. We know how to be good parents." *To your unwanted child*, Deborah thought.

"Well, don't blame me if she gets an upset stomach."

Deborah walked away, knowing if she said anything it would be insulting.

When Friday night Shabbos arrived, Miriam asked Deborah, "Do you think it would be strange if we left *shul* right after services? I don't really want to introduce Ruth to our friends."

Deborah snickered. "I guess you're coming around to my way of thinking."

"I guess so. She's tiring me out."

On Ruth's last day in town, Miriam suggested a visit to the Swan Boats. "It's probably the last time we could go this season. It would be lovely for Sylvia."

"Why should we do something just because Sylvia would like it?" Ruth asked.

Deborah held her breath and said nothing.

They headed to the subway, which was clearly not to Ruth's liking.

"Are there any available taxis?" she asked. When ignored, she continued, "Are taxis expensive in Boston?" Then she boldly asked, "Is there anyone who could drive us to town?"

Miriam answered Ruth politely. "We always take the subway."

Ruth was clearly unhappy. Deborah didn't care and stayed out of the conversation.

Once they arrived at the Public Garden, Miriam pointed to the brightly colored chrysanthemums in abundance along the curvy walking paths. Ruth's response was, "I hope I can keep my dress clean in this park."

When the Swan Boats came into view, Deborah pointed enthusiastically, helping Sylvia focus her attention on the lagoon. Ruth commented, "The pond has a foul smell. I wonder if it's the ducks or the pigeons."

Deborah turned away, hiding her smirk as Miriam made no comment, though she too was becoming increasingly disgusted with Ruth's behavior. Deborah took Sylvia out of her stroller and brought her to a grassy spot near the water's edge. She took some bread crumbs from her pocket, and the area quickly filled with pigeons. Sylvia delighted in the noisy birds, and Deborah delighted in the disgusted look on Ruth's face.

By the end of Ruth's visit, Miriam admitted to Deborah, "Ruth is behaving exactly as you described, and similar to how she behaved in Great Barrington. But now she's worse than ever. I made excuses for her then, but now I'm annoyed."

Deborah shook her head. "She has also been insulting, telling you how to parent Sylvia. I can't believe you invited her here. What did you expect?"

Miriam was silent with no answer for Deborah.

They were both thrilled to see Ruth depart, with Deborah hoping this was to be the last visit between the two old friends.

As they moved Sylvia back into her own room Deborah questioned why Miriam had continued a friendship with such a self-absorbed girl. She didn't want to be angry with Miriam for her naiveté, so she wrote about her feelings.

SELF-CENTERED

Why would someone choose a friend who cannot reach outside her own needs? There are no excuses for such egotistical behavior.

Is Ruth's weakness a reflection of an internal need to be accepted? She was raised with minimal affection and little attention. Her mother was a gadabout, scouring the world for appreciation, never imagining that adoration might be awaiting her at her very own home. Was the vacuum of emotion and attention the cause of Ruth's self-centeredness?

Even knowing the cause does little to absolve her of such shallow behavior. Ruth talks of her own world, rarely noticing others' existence. Her own feelings are paramount, her reactions the only ones that matter, her views the only ones with validity. Pain has created a villain.

Deborah knew she would never share this writing with Miriam.

CHAPTER EIGHT

Secrets and Lies

Late October, 1913

"Deborah, please do not tell anyone you are taking me to the doctor. I want you to make an excuse why you have to leave the shop in the middle of the day," begged Mrs. Cohen.

"Why the secrecy?" asked Deborah, suddenly aware of the dark circles under Mother's eyes.

"Do not worry about it. Please do not tell Miriam or anyone else."

All the way to the doctor, Mrs. Cohen was distracted, unable to carry on a reasonable conversation. Her tightened face showed how worried she really was. Deborah watched as Mother cautiously stepped into the doctor's office, holding the railing tightly for support. Waiting in the car as instructed, Deborah imagined possible reasons for this appointment. When Mrs. Cohen returned to the car, Deborah detected a stuffy nose and bloodshot eyes, but there was no conversation.

Mrs. Cohen was generally a cheerful woman. After her husband had died, she had become temporarily sullen, as expected, but over time she had regained her old demeanor. But lately, Miriam noticed her mother was slipping back into a more solemn state. A few days after Mother's stealthy trip to the doctor, Miriam was surprised when she arrived home to find her mother weeping.

"What's wrong, Mother?" Miriam said, placing her hand on her mother's shoulder.

Mrs. Cohen wiped away her tears, surprised she'd been caught in a moment of weakness. She hesitated, collecting herself. "I am beside myself. I hardly know what to do." She shook her head, continuing "You know my friend, Mrs. Shulman, from temple?"

Miriam nodded.

"She told me today she's very ill. The doctor implied she doesn't have long to live. He didn't tell her what is wrong, but he told her to get everything in order."

"I'm sorry, Mother. Illness and death are difficult, and you have dealt with more than your share. I wish there was something comforting I could say to you."

"It is just part of getting old. Last year, just before your father died, I lost my friend Mrs. Rosenberg. And the year before, Mrs. Singleton was very ill, though luckily she recovered. Getting old is not for the faint of heart; illness is the price one pays for living long. All this illness and death are inevitable."

"Please take good care of yourself so you can live a long time. I want you to watch Sylvia grow up." Mrs. Cohen's tears returned, despite her best effort to avoid them.

That evening, after putting Sylvia to bed, Miriam turned to Deborah. "Let's take advantage of this fairly warm evening and take a walk around the neighborhood. There won't be many more evenings like this. The fall air is getting quite crisp."

Deborah put on a shawl and the two of them headed out for a stroll. But as soon as they'd passed their own house, Miriam approached her with concern. "I wanted to get out of the house to talk in private. I'm very worried about Mother. She's been looking very peaked lately, and today I found her crying."

"I'm worried about her too," Deborah said, not disclosing a word about their trip to the doctor.

"Do you think she's suffering from some serious illness? Could she have consumption, which has taken the lives of several people from the temple?"

"I hope not. Some whole families die from it, but I think coughing is the primary symptom and she's not been coughing at all."

"What about dropsy?" Miriam asked. "There's no coughing with that illness. I noticed she dropped a spoon the other day."

"The women I met with dropsy had puffy faces and extremely swollen ankles. Again, that's not the case with Mother. Also, dropping one thing wouldn't be a good indicator. If so, you should also question whether I'm ill since I drop things all the time." Deborah laughed.

"What do you think could be making her so frail and weak?"

"I have no idea, but I think we should keep an eye on her and see if we notice any specific symptoms."

"I'll talk it over with Hannah when she comes to dinner tomorrow."

They continued their walk in silence.

Deborah's Journal, October 21, 1913

I hate having a secret. I felt awful, being unable to tell Miriam I took Mother to the doctor. It would have worried her, but it was awkward having the conversation about Mother's health without disclosing such pertinent information.

I wonder what's wrong with Mother. Would the doctor even tell her? He might withhold information because she's a woman. Had Mr. Cohen still been alive, the doctor might have shared the truth with him. Having a home headed by women has left us vulnerable to a protection we don't seek and don't want.

The next night Hannah and William arrived in buoyant moods, not noticing the sullen faces greeting them. They were fidgety, trying to gather everyone together. Their behavior soon became clear.

"We have wonderful news. We are going to have a baby!" Hannah blurted out the moment Bubbie joined them in the parlor.

Despite their concerns, they were all able to congratulate the couple, giving hugs all around. Hannah was absolutely glowing. She hugged her sister an especially long time, whispering, "Thanks to you," in her ear.

Miriam realized it wasn't so long ago that Hannah thought she was barren. When they were alone, she asked her sister, "How far along are you?"

"I think I got pregnant last night. I feel different today." Miriam was shocked by this revelation and doubted Hannah.

Deborah and Miriam stifled their need to discuss their concerns regarding Mother's health and let the jubilant mood continue through dinner. Without saying so, they decided to let this evening be about the good news.

Miriam's Diary, October 23, 1913

Deborah and I are watching Mother's every movement. We watch her face for signs of pain, her walk to see if she's unsteady, and her sleep patterns to see if she's losing strength. Mother hasn't noticed our constant attention, something she wouldn't tolerate should she become aware.

What will happen if Mother is really sick? Will she weaken more each day and soon not able to make it up the stairs or pour her own tea? Will Bubbie again be the caretaker, despite reaching her own elder years? Will Deborah and I take turns caring for her, leaving the business in ruins?

Hannah has always been tender, unable to handle the stresses of life. I think she's indeed pregnant, as evidenced by her morning illness the past few days. I don't know if I can care for her while caring for everyone else. I wonder if I'm strong enough for this. I worry Deborah and Sylvia will suffer as I distribute my caretaking. But I can't give my baby any less than full attention.

Is there anything I can do differently? My heart is big enough, but can my arms stretch to enfold so many? I must think of answers before I'm too worn out to be of assistance. I'll turn to Mrs. B. for advice, the one person I can always count on in my time of need.

October 24, 1913

Dear Mrs. B.,

I feel ashamed that I've been such a self-centered correspondent and haven't wished your family well lately. But as you read on, you'll understand what has been on my mind.

Our wonderful little girl has brought many decisions and concerns to us, though she also gives us tremendous pleasure, especially when she laughs. The vitamins and extracts the doctor ordered for her have done her no harm, but I see no positive effects either.

Yet this season has brought several new issues to our family. The good news is that Hannah is with child, though she's begun to suffer with severe morning illness. She's not been able to work regularly so it's been more difficult than ever keeping up with increasing orders at the shop. Bubbie is getting frail, so Deborah and I are extremely concerned about her, but that's not my greatest concern. My mother is. She seems weak and unwell, so we're filled with dread regarding her.

My life is filled with worry, and I fear I may not be strong enough to handle everything at once. My youth seems to be slipping away. I'm in disarray. I could use some of your comforting words.

> *Love,*
> *Miriam*

As soon as she received the note, Mrs. B. called and said she would come for a visit. Deborah picked her up at South Station just a few days later.

"Thank you for coming," Miriam said as she entered the house, greeting Mrs. B. with a huge, teary hug.

Once they were composed, Mrs. B. spoke. "I'm sorry I can only be here for three days, but I worry about leaving the four girls in our governess Bridget's care. This is mostly because Fannie has had a dramatic attitude change lately, and I don't feel comfortable leaving her unattended. She's been defiant, refusing to do the simple things I request of her. It surprises me that I'm more concerned with my thirteen-year-old than the younger children, but the problems she could create might be more than Bridget can handle."

"We're grateful you took the time to be with us. Your presence always makes us feel better," Deborah said.

During their visit, the three of them spent many hours talking. Mrs. B., as always, not only was a good listener, but also had many suggestions. "You need to find others to help you, both at the shop and at home." Mrs. B. also volunteered a way they could support one another. "I want you to talk with each other every night about what's worrying you the most. You must ask each other for whatever will help, be it a listening ear, a back rub, or an hour alone. Mr. B. and I do this each evening, which is how we've coped with everything we must face."

"I never think of you as having problems," Miriam said.

"Certainly we do. Everyone does. But we remember to have a serious conversation each evening about what we can do for each other. It helps a lot."

"You two are the most calm and loving people I know, so I'm happy to listen to your advice," Miriam said.

"Remember," Mrs. B. said, "This is every night, even if you're angry. You must be committed to be there for each other."

"I can do that. Can you Deborah?" Miriam asked.

"I'm not certain. I'll need your patience and maybe some reminders."

Miriam smiled a half-hearted smile, the most she was able to do. "I trust we can be there for each other."

"It is about trust," Deborah said.

"Yes, it is," Mrs. B. said.

Deborah and Miriam tried practicing what Mrs. B. suggested and reporting their success to her the next two mornings. They were both sad to see her leave to return to her children as she often felt like part of their family. They were greatly relieved when she agreed to come back with the four children in tow in a few weeks. It was good to have something to look forward to.

Focused on their family issues, both of them forgot about her suggestion they bring in more help for the business. They did remember that she suggested they get out together once in a while.

One Sunday they asked Bubbie and Mother to watch Sylvia while they went to a movie called "The Jew's Christmas," a short film about a Jewish couple whose children were forced to work on the Sabbath. This wasn't a cheerful story, but they were pleased to discuss it.

"I'm glad we get to practice our religion without restriction," Miriam said. As they headed home, she pulled her heavy sweater closed in the cool fall air.

"That's because we're the bosses!" Deborah snickered and Miriam smiled.

"I know a couple of the girls from temple aren't able to come to services anymore because they need to work. It's sad that employers don't recognize their desire to honor the Sabbath."

"But we're Jews. Christian shop owners don't respect us."

Miriam was lost in thought for a few minutes. "I don't know if I could work for Christians."

"Because of having to work on Shabbos?"

"I think they're just too different from us. I don't think I'd understand their ways."

"That's what they think about us."

"We're very fortunate," Miriam said wistfully. "We've been able to live our lives in a totally Jewish community, other than the friends we've made at the settlement house."

"Are you uncomfortable with them because they aren't Jewish?"

"Not really. Maybe because they're like us, choosing to be with other women."

"I think," Deborah said softly, "that it's human nature to choose people like ourselves."

"I agree."

"I also think," Deborah said before opening the door to their home, "That it's really good for us to get out on our own, like tonight. It's important that we talk about things other than Sylvia or the shop."

"Yes. But let's choose something more cheerful for our next movie. I'd like to come home with smiles."

"I know how to make you smile," Deborah said with a wink. They headed upstairs, finding Sylvia asleep for her nap. They managed a short session of loving while almost fully clothed. They hoped their wrinkled dresses didn't give away that they'd had an afternoon tryst, but it was actually the blush on their faces that told of their frolic.

CHAPTER NINE

Intimacies

Early November, 1913

The first of November was like any other Saturday, except it was Miriam's birthday. She and Deborah spent the morning at temple and took a brisk walk with Sylvia in the stroller in the afternoon. Although Sylvia was 17 months old, she had just learned to crawl and she did not have any words yet. But she was always cheerful. Miriam thought she smiled more than any other child she had ever seen.

"Does Hannah ever forget your birthday?" asked Deborah, soon after they'd cleaned up from the *Havdalah* service and dinner.

"She never has before, but this pregnancy seems to have thrown her off."

"I was certain she'd show up for services or dinner or—if she sent William without her, as she did—there would be a gift or a birthday greeting awaiting you. But William left without a word."

"It's fine. She has other things on her mind."

Just then William crashed through the front door, pulling a badly wrinkled package from his overcoat pocket. He exclaimed loudly, "Miriam, I almost forgot to give you this. If I had not dropped off your present, Hannah would have been upset with me."

"Why thank you, William. Can you wait while I open it?"

Miriam opened the parcel, finding a lovely embroidered shawl. She wondered how Hannah had shopped for the gift since she rarely left the house these days except to occasionally go to work. "Please thank Hannah for me. It's a lovely gift. I'll enjoy wearing it."

With a blush William said, "I picked it out."

"You have lovely taste," said Deborah, honestly impressed with his choice. "Maybe I'll send you to pick things for me too."

Concern was evident on William's face, so Deborah said, "I was joking, William. That was my way of acknowledging your skill in finding such a lovely shawl."

William blushed an even darker shade of red and headed out the door without further discussion. The door had just latched shut when it opened again, with William peeking in and quietly saying, "Happy Birthday, Miriam."

They all smiled at this sincere, yet awkward, man.

After William had left, Bubbie signaled for Miriam to come close to her and sit on the chair in the kitchen.

"I tell yu my gift," said Bubbie. "It be lesson to make *munn* cookies."

"What a sweet gift, Bubbie. It's the best thing you could offer me. Can Hannah learn too?"

"She no good cook. You learn fast."

"That may be true, but she loves your cookies as much as I do, and she'd be thrilled to have your recipe. I'd like her to join us."

"That be fine, but I give yu cookie cutters when I not make cookies anymore."

"That's very sweet, Bubbie. I'll treasure them forever."

They'd arrange a time for both granddaughters to come for their cookie-making lesson once Hannah was feeling up to it.

"Miriam. Please come to bed now," said Deborah, hoping to entice Miriam for a night of pleasure, as she knew Mrs. B. would encourage.

"In just a few minutes," Miriam said distractedly, as she arranged her clothing for the next day.

"I think you should put those clothes down and join me. After all, it's your birthday! We both seem to make everything else more important than being together lately."

"You are right. I'll be there in just a minute."

The minute turned into five minutes. Deborah sat on the bed with her carefully wrapped gift, awaiting Miriam. When Miriam finally joined her, Deborah handed over the small satchel and watched, wide-eyed, as she unwrapped the small gift.

"A book of poetry. How lovely."

"Not just any poetry. The man at the *Brattle Book Shop* on West Street told me this is an especially wonderful collection written by a newly published poet named Joyce Kilmer."

"*Trees and Other Poems*. It sounds lovely."

"I hope you'll enjoy it."

Just then both girls heard the sound of Sylvia waking up. Miriam shrugged and went to check on the baby. Deborah took a deep breath and let it out slowly. She was saddened they so infrequently made time to be intimate. Their short session following the movies had reminded her how much she missed it. They were always too tired or distracted. And they'd both been consumed with worry about Bubbie, Mother, and Hannah. Deborah had really wanted this night to be different, a celebration.

All evening, Deborah had been thinking of climbing into bed together and running her hands down Miriam's torso. She'd kiss Miriam deeply, signaling her interest in an intimate connection. She thought of how wonderful Miriam's lips would feel as they nibbled at her neck, which always made Deborah's nipples hard. As she rubbed her breasts against Miriam's, she'd feel the familiar feeling of arousal. There would be a tightening between her legs and she'd feel moisture in her private parts. She'd feel the familiar urge, as her focus became directed to her lower region.

Deborah was anxious to be loving with Miriam tonight. She wanted to watch Miriam's face change as she too became interested. She knew Miriam would rub her body against her, making sure to awaken every inch of skin.

She'd slowly circle Deborah's breasts, softly pinching her nipples until they became erect. She could imagine her breathing deepen as Miriam moved her hands lower but took her time in reaching the special place that felt so good. Miriam would come closer and closer to that sweet spot yet she'd make Deborah practically beg before she got there. She'd touch the area lightly to ensure there was wetness, then she'd move her hand away. Deborah would try to position herself to connect Miriam's fingers with the swollen part, which was ready for pressure, but Miriam would make her wait. Another light touch, more slippery than the first, would be followed by Deborah's squirming.

Finally, Miriam would run her fingers firmly along the special spot, then stop again. Deborah's panting would increase, and Miriam would glide her fingers again. By this next pass, Deborah often grabbed her hands and directed them to the exact spot where she wanted to be caressed. Within seconds Miriam would feel Deborah tighten, and the first of several flashes of passion would be done.

Next, it would be Miriam's turn. Miriam was always ready for Deborah's fingers. A quick stroke would prove her eagerness; she was always sticky and moist. Miriam liked to be touched firmly, rubbing herself against Deborah. She liked long strokes with the side of Deborah's hand, moving the wetness along the length of her tender area. Her excitement would reach a very quick peak, and soon she'd be stifling a scream.

While she waited for Miriam to return, Deborah reached down to soothe the throbbing between her legs. She stroked her own wetness and let out a soft moan, getting lost in the wonderful sensations. She didn't notice Miriam reenter the room. As she began to rub harder, Miriam silently climbed into the bed to join her. Miriam snuggled closely and began to stroke alongside Deborah's hand. Soon, Deborah removed her fingers and let Miriam take over. They had an exciting session of loving, a wonderful celebration of Miriam's birthday.

Deborah's Journal, November 2, 1913

Last night was lovely. It had been so long since we had intimacies that it felt almost new. I was ready for the connection yet I'm unsettled this morning. Although I wanted Miriam desperately, I'm feeling irritable, even when there is no apparent trigger for my reactions.

I find it easier to meet Miriam's demands. She often asks for a back rub, which I'm pleased to do. Her needs seem so simple; I wish my feelings weren't so complex.

I'm looking forward to the Berkowitzes' visit next weekend, though I assume Mrs. B. will ask for an update on her suggestion of our nightly asking for what we want from each other. My honest answer won't please either of them.

Fannie

CHAPTER TEN

Secrets Revealed

Mid-November, 1913

The weekend with the Berkowitz family was delightful, though everyone was exhausted from the commotion of the four young girls each vying for attention. Even though the family stayed at a hotel, there were many hours of noisy, excited play at the Cohen household. There were several sighs of relief as the car pulled away and peace and quiet returned.

The following Wednesday after dinner Deborah and Miriam strolled in their neighborhood, wrapped in many layers. As they walked, Deborah exclaimed, "Miriam! I fear we have a problem on our hands. Now I understand Mrs. B.'s concerns regarding Fannie. She's become a difficult adolescent, and now there's an issue affecting us."

"I was aware of the changes in Fannie when they visited. She had a negative attitude about everything, making faces at comments that would have previously entertained her. But why do you say that's a problem for us?" Miriam questioned.

"Just as I came upstairs to collect my scarf from our room, Mother told me something—."

Miriam cut her off. "I love that you call her 'Mother.' She certainly treats you like you're another daughter."

"Yes, thank you. But listen to me. She was telling me something she overheard at a temple meeting today. Two of the ladies were speaking our names, which caught her attention. Two women were whispering that we're more than friends. From their conversation she deduced that Fannie had talked to one woman's daughter when we were at *shul* Friday night. Fannie was explicit about us…sharing a bed."

"Oh my," Miriam said, clearly upset. "That is a problem. People at the temple have accepted us recently, but if they hear details of our sleeping arrangements they might not be so forgiving."

"She also overheard the women call our arrangement a 'Boston Marriage.' I never heard that term. Have you?"

"I have," Miriam said. "It was used in Henry James's novel *The Bostonians*, which I read years ago."

"What does it mean?"

"The book is about feminism during the mid-to-late 1800s. It's about a connection between two unmarried women, who, despite the admiration of a man towards one of them, choose to live together. There is speculation as to the true nature of their relationship."

"I'll get it out of the library and see what the book infers. But what are we going to do about Fannie?" Deborah shifted in her chair.

"Mrs. B. showed more stress than I've seen before. I'm certain it was due to Fannie."

Deborah agreed, nodding. "I'm concerned for Mrs. B., but we must tell her what Fannie said so she can stop Fannie from spreading more personal information about us when she comes to visit."

"Also, Mrs. B. would want to teach her about the inappropriateness of her behavior."

They considered a telephone call between the three of them, but worried about such a sensitive conversation being overheard by the switchboard operator. They decided to write a letter together, explaining the problem.

November 23, 1913

Dear Mrs. B.,

It was wonderful to see all of you last weekend. The girls have grown so much since our last visit. Sylvia remembered each of them and was comfortable with their cuddles. We're glad you all saw how much she's developed.

We were also glad you got to spend some time with Mother. Your perspective on her declining health was helpful to both of us. We'll keep in mind your focus on what she's still able to do, rather than our constant worry about what she's no longer capable of.

We're writing to tell you of a concern we have regarding Fannie. We both noticed how much she's changed and understand why you're distressed with her behavior. We hate to add to your concern, but we must bring up something difficult.

Over the weekend we introduced Fannie to one of the young girls at shul, thinking it would be pleasant for her to have another girl her age to talk with. It seems she told this girl we two share a bed.

Until now, no one at the temple has asked us about our relationship. Now, Mother overheard them mentioning "Boston Marriage," what we think was a term for two women living together. We don't know how this will affect their treatment of us, but we're concerned.

Please discuss this incident with Fannie and let her know this kind of talk could harm our reputation in the community. We know you can't assure us she'll desist from such behavior, but we'd like you to try.

We want very much to see you all again, including Fannie, though we'd appreciate some assurance this has been dealt with before your next visit. It's difficult to bring up such a delicate subject, and we hope we haven't caused Fannie punishment. We love your whole family and plan to remain close to all of you.

We hope you have a wonderful Thanksgiving.

With Love,
Deborah and Miriam

"Thanksgiving will be a pleasant, though quiet, affair," Miriam explained. "Just the immediate family, so it will be similar to a regular Shabbos meal, except we'll have turkey with stuffing instead of roasted chicken. Does that bother you, Deborah?"

"Not at all. The only thing I'll miss from a traditional meal is the pumpkin pie, but I know it can't be served with a meat meal because it contains dairy."

"But we'll have Bubbie's delicious apple pie instead."

"Then I'll be happy."

Hannah, who was finally feeling better, helped Bubbie bake the pie, though Bubbie clearly didn't approve of the messy crust she made. Also, it took Hannah a great deal of time to cut the apples, causing many of them to turn brown.

They talked of being thankful they were able to celebrate together. Yet for the girls and Mother there was an unspoken concern on their faces, reflecting their worry about what would face them at temple this weekend.

The day after Thanksgiving, the publishing shop was closed, so this was the day Bubbie arranged to teach her granddaughters how to make her *munn* cookies.

When Miriam came into the kitchen after breakfast, she said, "Bubbie, you look so tired. Are you feeling all right? You worked very hard to make us a wonderful Thanksgiving meal. Maybe we should choose another day for our cookie making lessons."

"No. We do today. Hannah come soon. I show you both."

Hannah arrived just a short time later, very excited to be part of this special class. Bubbie gathered all the ingredients and set them on the kitchen table. She began by grabbing a handful of flour, announcing, "Yu take this much flour, two time."

"But how much is that?" Miriam asked.

"Just right. Yu look, then yu do the same."

The lessons continued just like this, with two handfuls of flour to one smaller handful of sugar. Then a pinch of baking powder and a smaller pinch of salt. Miriam and Hannah both wondered how they'd ever make Bubbie's recipe, yet they knew they'd have fun trying.

After they were done adding the poppy seeds, rolling the dough, and cutting the cookies into flower shapes, they waited impatiently as the wonderful baking smell made their mouths water. When they took the cookies out of the oven, both girls reached out to grab a hot pastry. Bubbie batted both their hands, "Yu wait."

"I can't," Hannah said as she grabbed a hot cookie. It fell apart onto the floor.

"I tell yu wait," Bubbie insisted. They waited.

Once they'd all filled themselves with more cookies than they usually ate at one sitting, Bubbie announced, "I got something for yu."

She reached into her apron pocket and pulled out two copies of the recipe that her friend's daughter had written for the girls. They couldn't figure out how this young woman had figured out the measurements, but they were appreciative that they'd be able to replicate Bubbie's most special cookies.

(See Addendum for MUNN COOKIE RECIPE)

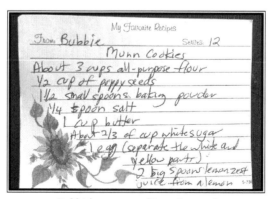

Bubbie's munn cookie recipe card

CHAPTER ELEVEN

Rejection

Early December, 1913

At temple the weekend following Fannie's announcement about their sleeping arrangement, Deborah and Miriam noticed several people looking directly at them and whispering to one another.

"People are obviously talking about us. What should we do?" Deborah said quietly to Miriam as they sat in their seats awaiting services to begin.

"Absolutely nothing. I think we should just continue to be ourselves and hope this attention is short-lived," Miriam said, stroking Sylvia's hair.

"I'll do my best, though I suspect there's going to be a fuss. I wouldn't be surprised if everyone rejects us."

"Let's not make assumptions."

Sadly, Deborah was correct. When they went to see their friends after services, the other girls didn't show up at the regular meeting spot. No one even stopped by to make excuses.

I think we have our answer," Deborah said, gazing at the empty room with a tightly clenched mouth. She shifted the baby to her other hip.

"I'm afraid you're right. But here comes Marjorie."

"Hello," Marjorie said with an insincere smile.

"What's the story?" asked Miriam.

"I'm sorry, but everyone seems busy tonight. Too bad. I always look forward to our gatherings after services," Marjorie said, a slight tremor in her voice.

Deborah cocked her head and with a lilt to her voice said, "Marjorie, we're not ignorant. We know Fannie talked to people about us last weekend, saying we shared a bed. I assume that has a lot to do with everyone suddenly disappearing."

Moisture reflected in Marjorie's eyes. "You're right. I'm afraid several of the women asked their daughters to stay away from you. They think you're a bad influence."

"Miriam is the same person they've always known. Nothing has changed, except the obvious has been stated," Deborah said forcefully.

"I don't know what to do," Marjorie said apologetically.

"I think you were brave to come to us," Miriam said in her typically sweet manner. "Thank you. I know you're risking their rejection by talking with us."

"If they rebuff you for loving each other, they can rebuff me too."

Miriam put her arm on her friend's shoulder. "Oh, Marjorie. You're a true friend."

"They better not reject you for talking with us," Deborah said, trying to be strong.

The three of them talked for a while, standing quietly on the stone steps of the synagogue as Sylvia slept in Miriam's arms. They resolved nothing, but Miriam felt better, having discussed the situation openly.

But on the way home, Deborah became irritable. "I don't think we will ever fit in here. I've ruined your life. Everything used to be calm for you. Then I arrived and upset your peaceful existence. Maybe I should leave."

"Deborah, no! I don't want you to leave. I'm pleased with the changes in my life since I met you. Obviously I don't like this situation, but I'm certain it will pass."

"It's hard to believe that you like the way things have changed. Everyone used to love you. Now I'm certain they think less of you because you're with me."

Sisterhood woman

"I don't care what they think. I love you, and I believe things will change over time."

"If they don't run you out of your own home. Or run me out."

There was no calming Deborah, so Miriam said no more. She thought that after Deborah stewed for a while, she'd be less cantankerous. At least she hoped so.

When she got home, Miriam wanted to talk with Mother about how people had treated her, but Mother headed to bed right after they walked in the door. And so did Deborah. Miriam remained in the parlor, gently rocking Sylvia and wondering how people could be so unkind.

A letter came in the mail the following week.

November 29, 1913

Dear Deborah and Miriam;

> *My parents made me write you this letter. I am sorry I caused you problems. I didn't think that by telling one girl everyone would know. I won't do it again. I promise.*
> *Say hello to Sylvia for me.*

> *Fannie*

Deborah and Miriam were glad Fannie knew she had been wrong and vowed not to talk about them to others anymore. But they still feared that the women of the *shul* would continue to shun them. They hoped this wouldn't affect Mrs. Cohen, who already had much to be worried about.

The next day there was a knock at the door. When Miriam, holding Sylvia, opened it, she found three women from the Sisterhood standing there. They all seemed startled by Miriam's presence, even though they had come to her home. They quickly asked if they could talk with her mother. Miriam seated them in the parlor and went to get her and also Deborah, figuring Mother needed fortification in what Miriam assumed could be a nasty verbal exchange.

As Mother and Deborah entered the living room, none of the guests noticed Mother lowering herself onto the chair quite slowly, a shift from her normal manner. Both Deborah and Miriam saw her discomfort.

"We wish to speak with your mother alone," one of the women said in a stiff, insistent manner as the three of them, plus Sylvia, sat down.

"We'd like to be present for this conversation," Deborah said briskly. "We want to hear anything you have to say, since we assume it's about us." She looked at Miriam.

"Well, fine," said one of the other women, with a huff. Turning to Mrs. Cohen she said, "We would like to discuss the issue being talked about at the *shul*. It seems Deborah and Miriam are a bad influence on our daughters."

Miriam interrupted, "We're right here, so you can talk directly to us. You don't need to talk about us."

Deborah nodded approvingly.

The women were obviously not expecting Deborah and Miriam to be present, so their prepared speech wasn't going to work. The same woman stammered, finally saying, "We are not comfortable with our daughters being in the company of young women with questionable morals."

Deborah laughed out loud. "My morals are just fine, thank you. I'm honest, sincere, and just in all my decisions. I hope your daughters are the same."

"I agree," Miriam said, a little timidly but with purpose.

"And we have no intention of corrupting anyone," Deborah said a little too loudly, staring directly into the eyes of each of the three women, making them squirm.

After an awkward pause, Mrs. Cohen shifted in her chair, sat up straight, and then spoke. "I too was a bit dismayed when I learned of my daughter's connection with Deborah, but I have learned to love Deborah, like she is another daughter to me. She is a lovely person—kind, supportive, and certainly honest. I couldn't have asked for more for my Miriam. Deborah is a person of high moral character, who has taken on my husband's business as if it were her own family she was rescuing. And she is parenting a baby who would otherwise be in an institution. She is an upright citizen, a practicing Jew, and the person my daughter has fallen in love with. I would wish such happiness for any of you."

Miriam and Deborah spontaneously reached over, each grabbing one of Mother's hands in her own.

"Thank you, Mother," Miriam said. "And I need to tell the rest of you that I've found more love in this relationship than I ever dreamed. Deborah was a wonderful support when my father rejected me, as you wish to do. I love her, and I'm not ashamed to say that."

The whole room went quiet. Everyone looked at one another, but no words were spoken for a very long and awkward minute.

Finally, Deborah broke the silence. "I've fallen in love with the sweetest girl I've ever met. I have an adorable baby, a lovely home, and a successful business. I won't allow your attitudes to break my happiness."

More silence. Mrs. Cohen stood, ready to escort the women out of her home when Bubbie arrived with tea and *munn* cookies. Everyone looked at one another, trying to decide what to do as Bubbie poured the tea into cups. The Sisterhood women began chatting about the treat and the tension seemed broken. They all made an effort to be sociable, though this was clearly not the end of their concerns.

Once the women walked out the door, Miriam plopped on the couch and signaled for her mother and Deborah to sit beside her. The three of them held hands and quietly talked of what had happened.

"I'm so glad they're gone. I could hardly wait for them to leave," Deborah said. Miriam and Mother nodded in agreement.

"Thank you for your kind words, Mother," Deborah said.

"I meant every word I said. I have learned to love you like another daughter."

"I thank you sincerely. I don't think we persuaded them we're behaving like proper young women, but it felt good that we each spoke up."

"I wonder if they'll still require their daughters to refrain from contact with us?" Miriam said.

Before they could continue the conversation, Bubbie came to the doorway, announcing, "Sylvia need diaper change." Things went on as if there had been no crisis looming just a short time before.

The next Friday night, Deborah and Miriam headed to shul, both nervous but determined to handle whatever happened.

"Hannah and William won't be there for support tonight," Miriam said wistfully.

"I would've appreciated having them there, but I know Hannah is still occasionally ill from her pregnancy," Deborah said.

"She's having a difficult first few months."

Mother almost declined coming, until Miriam said, "Mother, I'd like to leave early and take a slow, casual stroll to temple." Miriam didn't mention this was to accommodate her mother's slower pace, but it did help to change Mother's mind.

During the walk, Miriam wondered how many more times Mother would be capable of making this short trip. When the trio arrived, they looked around the sanctuary with stealthy glances but only noticed a couple of women look-ing their way. As the services ended, Deborah and Miriam each took a deep breath as they made their way to their regular meeting spot. Marjorie was waiting for them.

The three of them stood silently, wondering what would happen. Then, one by one, their friends arrived. None of them spoke of their previous absence, of the meeting with the girls' mothers, or of anything that might have been said to them during the week. Both Deborah and Miriam smiled warmly, greeting each girl with a hug. At first, conversation was slightly awkward but soon settled into their regular, warm rhythm.

Mrs. Cohen's reception at the Sisterhood meeting the next Tuesday was less successful. When she got home, she explained. "Everyone was polite to me, but there was coldness in the room. I noticed no one addressed comments or questions directly to me. I wonder if I'll be an outsider from now on."

"I certainly hope it will pass," said Miriam.

"But I was proud I defended my family, no matter what the outcome."

"I love you, Mother."

"I love you too," said Deborah.

Later, Deborah and Miriam talked about Mother and how she would need the support of her friends if she became weaker. And how they hated the thought that their relationship might get in the way.

CHAPTER TWELVE

Allies

Mid-December, 1913

One evening, a week after the Sisterhood women came calling, there was another knock at the door. Deborah and Miriam, sitting in the parlor with Sylvia when they heard the rapping, looked at each other with wide eyes.

"Who might be at the door this time?" asked Miriam. "I hope it's not another posse from the Sisterhood, hoping to be more successful in rejecting us than the first group."

Deborah walked with a quick step, determined to greet the newest intruders assertively. At the door she found a young woman, looking uncomfortable.

"I'm Chava. I go to the same *shul* as you. I was a couple of years ahead of Miriam in school," the young woman said in a halting manner.

"Come in," Deborah said, glancing at Miriam, shrugging her shoulders when she was out of Chava's sight.

Deborah motioned to a seat near the couch where she and Miriam had been sitting together. Deborah sat and waited for their unexpected guest to open the conversation. Miriam looked her over, noting her light-colored, curly hair carefully pinned under her full-brimmed hat, and a stylish, peach-colored dress, which would have been to Ruth's liking.

With glistening eyes, which didn't go past Deborah's observance, Chava said, "I've come here today to talk with you both." Deborah and Miriam nodded and waited.

"This may be too forward, but I'm going to say it anyway. I've heard the talk about you two at *shul*." Chava hesitated, gulped, and continued. "I hope what they say is true because I think I may be like the two of you."

This comment certainly got the girls' attention, and they both leaned forward. Miriam's mouth fell slightly open as Deborah's lips curled into a wide smile.

"Thank you for telling us," Deborah said. "It's wonderful to know you're a friend, rather than a foe."

"I've never said that out loud before," Chava said with a shiver. "I barely even admitted it to myself. Hearing about you helped me to accept my truth."

"I'm so glad you were brave enough to come here to tell us," Miriam said.

Tears streamed down Chava's face, and Deborah held her hand as she told her tale. "I've always known I was different," Chava began, telling them a bit about her life and her fears.

Once she relaxed, the three of them chatted excitedly, as each told a short version of her own story of self-discovery. Chava explained that she'd had lots of attention from boys, though she never took a fancy to them. But when a new girl arrived at her school, she was immediately smitten. She realized then she was different from her friends.

After a short while, Bubbie arrived with a pot of tea and a plate of cookies. Despite her poor hearing, she'd figured out there was a guest and she was ready to entertain.

"Please excuse me," Miriam said once they finished the treats. "Sylvia has fallen asleep in my lap. I'll put her to bed. You two can keep chatting."

Deborah stayed to talk further with Chava. The two girls talked with familiarity, despite just meeting, discussing the loneliness they felt growing up and of their current situation. They made plans for Chava to return in a few days. When she left, Deborah realized she had just made her first friend in Boston.

Chava

Another week went by and again there was a knock at the door, this time during the daytime. Miriam, who had stayed home from work to care for their sniffling daughter, sat in the parlor with the baby. While Bubbie cooked and Mother rested in her room, she headed to the door wondering who was knocking this time. She thought it might be someone delivering Chanukah wishes, since the holiday was about to start.

"Good afternoon. I'm Marilyn. May I talk with you?" asked the dark-haired stranger with a gravelly voice.

Miriam didn't know her but had seen her at *shul* a few times. Miriam welcomed her inside, and immediately Bubbie peeked into the room and headed back to the kitchen to prepare a snack.

Miriam took a good look at this girl, thinking her attractive in a wholesome way, with a round face and a substantial body fitted comfortably into tailored clothing.

"We live in the West End of the city but I often visit my parents, who attend your *shul*. I came to spend the first night of Chanukah with them this evening. We were already living on our own when they moved here, so we don't know many people in this area of town."

Marilyn and Julie

"Where do you and your husband live?"

Marilyn smiled and boldly said, "I live with my girlfriend, Julie."

Miriam's eyes widened, realizing this was about to be another woman admitting she was in a relationship with a woman instead of a man.

Marilyn said, "We are 'Lesbianke.'" When Miriam looked confused, she explained, "That's Yiddish for 'lesbian.'"

It didn't take long for the two girls to begin discussing their friends and reactions of others to their lifestyle.

Marilyn explained, "My girlfriend and I set up housekeeping together several years ago. We've found several other lesbians living in 'Boston Marriages.'"

This time, this term was welcoming rather than chastising. Marilyn freely used the word "lesbian," which neither Deborah nor Miriam had adopted after they learned the term from Abigail and Margaret at a suffrage meeting.

Bubbie arrived with the goodies and quickly retreated so the women could resume their conversation.

"I work at Denison House, a settlement house founded by a group of female professors from Wellesley College. Have you heard of Emily Green Balch?"

"No."

"She's a pacifist and well-known social reformer. She, plus Katharine Coman and Vida Scudder, well-known progressive lesbians, are founders of Denison House. This organization attracts many others like us."

"This is very exciting," Miriam said. "I volunteered in a settlement house when we were living in New York, and I've been looking for a place to volunteer since I moved back to Boston."

What she thought, but didn't say, was that she was equally excited to have met another female like herself who might connect her with others. In their excitement Marilyn and Miriam consumed two plates of Bubbie's *munn* cookies as they got to know one another. By the time Marilyn left Miriam could hardly wait for Deborah to come home to tell her the good news.

Miriam was especially buoyant lighting the Chanukah candles soon after Deborah returned from work. Deborah noticed her excitement and wondered what could have stimulated Miriam while she was caring for their ill child. She got a hint when Miriam said, "We had a guest this afternoon, Marilyn Swartz. She and her girlfriend live in the West End and visit Marilyn's parents frequently. Her parents have attended our *shul* since moving to this neighborhood. Do you know the Swartz family, Mother?"

"No, I don't. But I'll be certain to make their acquaintance, knowing they are new to town."

Deborah, who noticed Miriam's mention of Marilyn living with her girlfriend, simply said, "I look forward to hearing more about your new friend." Miriam winked, letting Deborah know that she'd properly heard the message.

When Miriam brought Sylvia upstairs to get her ready for bed, Deborah followed, anxious to hear the whole story about Marilyn. As soon as they were out of earshot of the others, she said, "So tell me about Marilyn."

Miriam spilled out the tale in rapid sentences. "She called herself 'Lesbianke.' That's Yiddish for 'lesbian'! And just as important, she works at a settlement house, where I could volunteer. And there are many other 'Lesbianke' girls there."

"Slow down. I know you're excited, but I want to hear all the details."

"Oh, Deborah. I'm so excited. I don't know if I can be slow, but I'll try. And the best part is that I really liked Marilyn. I think we might have another friend."

Miriam again was speaking quickly until Deborah said, "You're so worked up. I haven't even met her and you have already decided we're going to be friends. Maybe you should let me choose my own friends."

"I'm sorry. I didn't mean that you need to be her friend."

"I'm going to decide on my own anyway, so don't push me. And right now I think you're too excited to calm down our baby for bedtime. You should go back downstairs while I settle Sylvia. I don't think she'd ever fall asleep for you."

Miriam left, upset. She'd been so excited and wanted to share her good fortune, but now Deborah was annoyed with her as was the case quite often these days.

The next day, Miriam suggested something fun for them to do together, hoping it would raise Deborah's spirits. "Let's go skating on the Frog Pond this weekend. It's something we've always talked of doing."

"Why now? Have you heard that your new friend, Marilyn, is going?"

"Deborah! I have no motivation other than to have a nice time with you. You seem on edge so much of the time lately that I thought a fun afternoon might help. I'm certain Bubbie or Mother would watch Sylvia for us on Sunday afternoon."

But, as it turned out, the weather was unseasonably warm and never reached freezing so there was no skating.

Denison House, 93 Tyler Street, Boston

CHAPTER THIRTEEN

Volunteering

· *Early January, 1914*

However, by the first Sunday in January, Bubbie offered to watch Sylvia so Deborah and Miriam could go skating on the Frog Pond. They'd passed it many times, eying the skaters with envy as they floated across the glassy surface. Now they'd be skating there themselves.

Deborah and Miriam put on their skates, and immediately it was clear Miriam was not used to balancing on the thin blades. "I bet you fall first!" said Deborah as she skated smoothly into the middle of the pond.

"I bet I do, too," said Miriam, teetering precariously. It was under five minutes before she fell, landing in an unbecoming manner. "Oops."

Deborah helped her back onto her feet, pleased to have an excuse to hold Miriam upright. It wasn't long before the two of them were gliding along the cold surface with ease.

"I like this!" Miriam said enthusiastically.

"I like it too as long as you remain upright," Deborah said sarcastically.

"Can we come back again?" Miriam barely got the words out of her mouth when she slipped again, pulling them both down onto the ice.

"Maybe. Or maybe we can try skating on Jamaica Pond. I've heard that it's much bigger," Deborah said as she brushed the ice crystals from her clothing.

"More room to fall ungracefully!"

Miriam missed her work at Henry Street Settlement House, where she believed she made a difference in the lives of the children. Since Marilyn had mentioned Denison House, Miriam could think of little else. She'd need to steal precious time from her family to fit in charity work but, with Deborah's encouragement, she signed up to go weekly.

On Miriam's first day of volunteering Deborah said, "I'm glad you're excited, Miriam. So much of your life is heavy with worry these days, and I believe you need something positive."

"Thank you for your encouragement. Volunteering is enriching for me. I'm anticipating my Wednesdays with enthusiasm. I'll enjoy spending the evening being of service."

Deborah encouraged Miriam to bundle up before she ventured out in the cold winter air, heading to 93 Tyler Street. She had to walk a distance to Dudley Station to take a bus or trolley downtown. Deborah used the evening without Miriam to write.

Deborah's Journal, January 7, 1914

I just sent Miriam off to her first evening at Denison House, a wonderful opportunity, which she's been anticipating for weeks. I'm excited for her, but I also have a sense of foreboding. I never worried when she was at Henry Street, but knowing Denison House has many others like us concerns me.

I feel insecure these days. My mood has been foul, and I've not treated Miriam with respect. I fear she'll find someone sweet like her to lure her away.

Why have I been so disagreeable?

Providing for Sylvia feels troublesome. Likewise, the business is stressful. It takes a huge amount of attention to keep everything working smoothly, and lots of the coordination falls on me. Also, I still have strong feelings about my father's rejection. I wonder why I haven't heard from him at all, except for that one sweet telegram. Then I wonder—could my frustration be loneliness, since I have no friends here in Boston other than my new friend, Chava? This is Miriam's world I'm living in –her city, her family, her business, her friends. Maybe I'm prone to frustration, since I felt similarly when in New York. I worry this discomfort will last my lifetime. Is there something I can do to calm my disgruntled state?

I must behave differently, especially tonight, when Miriam will be excited with her new adventure. When she returns, I'll greet her with cheerfulness and encouragement. I can do that for her. And maybe her excitement will encourage her toward some physical play, something I've missed greatly. I'm pleased some of the spark has returned lately.

Following her first evening of volunteering, Miriam came home elated as Deborah had expected, barely getting off her coat before telling Deborah of her experience.

"I had a wonderful time. Denison House is like Henry Street in many ways, and I felt very at home there. It serves mostly immigrant families, predominantly Italian, Syrian, and Greek."

"Are any of the families Jewish?" Deborah asked.

Miriam shrugged. "I met only a couple of Jewish volunteers so far, but no Jewish families. One of the Jewish volunteers is Sadie, who is about my age. She lives in this neighborhood, so we can travel back and forth together."

"How nice you have a new friend so you don't have to be alone on your way home. Tell me more," said Deborah with wide eyes and a grin.

"Denison House was founded by a group of Wellesley College faculty who wanted to provide education to the poor. It's run by women, which makes it unique."

"What kind of classes do they offer?" asked Deborah, motioning to the couch so they could sit together.

"I heard about a woman who studied nursing, and now she has a good paying job at Boston City Hospital. She brings home enough money for her family so her poorly sighted grandmother no longer has to take in sewing projects."

"What a great story. What else do they offer besides nursing? Not everyone's suited for that."

"There was a long list of classes, including literature, woodworking, and many others I can't remember. They want to help women get jobs."

Deborah changed the subject. "Did you see Marilyn, who came by our house? She works at Denison House."

"I was hoping to see her, since she's the one who told me about it, but she wasn't around."

"What does she do there?"

"She's a social worker. I don't think I'll see lots of her since I'm working during the evenings and she works during the daytime. But I'm certain I'll see her at the festival this Friday."

"What festival?"

"At Denison they encourage the women to celebrate their heritage. They hold cultural and craft exhibitions, which sound like great fun. This week is Greek Festival. Would you be all right if I go on Friday afternoon? I promise I'll not take a lot of time away from work or from our family, but I'm excited about this."

"Fine to go on Friday, as long as you're home in time for Shabbos, which is early this week. Sundown is 4:36 p.m. And I won't mind an evening alone with Sylvia each week while you volunteer."

"Oh my. I didn't even ask about Sylvia. How was she this evening? Is her earache gone, and did she go to bed easily without me?"

"She's just fine. I wondered when you would remember you had a daughter. I think this volunteer job is making you forget your responsibilities."

"No, it isn't. Well actually maybe it is. For a few hours I leave all my concerns behind. I think it's good for me to have a break, just as you suggested. I don't want to upset you, Deborah."

"Maybe it's good for you and I should be more understanding."

Miriam sighed. "Please tell me how your evening went."

"Sylvia and I had a lovely time together," Deborah said. "Now I think we should get ready for bed. I anticipated you would be too excited to go to sleep, so I took a nap when I put Sylvia down. I think we should take full advantage of both of us being awake for a change. I'd like to harness your enthusiasm and see what we can do beneath the sheets tonight."

"What a wonderful idea!"

When Miriam got to the Greek Festival on Friday, she looked around, hoping to find Marilyn. She spotted her talking with one of the mothers. As Miriam approached, Marilyn excused herself from the parent.

"How wonderful to see you here," Marilyn said. "I didn't know if you followed my suggestion that you volunteer here."

"I'm embarrassed I didn't contact you before now to thank you for telling me about Denison House. I started just this week."

"No need for shame. I'm just pleased you're here."

Marilyn introduced Miriam to several other staff members, commenting after several introductions, "This woman's a lesbian, too." Miriam was pleased to be in the company of so many like her. She wanted to tell Deborah about all these other women, but she feared Deborah might be jealous of her connections, so she decided to keep her enthusiasm to herself. When she got home, she asked about Sylvia, then talked just a bit of the festival and Marilyn.

Miriam's excitement continued during her second week at Denison House. She arrived home with stories to tell and satisfaction she'd done something worthwhile. "I worked with a sweet little girl tonight who was just learning English. I was surprised how well we were able to communicate. Children seem to pick up new languages quickly."

"Tell me more."

After hearing more stories of Miriam's evening, they climbed into bed. Miriam made the first move toward intimacy. She began to caress Deborah with sensual fingertips and kissed her with promise. She undressed Deborah completely, snuggling deep under the covers so they could both stay warm. Deborah slid Miriam's nightdress off and they were soon kissing passionately.

As soon as their hands moved southward, they were both caught in a frenzy of touches. Without awaiting their customary period of slow seduction, Miriam moved quickly to very intimate strokes of Deborah's private parts. Finding her ready, Miriam reached inside Deborah, rubbing rhythmically. Deborah took a deep breath, making guttural sounds, which signaled she'd quickly reach the pinnacle of pleasure. Miriam slowed her movements for a moment while Deborah caught her breath, then continued. Within just a few seconds, Deborah's breath increased again and she began rubbing herself along Miriam's fingers. Miriam reached deep inside, then withdrew her fingers, almost coming completely out of Deborah. Then she thrust in again, this time inserting two fingers together. Deborah writhed and ground herself against Miriam's digits. This next time, the pleasure was more extreme and Deborah called out a little too loudly, clenching her teeth and moaning. Miriam rubbed her until all shudders ceased and Deborah's breath returned to normal.

Miriam then reached over and grabbed Deborah's hand. She kissed her fingers, then lowered them to her own private place. She let Deborah rub her slowly, moving the wetness along her woman's spot. Miriam was silky wet by this time and almost ready to explode. Deborah kept the pace very steady, rubbing the sweetness as she felt it grow harder under her touch. It was Miriam's turn to moan, but it was the sound of pleasure, not release. Deborah continued to rub firmly, just as Miriam liked. Several times Miriam came close to the final point of not being able to stop, but she slowed Deborah before that happened. She held out as long as she could, treasuring the repeated sensation of being on the brink. When she could finally stand it no longer, she reached down and moved Deborah's fingers quickly along her special parts with great firmness. They rubbed hard together until Miriam arched her back and whimpered with sounds of pleasure. She lay on her back, and Deborah continued to stroke her until she was finally relaxed. Miriam then turned over and asked Deborah to stroke her back gently. After what seemed like a very long time to Deborah, Miriam turned around and they fell asleep in each other's arms.

Miriam's Diary, January 15, 1914

My tutoring work with the children was rewarding yesterday. But the best part of the evening was when Sadie and I stayed after all the other volunteers had left. We sat on small green chairs in a tiny back room, which was loaded with books and school supplies the volunteers had provided. We chatted quietly so no one would notice us, sharing our life stories and dreams.

Sadie comes from a family with similar practices to those of my family; they attend the Vilna Shul in downtown Boston. I love our similarities. I felt comfortable enough with my new friend to tell her that I live with Deborah. I never explicitly said we share a bed, but I made it clear we were closely connected. She didn't seem uncomfortable.

Sadie is a very pretty girl, with soft, fair skin; a rosy complexion; full lips; and thick blond hair pulled into a soft bun. She dresses in unsophisticated, simple dresses in warm colors, quite similar to mine. She also has a similar figure, with a small waist and full breasts, and she possesses a quiet and cheerful manner. I found her pleasing.

Deborah's Journal, January 15, 1914

I was encouraged that Miriam's happiness led us to frolicking in bed again. While being intimate, I stopped worrying Miriam would find someone sweet to whisk her away. After all, I'm becoming easier to live with than I've been in the recent past, so Miriam will have no reason to stray. At least, I hope not.

After their next volunteer night together, Miriam and Sadie sat in the back room again, discussing an especially trying time with a new child who spoke no English. Miriam said, "It was difficult this evening with the little girl who cried the whole time we talked with her. She didn't understand what we said and wouldn't let us get someone who spoke her language."

"I know how she felt," Sadie said.

"What do you mean, Sadie? Have you ever been somewhere you couldn't converse in the same language as everyone else?"

"No, I haven't had that same experience, but I have felt as overwhelmed as the little girl. Until I met you, I couldn't communicate my thoughts and feelings with anyone about liking girls."

Miriam looked surprised, yet pleased, since Sadie had not shared her feelings about girls before. "Has there been anyone you could tell?"

"Sadly no. I certainly couldn't tell my friends. They'd be scared away. You're the first person I ever told. I've never had a special girl in my life, though that's something I always wanted."

"I'm sorry," Miriam said softly.

"I've always wanted the experience of being close to another girl, but that never happened until I met you," Sadie said, looking directly into Miriam's eyes.

Miriam turned her head and took a big gulp of air and held it a long time. She was unsure what Sadie was saying, but she didn't want to risk asking. The words she heard made her nervous. Was Sadie saying she felt something special toward her? Would this change their connection? Was Sadie expecting Miriam to say the same to her?

"Where'd you go, Miriam? You seemed to disappear."

Miriam let out her breath in a rush and said, "I'm sorry. I guess I'm really tired. I think it's time we leave. I need to get home."

Miriam's staccato comments did not go without notice. Sadie wanted to ask more questions but didn't want to upset Miriam, nor did she want Miriam to know how deeply she meant those words. She was feeling closer to Miriam than she'd ever felt toward anyone before.

Their trip home this night was different. They strode down the quiet streets with a quickened pace and little conversation. It wasn't the cold air that stiffened them. Both girls were a bit afraid—Sadie afraid she had said too much and Miriam afraid of Sadie's feelings. Miriam didn't dare think about her own feelings.

As on other Wednesday evenings, Deborah checked on Mother to see how she was doing. Then she put Sylvia to sleep, took a short nap, and spent the rest of the time writing in her journal, waiting for Miriam.

Miriam took the time while she walked home from Sadie's to calm herself. She walked into the house cautiously, afraid her confusion might be obvious. She began talking nonstop, trying to steer the conversation to less personal topics than the one she was dealing with in her head. "Tonight I learned more about the women who founded this program. They and their friends are accepted as couples, just like us. Tonight, some of the other workers talked about their relationships with one another. I felt safe admitting our situation for the first time."

"I don't feel comfortable with you telling people about us," Deborah said harshly. "You know how badly it went for us when the temple women heard about us."

"It isn't like that at Denison House. And I only told the women who are like us."

"It still makes me nervous. I just hope no one tries to steal you away."

"Deborah!"

Deborah's Journal, January 22, 1914

When Miriam came home from her volunteer job this week, she spoke quickly and insistently, as if she didn't want me to ask questions. She spoke of the women who founded the program, but I noticed that tonight she didn't talk of the other volunteers as she did on other evenings. I wonder what has changed.

CHAPTER FOURTEEN

Writing with Purpose
Late January, 1914

One evening, Miriam returned from volunteering with a tale to tell. "I finally met Jewish girls at Denison House! The eleven-year-old girl I'm now tutoring, Rivkah, lives with her mother and four sisters in one room. Rivkah, a dark-haired beauty, has the saddest eyes I've ever seen. There is no joy in her face, and there was nothing I could say or do to coax a smile."

"How unfortunate," Deborah said.

"It got worse. Rivkah's oldest sister, Rachel, 16, arrived to collect her at the end of our session with tears in her eyes. I asked why she was so distraught, and she began to cry in earnest. After I calmed her, she told me she'd been asked to write the story of how she arrived at Denison House after spending a year as a mill girl at the Lowell textile mills. Do you remember the mills of the widely publicized "Bread and Roses Strike" two years ago?"

"Was that about the newly immigrated workers who went on strike when their salaries were cut by two hours per week, reducing money sent home to their families? Wasn't that the Lawrence textile mills, not the Lowell mills?"

"Yes. You remembered it more accurately than I did," Miriam said. "Well, Rachel was pleased they wanted her to tell her story, but she was ashamed she couldn't write well enough to put her tale on paper. She explained she left school at age ten to help her family. She didn't want to disappoint the staff person who had requested the article for their newsletter."

As soon as Deborah heard of this situation, she lit up. "What if I help Rachel write the story?"

"I'd hoped you would say that. Actually, I expected you to offer, so I already arranged for a meeting between you and Rachel."

"You're so clever, my love, and know me so well."

Rachel and Deborah worked together on many occasions to write Rachel's story.

"I'm pleased to use my writing skills for someone's benefit, especially for Rachel, whom I've come to like a great deal," Deborah said to Miriam as they went for a walk on a cold January evening.

"My dear, I'm very proud of you for doing this."

"You haven't even read it yet. Save the accolades until you've seen it. I'd like you to review it before we submit it to the newsletter."

When they got home, Miriam read it. "I'm touched by Rachel's story. I knew very little about the horrible conditions at the Lowell mills for the girls who worked there. This story makes their suffering very clear. I'm pleased you were able to tell her tale so eloquently."

"Thank you. I wanted to make her situation vivid, but not pathetic. Do you have any suggestions for my writing?"

"No. You did a wonderful job. I'm also glad to see you involved in something meaningful outside of work."

"This is the second time I've asked you to help me, and you have refused. It makes me so mad."

"I did not refuse. I just didn't have anything to suggest."

"Well, I'll never become a better writer unless I get feedback. I guess I'll have to find someone else."

"Sorry I couldn't help you."

Deborah stomped off and sulked for the rest of the evening.

Rachel

The next day, Deborah read the completed story to Rachel, and there were tears in the young girl's eyes.

"You did a wonderful job of telling my story," Rachel said. "I was so exhausted that I stopped feeling anything, and I think you captured that."

"That's a wonderful compliment, Rachel. I was really pleased to write this for you."

Deborah had made a nice connection with Rachel. After their joint task was done, she invited Rachel to their home for dinner.

"I want to invite her sister, Rivkah, too." Miriam said over breakfast.

"But if you invite one child you tutor, shouldn't you invite them all?"

"You're right. Please invite only Rachel."

When Rachel walked into their house, she was immediately drawn to Sylvia. She knew just how to treat this baby, getting her to smile and interact in ways that most people weren't able to do.

Deborah and Miriam talked that night about Rachel's natural talent with children. Miriam said, "I'd be comfortable having Rachel watch our baby if neither Mother nor Bubbie were able to handle our child care needs."

"Given the poor health of both of them, this is a comforting thought."

Soon, Rachel became a regular dinner guest. Deborah and Miriam both enjoyed her, but more importantly she was getting to know their daughter. They decided this was a wonderful opportunity to hire her for some child care, to relieve Bubbie from some stress.

Lowell Mills

Rachel began coming one afternoon per week, though within a couple of weeks they increased this to twice a week. They told Bubbie that Rachel badly needed the income, which Bubbie accepted, though it was probable she guessed their real motivation.

While Rachel was working one day, she took Sylvia on a walk where they met a small dog belonging to a neighbor. They played together for a long time, but every time Rachel tried to leave Sylvia cried. Finally, after many attempts, she returned home with a tearful child.

Deborah and Miriam had just gotten home from work when Rachel walked in with the crying girl. Rachel asked Sylvia about the dog to which she had grown so attached. "Did you like the doggie?"

Sylvia sniffled and nodded, but Rachel insisted that she speak. "Woof."

Deborah and Miriam were thrilled that Sylvia had said something and were doubly pleased she linked the animal with a sound, something she'd never done before.

"Sylvia really loves animals," Rachel said.

"Thank you for figuring this out," Miriam replied. "And thank you for encouraging her speech."

"Would you like to go to the zoo with us, Rachel, where Sylvia can visit many animals?" Deborah asked. "Maybe you can get Sylvia to say some other animal sounds."

"I'd love to, but it's very cold outside. Maybe we should wait until the weather is better."

"Let's go on a short visit to Franklin Park Zoo now since it's so close by, and a longer trip when the weather improves," Deborah said. They all agreed to go on Sunday.

On Sunday, Rachel arrived early, dressed for inclement weather. Deborah came downstairs with Sylvia wrapped in her heaviest outside clothing.

"Zoo. Zoo. Zoo," Sylvia said excitedly.

"Time to put on your coat, Miriam."

"We should cancel our plans to go to the zoo today," Miriam pleaded. "It's too cold, and I fear it might snow."

"How could you disappoint your daughter like that?" said Deborah.

"She'd be just as happy to go another day."

"I can't believe you would cancel this trip. Sylvia has been so excited. And it's only a few blocks to the zoo. Rachel and I are going. You can stay home and remain warm. We'll talk about this later."

"I guess I could go," said Miriam sheepishly.

"No. We'll go without you." Deborah grabbed their daughter and the travel bag with her diapers, and headed out the door without looking back.

About an hour later the door opened and the trio arrived home.

"Oh my, what an odor. Why didn't you change Sylvia?" Miriam asked.

"What a lovely greeting. Couldn't you ask how our trip was before complaining?" Deborah asked.

"Well, I wondered why she came home with a dirty diaper."

"It so happens that I tried to change her, but she was unwilling to get undressed in the cold weather."

Rachel stood by, saying nothing.

"Give her to me, and I'll change her," Miriam said.

"No, I'll take care of her." On the way up the stairs Deborah said, "Did you have fun, Sylvia?"

"Woof. Woof."

"No honey. Those were not dogs. Those were sheep. What do the sheep say?

"Woof."

Rachel left quietly, trying not to take sides.

Miriam tried to talk about the zoo with Deborah, but that whole day Deborah stayed clear of Miriam. Any time their paths crossed, it was obvious that Deborah was still annoyed with Miriam for not going.

Rachel's story was distributed by newsletter to staff, board members, volunteers, and anyone interested in giving money to the organization. This created lots of talk at Denison House. The tale was so well received that the same staff person who approached Rachel for her story asked Deborah to meet with another girl with an interesting experience. Deborah was proud her writing was doing some good and happy to work with another girl. She wondered who this new child might be and what had happened during her young life.

(See Addendum for the story of "RACHEL: THE LOWELL MILL GIRL")

Franklin Park Zoo

Franklin Park Zoo Bird World

CHAPTER FIFTEEN

Jealousy

Early February, 1914

Miriam was arranging her hairdo for her volunteer job one evening when Deborah came into their bedroom. "Lately you're spending a lot of time choosing your clothing and fixing your hair for your volunteer work."

Miriam blushed. Before she responded, Deborah continued in a mocking tone, her lips noticeably pursed. "I think you're fixing yourself for your friend, Sadie."

"I want to look nice. It's the only place I go other than work and temple," Miriam said.

"Good excuse. I've noticed a change in you, and I don't like it. Not only are you dressing up for your volunteer work, but you're daydreaming a lot."

"Nothing has changed."

"I think the change is in your attitude. I hope it's not in your behavior."

"Deborah. I'd never do anything you wouldn't approve of. I love you."

"I hope you love only me."

"Certainly, it's only you. And you have a new friend too, Chava. You have seen her several times, and I've never been concerned about your friendship."

"Miriam, you know that Chava is just a friend. I don't see her as often as you see Sadie, and I don't daydream about her."

"Deborah! You are wrong."

"We'll see. But I don't like it!"

That evening, as Miriam walked out the door to pick up Sadie, Miriam thought of Deborah's words and wondered if Deborah was right. Miriam decided she'd have to make certain it was not true.

When she arrived home, Miriam noticed Deborah didn't smile, nor did she say much. Miriam went directly to Sylvia's room to kiss her goodnight, and then to their bedroom. Deborah asked, with a taunting lilt to her voice, "So how was your new girlfriend tonight?"

"Deborah! She isn't my girlfriend. You are!"

"I know you're thinking about her a lot. I see you daydreaming and I know she's on your mind," Deborah said, mimicking a dreamy-eyed look, with her eyes upward and hands clasped.

"You can't know what I'm thinking. I have thoughts of you, a baby, a sick mother, and an old grandmother to occupy me."

Deborah raised her voice. "Miriam, you're thinking of Sadie. I can see it in your eyes when you talk of her. And I noticed you're talking about her less these days. Maybe you're keeping things from me."

"Deborah! There's nothing to keep from you. I've done nothing to upset you. You're being jealous for no reason at all!"

"Time will tell," Deborah said firmly. Then, while looking directly into Miriam's eyes she said bitterly, "If you whisper Sadie's name when we're being intimate, I'll know the truth."

"Deborah! There's nothing going on with Sadie and me. We're just friends."

"As Shakespeare said, 'The lady doth protest too much,'" Deborah taunted.

"Enough talk about this. Tell me about your evening with Sylvia. Is she getting over her earache finally? She gets ear infections often these days."

"I'll let you change the subject for now, but we'll continue this discussion when I notice you daydreaming. And yes, Sylvia seems to be doing better. Those drops the doctor gave us are helping."

But as they lay in bed that evening, Miriam's thoughts returned to her time with Sadie. She could do nothing to prevent it.

The next day, when they got to work, Miriam stayed focused on the tasks at hand, not on her argument with Deborah nor on thoughts of Sadie. But late in the afternoon, Miriam got lost, thinking of what Sadie might be doing right then and what they'd discuss during their next volunteer night.

Just then Deborah called to her, "Miriam. You're daydreaming again. Can't you focus on your work anymore?"

"I'm sorry. I was thinking about work. And about Sylvia. And Mother."

"Stop. We both know what your starry-eyed thoughts were about."

"Deborah!"

Soon after Deborah walked away, Marjorie approached Miriam and guided her into the back room so they could talk privately. "What's going on with the two of you?" Marjorie asked. "You're arguing a lot lately."

"It's nothing. Deborah thinks I'm daydreaming too much. She's jealous I have a new friend at my volunteer job."

"Is it that girl, Sadie, who you keep talking about?"

"Well, yes. Have I been talking about her a lot?" Miriam asked.

"Miriam. You talk about her all the time. It's no wonder that Deborah is jealous. I would be too, if I were her."

"Oh Marjorie. I'll try to stop, but I have been thinking about Sadie. It's hard not to have thoughts about someone so sweet and accepting when Deborah is so irritable these days."

"Has anything happened between you and Sadie?"

"Certainly not. Well, Sadie said a few things. But it was really nothing."

"Miriam, you have to stop this before it gets out of hand. Deborah is a fine girl and the other mother of your child. She's also your business partner. You can't do anything to jeopardize your relationship."

"You're right. I must put all those silly thoughts out of my mind. It's only Deborah whom I love."

"That's more like it," Marjorie said, repeating. "You love Deborah."

"Yes, I do. I only wish she wasn't so hard to live with these days."

"I think you need to change your ways a little, my friend. Otherwise you might lose the best thing that ever happened to you. I love you, Miriam. I want what's best for you, and I'm certain Deborah is what's best."

"You're right. Thank you for being such a good friend, Marjorie. Now let's get back out there before Deborah thinks there's something going on between the two of us!"

Miriam's Diary, February 11, 1914

When I arrived at Denison House tonight, there was a lot of excitement among the volunteers about a Valentine's Day party for the staff and volunteers to be held at the house of some lesbian couples. Some of the volunteers were curious, others elated, and still others fearful, not knowing what to expect. I heard people wondering if this would be a house of sin or a regular home occupied by proper professors. Staff members I know to be lesbians, as well as some I suspected, were the women most enthusiastic about this upcoming get-together. I look forward to going to this party with Deborah.

During this past week, I willed myself to think less about Sadie. It isn't good for my relationship to have these thoughts. Each time my mind focused on Sadie I turned my thoughts to Sylvia, our work at the shop, or how Mother is doing. When I was dressing for my volunteer

work, I got ready quickly, rather than spending extra time fixing myself.
I'm determined to squelch any unacceptable thoughts and to reduce
Deborah's jealous rants. If only it was that easy.

The next morning before work Miriam told Deborah about this Valentine's Day gathering.

"Do you really think I'd go to an event like this?" asked Deborah, after listening to Miriam's explanation of the party.

"I thought you'd be thrilled to be among a houseful of others like us. And I'm certain Marilyn and her girlfriend, Julie, will be there," responded Miriam with a fallen expression.

"And Sadie? I'd never want to spend an evening with her!" Deborah blurted out. "Could you promise me she wouldn't appear?"

"I assume she'd attend. After all, she's been wanting to meet others like herself."

"So now you admit she's one of us. Until now I merely assumed that. I won't go to the party, no matter how much you beg. And I hope you won't attend either." Deborah walked outside to the car with her back to Miriam, never looking back.

For Deborah and Miriam, Valentine's Day was like any other day. They left each other cards on their bed, but neither offered a gift and neither mentioned the holiday.

The Valentine's Day party of the women from Denison House came and went without mention. Miriam heard news, when she volunteered the next week, that it was a wonderful party. This saddened her. She was upset that she and Deborah didn't have this opportunity to be with other couples.

Miriam's Diary, February 15, 1914

It has been difficult to be around Deborah. She's on edge because she's so jealous. She worries about Sadie, and I must admit that there is some validity to her concerns. It's hard for me to differentiate whether my feelings for Sadie have to do with her sweet personality and the ease I find being with her, or whether my attraction is in retaliation for the stress Deborah has caused in my life. Or maybe Sadie is tempting because I've never had an opportunity to be with anyone other than Deborah.

I'm all at once excited and worried. I don't want to disrupt my relationship with Deborah, yet if things continue to progress in the direction they have been going lately, I'm not certain I can maintain things. I love her, yet I'm increasingly frustrated with her.

It was sad that we barely acknowledged Valentine's Day.

SKATING ON JAMAICA POND, NEAR BOSTON.

Winslow Homer's SKATING ON JAMAICA POND, NEAR BOSTON

CHAPTER SIXTEEN

Mothering Sylvia

Mid-February, 1914

Shortly after Valentine's Day, Deborah suggested that they go skating on Jamaica Pond.

"We can bring Sylvia with us," Miriam suggested.

"But she doesn't walk well, so I'm certain she won't skate well either," Deborah said.

"It doesn't matter. She'll be easier to pick up than I am," Miriam replied, smirking.

"Let's try." Deborah took charge of planning the adventure.

They all put on many layers of clothing, climbed into the car, and headed the short distance to Jamaica Pond. There were huge numbers of families dressed in their finest winter outfits, couples enjoying the intimacy of holding each other as they skated, and children tumbling onto the ice with great regularity.

"It's crowded," Miriam said.

"This is certainly a popular place to be," Deborah said.

"The ice is cracked and sometimes uneven," Miriam said, wondering if she'd be able to stay upright at all.

They all ventured onto the cold ice, and Sylvia was the first to fall, even ahead of Miriam. But Sylvia enjoyed herself, licking her gloves each time she fell, enjoying the cold on her tongue.

"Dirty ice," Miriam said.

But Deborah shook her head. "Let her enjoy it. No one ever died from eating dirty ice."

"I hope not."

As Miriam buttoned Sylvia into her blanket sleeper that evening, she said, "I've been thinking about Sylvia growing up. The older she gets, the more she stays the same. I watched other children skating, and she seems so far behind the others her size. I wonder if she'll be further behind each year."

Deborah's forehead wrinkled. "I've had similar thoughts. When I take her to the park or skating, like today, she seems so different from others almost two years of age. Do you think there's more we can be doing?"

"I wish I knew. We both talk to her constantly, hoping she'll pick up language. Maybe we should talk less and give her a chance to learn one word at a time."

"I don't know which is better for her. It's so hard that we've no one to ask questions of."

Miriam put the baby down and brought up the subject that caused many arguments between them, "Maybe you were right and we should go back to The Experimental School again and talk with the nice doctor who examined her."

"No," shot back Deborah. "I thought that initially, but now I feel we should do our best without their help. I fear they'll hold her back since they'll have so little hope for her development. I want to continue doing what we're doing."

"But Deborah, we're floundering, just guessing what Sylvia needs."

"I think we know better than anyone else what our own daughter needs."

Miriam sighed and gave up. Deborah had stood firm on this same issue many times, but Miriam was surprised with her changed position. Then something happened which concerned both girls.

The next day, Deborah bundled Sylvia in many layers so she and Miriam could take her to the park. Sylvia tumbled many times, landing on the soft snow which had blanketed the ground overnight. Before they headed home, Deborah brought Sylvia over to the bench where Miriam was sitting. As Miriam retied the scarf around their little girl's neck, a man approached them and asked, "Which of you is the mother?"

They looked at each other, not knowing how to respond.

"I am certain you are avoiding my question because you know what I am going to say," said the tall, well-dressed stranger with piercing dark eyes. He looked back and forth from one girl to the other. "I am a strong proponent of eugenics. Do you know what that is?"

Both girls shook their heads, despite some knowledge of the disturbing term. They looked at the man while both caressing Sylvia, who was sitting comfortably on Miriam's lap.

"I believe the mother of this child should have no other children. We must keep our race pure and not bring additional children of lesser breeding into this world. It's your moral responsibility to avoid doing this. You must read the new book *The Kallikak Family* and learn the benefit of allowing only the finest specimens of the human race to reproduce. After reading this, whichever of you is the parent will have no more children. And you should have this girl sterilized so she won't produce more inferior children."

The man huffed and departed, leaving Deborah and Miriam stunned. Miriam knew she'd never read this book, but Deborah very much wanted to find out what it had to say.

"Oh, Miriam," Deborah said as she came home from the library a couple of days later. "I found the book the man at the park mentioned, and I sat at the library to read some of it. It was so upsetting I didn't bring it home."

"What was it about?"

"It was a study of a family with a feeble-minded child at a training school in New Jersey. The book claimed that her condition was hereditary. The book dictated that society should rid the world of such people by sterilizing all women with such a child so they would bear no more misfits. It also suggested the sterilization of all feeble-minded people so they wouldn't reproduce."

"What an awful thought," Miriam said. "It would be sad if Ruth was told she could never have another child. I may not be fond of Ruth anymore, but I wouldn't wish her a barren marriage. She has enough difficulties as it is, being lonely and in a difficult relationship. Life without a child would be devastating."

Deborah picked up Sylvia from her crib, an elevated bassinet to keep her away from the cold floors, and said, "We'd have a childless life if it weren't for our little girl."

"I know," Miriam said, looking at Sylvia with love and a deep sigh.

Deborah looked at Miriam with a soft, warm glance as she said, "You're a wonderful mother and it would have been sad if there was no child to benefit from your sweetness."

"That's very kind of you to say, but you're a wonderful mother, too. I know you never ached to have a baby, but you have taken on the parenting role with every bit of skill and concern I could ever want. Had my life included a husband, I wouldn't have such a loving and supportive partner in parenting."

"Nor one who argues with you so vehemently for what she believes is right for our child," Deborah said, eyebrows raised.

Miriam shook her head. "I disagree with that statement. A man, instead of arguing, would have overruled my decisions. You state your opinions but you don't require we always follow your way."

"Some days I'd like to. It's not in my nature to make demands on you, just to repeat my requests."

"And think about what life would have been like for Sylvia had Ruth placed her in an institution, as she'd planned. Sylvia wouldn't have the benefit of a loving family. And I doubt those at the facility would believe in her abilities."

"I know. She's as lucky as we are."

"Deborah, I know you prefer not to go back to that awful school, but I believe Dr. Kingsley is an expert on Mongoloids. I hope he could guide us."

"That's where we differ in our opinions. I think the people there are experts on those who live in their institution. Few of us have kept our special children at home so I fear they know little of what's possible for a child living with their family," Deborah said.

"I agree they aren't familiar with keeping a child like Sylvia at home, but I'd value hearing their ideas. They're more knowledgeable than us about what the children can accomplish and how they learn."

Deborah cocked her head, letting out the breath she was holding. After a moment she said, "I'll agree to another evaluation as long as you promise we'll not blindly follow all their recommendations. I don't want to subject Sylvia to their tests and I won't agree to anything that will be painful or uncomfortable for her."

"Agreed! Thank you so much. Even if we learn one thing to help her, it will be a worthwhile visit."

On their way to The Experimental School in Waltham, Deborah and Miriam first passed through Jamaica Plain, where they noticed signs pointing toward Forest Hills Cemetery.

"Is it possible for Jews to enter a non-Jewish cemetery?" Deborah asked. "I've heard it's a beautiful garden, both a place for interment and an arboretum."

"Where did you hear that?" Miriam readjusted Sylvia in her lap.

"Someone at a shop in Roxbury mentioned it. He was raving about it, saying that the grounds are magnificent, with rolling hills, a small lake, and beautiful plantings."

"They wouldn't be beautiful in the middle of winter! Did you really think we should stop there?"

"No, I don't want to stop anywhere. What makes you think that? We need to get to Waltham."

"I agree. But I'd be happy to come back another time."

"But what about my question about Jews going into non-Jewish cemeteries?" asked Deborah, frustration evident in her voice.

"Don't be so impatient. That's a tough question and one I'm not really sure about. I don't know if it's like going into a church, which we clearly can't do. But my parents never knew any non-Jews well enough to visit them in the cemetery."

"What about the milkman they had for so many years?" Deborah asked.

"They never mentioned wanting to go to his funeral or the cemetery."

"So do you think it might be possible for us to go there? I'd love to explore it. Obviously, not in the middle of the winter, but maybe during the summer when all the plants and bushes are in bloom."

"I'll look into this question. I'll have your answer by the time spring comes," Miriam said.

"I guess the question is not important enough to answer for the next several months."

"Deborah, if it's important to you, I'll get you the answer soon."

They both watched the scenery as they passed through towns they'd hardly noticed on their first trip. Miriam hesitated asking anything of Deborah since her mood seemed foul. She did comment on the beauty of Echo Bridge in Newton Lower Falls, but other than that she mentioned nothing on their journey.

Miriam helped with directions, looking frequently at the handwritten map, which Deborah had gotten during one of her trips to the library. There seemed to be no end to what she found at the Boston Public Library. Miriam was tempted to suggest that Deborah ask her question of the librarian, but she knew that bringing it up would annoy her so she remained silent.

Deborah was obviously on edge about this trip, but as they entered the doctor's office, they were both put at ease.

Dr. Kingsley greeted the girls with a large smile, and they assured him that there were no new problems since their last visit. He directed the conversation exactly as they wished. "You have a beautiful little girl. I'd like to make some suggestions for her care."

Both Deborah and Miriam sat up straight, both hopeful and worried.

"I can see that Sylvia's gait is unsteady so I'd like to encourage physical exercise to stimulate her brain. Creating a movement program for these children was suggested by a Dr. Seguin who believes physical activity will encourage development."

Deborah took a deep breath and spoke up. "We were so worried you would suggest more testing and institutionalization for Sylvia. It's nice to hear you give us some encouragement."

He went on, ignoring Deborah's concerns. "It would also be good to introduce her to music. You can teach her to keep time to the rhythm of songs."

"What a wonderful idea. That would be a pleasure." Miriam turned to Deborah. "I bet we could get Mother to play the piano or sing to her, and Bubbie can have her bang on some pots and pans."

"And as she gets older," the doctor continued, "we can create a calisthenics program, and you can teach her a skill."

"What type of skills do you teach these children?" Deborah asked.

"The girls here learn cooking, housekeeping, laundry, and sewing. We teach the boys woodworking, farming, shoemaking, printing, and broom-making."

Excitedly, Deborah said, "We own a printing shop. We could teach Sylvia some of the easier tasks a little at a time as she grows up!"

"Or, maybe we can teach her to make us all fancy shoes." Miriam smiled.

The doctor continued with a significant statement that put them at ease. "I assume you know you will never be forced to put Sylvia into our institution. It's voluntary to place a child here. Many families remove their children once they've reached the end of their school years so they can help on the farm or at home."

"That's the best news of all," said Deborah, excitement evident in her voice. "We were afraid you would make us place her here and you would want to keep her here forever, which is why we were afraid to come."

"Which is why *you* were afraid," said Miriam.

"No, girls," Dr. Kingsley reinforced. "You can keep her at home with you. I think she's a very lucky little girl to have the two of you to care for her."

By the time they left the office, both Deborah and Miriam were excited. They'd been shown a way out of their dark moods and been given some concrete tasks to work on with their child. Things were looking up.

Miriam's Diary, February 18, 1914

I'm greatly relieved. So often I wonder what our little girl will be able to accomplish in life. After talking with Dr. Kingsley today, I'm encouraged that someday she could develop a skill, which will make her a valuable member of society and be a benefit to our family. I know she'll probably always need supervision, but it would be so nice for her to be

good at something. Even if her talent is shoemaking, sewing, or printing,
it will give her a purpose to her day, and hopefully her skill will be
something useful to us or others. I want to focus on improving her
chances at having a productive life. I hope Deborah can remain calm
around her and not direct her bad moods toward Sylvia.

After dinner the next day, Miriam approached her mother with Deborah's question about Jews going to a Christian cemetery.

"I am not certain, Miriam," Mrs. Cohen said. "I think you should ask Rabbi Feldman. I am certain he would know the answer."

"Oh, Mother. I'm afraid to approach the rabbi. I had an upsetting experience the last time I approached him with a question, and I'm afraid he'll ask me about it."

"What could he have possibly said to upset you?"

Miriam hesitated. "After one *Yom Kippur*, I asked him about asking for forgiveness for being interested in someone of the same sex. I'm ashamed to say that I didn't tell him the question was about me, but for a friend."

"And what did he say?"

"He quoted Leviticus and told me that it was a sin against G-d. He became almost enraged. It really made me fear repercussion from Jews, much like we faced from the Sisterhood women recently."

"I am so sorry he made you feel badly. I am surprised. He is such a wonderful man."

"Yes, I think he is." Miriam turned away, thinking she'd have to tell Deborah she had no answer for her.

"What if I ask the rabbi your question?" Mrs. Cohen asked.

"Would you do that for me? But would he hold that against you if he thought you were the one who wanted to go to a non-Jewish Cemetery?"

"No, I do not think so, dear. I will ask him this weekend."

Mother attended temple with them on Friday night. After services, Miriam noticed her mother heading toward the rabbi, rather than talking to the Sisterhood ladies. During her entire time with Marjorie and her other friends, Miriam kept looking toward the Rabbi's office, wondering what he had said to her mother.

On the way home, Miriam turned to Deborah, telling her that Mother had asked the rabbi the answer to her question. Mother explained what she'd learned.

"Rabbi Feldman said that there is no actual prohibition for cemeteries, like for churches, as far as he knows. He explained that in Jewish tradition burial of the dead is an act of kindness. What we do for the dead is the most sincere act we can perform, so to help the deceased to rest in peace would be considered charitable."

"Sounds like a 'yes' to me," said Deborah.

"Thank you so much for asking," Miriam said as she hugged her mother.

"It looks like you and I will be heading to Forest Hills Cemetery in the spring, Miriam."

"May I go with you? I have always been curious about what it is like," said Mrs. Cohen.

"We will be happy to take you," said Deborah, smiling at Miriam.

Forest Hills Cemetery

CHAPTER SEVENTEEN

Published

Late February, 1914

"Miriam! Miriam!" Deborah shouted into the front hall.

Unused to such yelling, Miriam responded to the alarm by running quickly toward the front door with Sylvia in her arms. "What's wrong?"

"Nothing is wrong. I'm so excited! I've been published."

Miriam let out her breath and said, "Deborah, you frightened me."

"Sorry. I was so thrilled I couldn't help myself."

Mrs. Cohen lumbered down the stairs and asked, "What is all the commotion about?"

"I'm sorry to have upset everyone. Let's all sit in the parlor so I can share the letter and package I have received."

February 17, 1914

Dear Miss Levine;

I am pleased to tell you, my book, Youthful Thoughts, *is about to be published. I am sending you an advance copy so you can view your article in print. As you can see, I found it so significant for young women that I selected it as the first piece. I hope you feel gratified with this, your first publication, and I certainly hope there will be many more to come.*

Now that this project is done, I am excited to find other venues for your work. I found your article "Parenting a Special Child" engaging and informative but I am certain that publications would find your open communication about a special child, as you call her, too disturbing to print. People want to hear about healthy children. Most of your writing would appeal to their readers, but not that article. Please continue to send me more of your commentaries.

Sincerely,
Grace A. Hubbard
Associate Professor of English, Barnard College

Deborah made a sour face as she read Dr. Hubbard's notes regarding her article, but then smiled as she tore open the package containing the book. She couldn't control her excitement as she held out the book at arm's length.

"Oh Deborah," Miriam said with a wide grin. "No wonder you were so excited. I'm delighted." If it weren't for the baby in her arms, she would have thrown her arms around her girlfriend.

Mrs. Cohen joined in. "I am *kveling*, Deborah, so proud. I know you're a wonderful writer, and those were certainly lovely words from your professor."

Deborah didn't correct Mrs. Cohen, avoiding explanation that she'd never taken a class with this instructor and had not even met the woman who had become her mentor. Nor did she mention her disappointment about the wonderful article she'd written about loving Sylvia. She decided to pay more attention to her success than her frustration. Deborah sat back on the chair and thumbed through the book, marveling at her name and words in print.

Miriam handed the baby to her mother and sat next to Deborah so she too could see "Deborah Levine" written in the book. "Sweetie, you bring me as much *naches*, pride, as our baby does."

Pleased with her new status as published author, Deborah was motivated. She told Miriam, "Before Sylvia and the publishing shop entered my life, I had a daily writing practice, but lately I'm so busy I rarely take the time. Now that I've seen my name in print and I've a request for more articles, I want to begin again."

That afternoon, fueled by her enthusiasm, she worked on the piece, carefully avoiding the topic of having a special child.

BECOMING A PARENT

Nothing in my life has been so life-changing as becoming a parent. Having a baby has shifted my perspective on everything. I no longer look at things through my old eyes; I now imagine what my little girl sees.

I notice the dew glisten on the leaves of the tree outside our home. I notice the sun overhead at noon and falling into the horizon at day's end. I see the bright red of an apple and smell each flower as it blooms. My world is enriched by her presence and I love to share my views with her.

When a sound is loud, a light is bright, words are harsh, or attitudes are critical, my senses become alert. I do not want to control her world, yet my instinct is to protect her from the harsh realities of life. There will be plenty of time for her to learn to cope with stress, but for now, she deserves a protected environment.

"Miriam, please read my latest article. I think you'll find it interesting."

"I'll read it after we put Sylvia to bed. I'm really pleased you have begun to write again."

"It was very motivating to get the letter from Professor Hubbard. She made me feel accomplished."

"You deserve the compliments. You're a fine writer and you write about topics that many young women will relate to."

"But not about special children …."

Miriam cocked her head. "You may never be able to write about that one topic, but there are many other subjects that catch your fancy."

"What do you think I should write about next?" Deborah asked.

"How about writing more about being a parent?"

"How funny! That's exactly what this article is about."

"Then I'll certainly find time to read it."

"Maybe you can help me choose another topic. They used to come to my mind all the time, but lately I haven't been thinking about what to write."

"How about an article about being with a woman?"

"I'm not brave enough to do that, but I will write about being in love."

"I look forward to reading that one. You could also write about learning to drive or about your mother. Or you could write a whole book about Ruth. She's certainly an intriguing, though pathetic, character."

"That's an interesting thought. I never considered writing a book. Ruth certainly would be a fascinating character, though I'm not certain I could develop empathy for her from the reader. Who'd relate to such a self-centered person?"

"I did for a long while. There must be others out there who are duped into finding the good in people who have so little to offer," said Miriam.

"My, my! You're becoming insightful in your old age. And I'm impressed that now you're the one thinking about writing topics. I just might try your suggestions. Not the Ruth one for now. I'll save that for later."

"Later, when you've become a famous writer and Sylvia is all grown up, and you finally have time to pen a whole book?"

"Maybe then."

During the evening, after Sylvia was sleeping and all the chores were done, Miriam returned to their room to read Deborah's writing. She sat at their small desk, reviewing the article. As soon as she finished, she smiled up at Deborah and said, "I'm so glad you love being a mother as much as I do. I know Sylvia's medical condition adds concerns to our lives, but she brings us much joy. I wish others who are parenting a special child could learn from your writing, understanding children like her bring more pleasure than *tsoris*, heartache. It's sad that article won't be published."

After a moment of quiet, Deborah asked, "I guess loving a child like Sylvia will never be a popular topic."

"I was impressed with how similar your attitude about caring for our baby is to my own. You talk of wanting to protect Sylvia from challenges, which is usually my style. Typically, I feel your criticism when I become protective of her."

"Don't compare me to you."

"Sorry."

Realizing she would not get a critique of her writing, Deborah hid her sadness and said, "I'll write to Susan to tell her of my book. I'm certain she'll be excited for me."

With a yawn, Miriam said, "I'm glad Susan and Helen have remained our friends since we left New York. It's wonderful we've continued our correspondence. I wonder if we'll ever get to see them again."

"I hope so," Deborah said. "I really like both of them. You go to bed now, and I'll join you as soon as I've finished the letter."

February 24, 1914

Dear Susan,

I'm pleased to tell you I got a letter today from Professor Hubbard, the Barnard instructor who is helping me get published. She sent me an advanced copy of her book and it was a thrill to see my words and name in print. What was most exciting was that she chose my piece to be the first in the book! I wanted to share my excitement with you.

I'd love to hear more about how your life is going since you finished college. In your last letter you said you had not found any work since graduating, which I know is frustrating. I hope you've found something interesting to occupy your time.

When you write back, tell me how your visit with Helen was. She was due to visit you a few days after you last wrote. I assume you had a wonderful time together.

Fondly,
Deborah

Deborah's Journal, February 24, 1914

I was excited with Dr. Hubbard's book, but also annoyed with Miriam tonight. I thought I could distract myself by writing to Susan, but I've returned to feeling frustrated. Again, Miriam didn't give me feedback about my writing even after I asked for it. This has happened multiple times, and she always finds a way to steer the conversation away from what I asked. I have nowhere else to turn to ask for help, though I know I would benefit from guidance about my writing. I fear my style may be too stiff, and I'd like to be more polished when I send things off to Dr. Hubbard. I know no other way to ask for her assistance. I found it hard to lovingly ask again without anger in my tone. I doubt Miriam guessed my aggravation with her.

The next day, Miriam wrote a letter to Helen, informing her of Deborah's exciting news. Though their primary friendship had been with Susan, Miriam enjoyed Helen's calm manner and her artistic skills as well.

After her success with the article about Rachel, Deborah was enthused about helping another child write their story. The next article for the Denison House newsletter was about Mildred, a very sweet nine-year-old with long dark braids and a pretty face. Deborah met with her several times to discuss her experience of being on an Orphan Train, something previously unfamiliar to Deborah. Mildred cried a great deal while telling of her experience traveling to Missouri in search of finding a family of strangers to parent her. She was one of thirty orphan children paraded in front of potential mothers and fathers, hopeful a couple would select her to live with them. Yet, after hearing stories from other orphans, she feared she'd become their newest farmhand rather than a true daughter. Deborah was able to calm Mildred enough to hear of the traumatic process. Her heart broke for this unfortunate child who had lost both of her parents in a tragic accident.

During the two weeks they worked together, Deborah became close to this sweet girl. In an interesting coincidence, the same day Mildred was coming to their house for dinner to meet Deborah's family, the article was published. Mildred had several copies of the Denison House newsletter in her hands when Deborah picked her up. Mildred was thrilled to show her that their piece was featured on the front page.

Deborah's article was met with appreciation, and she was asked to continue working with children to tell their stories. This pleased Deborah, but Miriam worried that having her at Denison House frequently increased the risk that Sadie's name would come up, causing another bout of jealous rage.

(See Addendum for MILDRED'S TRIP ON AN ORPHAN TRAIN)

Mildred

CHAPTER EIGHTEEN

Friendships

Early March, 1914

March began with a huge storm. When it passed through Pennsylvania, the newspapers named it the "Billy Sunday Blizzard" because it hit the same day as a revival prayer service led by the famed evangelist. The *Boston Globe* reported that most of the 3,000 people who had come to hear his sermon were trapped overnight in the tabernacle where he spoke, with temperatures outside plummeting to zero.

Deborah read the newspapers and, with a deep frown, reported to the family, "The papers compared this storm to the massive Blizzard of 1888, with huge winds and significant snowfall. In New York, blinding snow halted trains yesterday, in one case stranding 200 passengers overnight at a Long Island train station."

"Are you worried about your family?" Miriam asked with concern.

"Yes. I wonder how they're managing. I'll try to call tonight if the telephones are working."

"Should we do anything to protect ourselves?" asked Mother.

"I don't think anything is necessary," Deborah responded. "The *Globe* says the storm shouldn't affect us badly in Boston."

There was no telephone connection in New York that night or any succeeding night. It was almost a full week before Deborah finally got a letter from her mother, assuring her that everything was all right.

Deborah also heard back from Susan.

March 8, 1914

Dear Deborah,

I'm not certain when this letter will get to you, since there's been no mail service since the storm struck.

Luckily, we had no destruction. I'm stranded in my home but the only difficulties we had were minor, like running out of milk and having no access to newspapers. We only lost electricity for a while and had to rely on candlelight. I hope you haven't had any problems in Boston.

Your letter contained such exciting news. I'm so happy for you. What a thrill it must be to hold a book that includes your article.

You asked about what I do at home. I volunteer with youngsters at a local school, helping with their writing assignments but that's just one afternoon per week. The rest of my life is dull. I haven't found any work nor much else to occupy my time.

My visit with Helen was wonderful, but it may be the last for a long time. My parents don't understand why we want to see each other or send letters so frequently. I don't know how we'll manage to maintain our connection with their restrictions, so I'm sad most of the time.

I wonder if you have been keeping up with the Suffrage movement, since you haven't mentioned anything about it in your letters. I've been reading the weekly newspaper, 'The Suffragist', which had an exciting article about National Suffrage Day. To commemorate the huge March 3rd Suffrage parade in Washington D.C. last year, they had another parade. It was a wonderful way to raise the national profile regarding this issue. I assume that you knew about Illinois passing the suffrage bill in June, the first state east of the Mississippi and the 11th in our country to do so.

According to the same paper, the Congressional Union announced in December that they had adopted colors, with purple representing loyalty, white as quality of purpose, and green as the color of light and life. Should we march in another parade, I'd be proud to wear these colors.

I look forward to hearing from you again soon. My parents haven't yet complained that we're writing too much!

Affectionately,
Susan

As was becoming the pattern, Deborah wrote back to Susan and Miriam wrote to Helen. They read each other's letters, often adding a comment or two (and then both signed each letter.)

March 11 was the festival of Purim, celebrated every year on the 14th of the Hebrew month of Adar. Purim commemorated the salvation of the Jewish people in ancient Persia, saved from Haman's plot to annihilate all Jews in a single day.

Bubbie presented a plate of fresh *hamantashen*, the special Purim pastry in the triangular shape of the three-corner hat worn by Haman. "Cum. U eat."

"I love the ones filled with prunes," Deborah said.

"That's great, since most of us like the ones with *munn*, poppy seeds, best," Miriam replied.

Mother's appetite had not been great, but she grabbed a *munn* pastry, saying, "If I cannot finish this, please save it for me for breakfast."

"Your *hamantashen* is safe," laughed Deborah.

After a celebratory meal, Miriam said, "Please stay at the table, Mother, and wait for us to come down in our Purim outfits."

Deborah, Miriam, and Sylvia went upstairs to dress in festive costumes for the Purim celebration at the *shul*. They took a large pile of scarves the family saved for this holiday, wrapped them around their heads and arms, and even tied them to their waists so they draped down over the plain clothing underneath. They covered Sylvia in as many scarves as they could fit on her little body, and she laughed each time they added a new one.

The three of them paraded down the stairs, a colorful, silly group. Mother smiled at all their clothing, especially Sylvia who was practically giddy with excitement, then headed to bed.

The small group wrapped their coats around them for the outdoor weather, then left for temple for the recitation of the *Megillah*, the story of Purim.

On the way home, Deborah said, "The event was so joyful, a welcome change from the recent challenges in our lives."

"Agreed," Miriam answered. "The best part of the festivities was when we found Marilyn, the girl from Denison House. I was glad to finally meet her girlfriend, Julie."

"Julie is a dark-haired beauty. Her eyes are piercing, and her skin appeared as soft as a feather."

"Should I be jealous?" asked Miriam, teasing.

"No. I can look, can't I?"

"I'll remind you of that, when you get jealous."

When they got home from temple, Deborah and Miriam put Sylvia to bed and then talked in their room. Deborah turned to Miriam, saying, "Marilyn and Julie are lovely girls. I felt an immediate kinship, much like when we met Susan and Helen."

Miriam smiled. "I'm so glad to hear you say that. I think it would be nice to invite them to our home one evening and get to know them better."

"I'd be happy to spend time with them. I'll leave it to you to take care of the invitation. It's interesting that, even though we've wanted so badly to meet others like us, we haven't contacted Abigail and Margaret, the girls we met at the Suffrage meeting almost two years ago," Deborah said.

"Even though they're like us because they were a couple, they aren't really like us in any other way."

"I thought you were going to refuse to talk with them when Abigail said she seduced Margaret right from her parent's home," Deborah said with a wide grin and a giggle. "And when they wanted to drink alcohol with us, you and I were both stunned."

"And then seeing their sparse, uncomfortable apartment made it clear to me they were too different from us. I think we really need Jewish friends."

Deborah said, "But Susan and Helen aren't Jewish and we like them."

"You're right. I guess it wasn't their religion but more of a difference in social mores."

Deborah changed the discussion a bit. "It's interesting we're discussing our choice of friends because I've written another article, and it's titled 'Friendships.'"

"Interesting coincidence."

"When you read it, I really want more than just approval, which is all I usually get from you. Talk to me about the writing. How it can be improved?"

"I thought I give you feedback," said Miriam, confused.

"No. You usually tell me how wonderful my writing is and just comment on the content. The only way I'll become a better writer is if I get constructive suggestions. I need ideas of how to make my language less stiff and my characters more real. You never do that for me."

"I don't know if I can. I love what you write. I don't know enough about writing to suggest changes."

"No. Forget it. I guess you can't do what I asked," Deborah said with annoyance.

"You're asking for something I'm not good at and then making me feel bad this isn't one of my strengths."

"This is a wasted conversation. Let's just go to bed and I'll find someone else to critique my work."

"Deborah, I don't want us to go to sleep frustrated with one another. I do think it's a good idea for you to get someone else to help you, but that doesn't mean I don't want to read what you have written, nor does it mean I won't try. Please don't give up on me."

Deborah looked at Miriam and noticed tears dripping down her cheeks. She realized Miriam was feeling insecure about her abilities. She wasn't refusing to offer suggestions, merely worrying she wasn't good enough. Deborah took a deep breath and placed her arms around her.

"Let's try. I'll show my 'Friendship' article to you and try not to have any expectations."

"Thank you," Miriam said through her tears. "If I can't come up with a brilliant commentary, I hope you won't be angry with me."

"I'll try to be patient."

"Now hand it to me and I'll get back to you tomorrow," Miriam said, sniffling.

"Thank you for bearing with my hostile style of asking for what I want."

Deborah handed over the article and left the room to wash her face and change into her nightclothes. Miriam took several relaxing breaths and began to read.

FRIENDSHIPS

How does a young woman select the people who will be important in her life? She begins with attachments to her closest relatives and then expands her circle of friends to neighbors and classmates. Later she chooses strangers.

When I evaluate the people I have befriended, noticing their differences and their similarities, I realize that as a young person I chose people most like me. Next, I branched out to anyone unlike my family members, as if retaliating against those people who were thrust on me. With these new friends I discovered new values to consider as mine. These friends showed me ways to think and behave which my family never considered.

Lately, a third phase of friendships has emerged. These are the people I choose, neither because they are like my family nor because they are opposite to them. These are the people who have values similar to my own...

After Deborah returned from the lavatory, she found Miriam deep in thought, sitting at their desk with the article lying to the left, a sheaf of paper on the right, and a pen gripped firmly in her hand. Miriam didn't acknowledge Deborah's entrance but remained focused on the notes she was scratching.

An hour passed, with Deborah trying to read, yet her attention was on Miriam, not on the book.

Suddenly, Miriam put down the pen and said, "I'm ready to discuss this with you now, if you would like. Otherwise, we can wait until morning."

"There's no way I could wait. I've spent a whole hour preparing to hear what you have to say. Go ahead."

"First, I must thank you for giving me the time to get my thoughts in order. Secondly, I want to thank you for your belief I'll have something of value to share. Thirdly…."

"Enough!" interrupted Deborah. "Just tell me your thoughts about my article. I can't wade through your apologies and self-demeaning lecture."

With a sideward glance and a huff, Miriam said, "I do like your article, but I've found places for improvement as you desired."

Miriam then began a series of comments, the first regarding the impersonal nature of the article, suggesting Deborah enhance it with examples from her own life.

Deborah fidgeted a bit, pleased Miriam was up to the task she had assigned but surprisingly uncomfortable with her suggestions of how to improve the article. She thought, "I find myself ready to justify the rationale for my writing, yet that defeats the purpose of my request. Instead, I'll listen to Miriam's suggestions. After all, there's nothing to lose. And maybe, just maybe, it will improve my writing."

"Thank you, Miriam, that was a great suggestion. I appreciate your input," Deborah said stiffly, pretending to believe her own words, and wishing Miriam was still the insecure young woman she had been when they first met..

"Sit back, my dear. That's not all. You have asked for help and I'm ready to offer more suggestions. You don't get off that easily."

Deborah squirmed. Again, changes in Miriam's behavior were surprisingly hard to accept. But Miriam pressed on and offered more suggestions.

The next couple of nights, while Miriam was spending time with Mother, Deborah worked on her article, tearing up page after page in frustration. Finally, Deborah had a draft to share.

"Would you read this over?" Deborah asked quietly, putting her pen down.

"Certainly, but please be kind when I comment."

"I'll try to remain calm, even if it's difficult."

Miriam read. Deborah watched her face for any reaction. Miriam said nothing and tried to keep her feelings from her countenance. Deborah began to pace impatiently. Miriam didn't look up.

Miriam took notes while reading Deborah's piece but said nothing until she'd read it several times. Finally, she said, "I don't think you captured what you wanted to say."

Deborah took a deep breath and opened her mouth to speak, but said nothing. She took the paper from Miriam's hands and tore it up. She then retreated to her bed with her hand across her forehead. Miriam was afraid to annoy Deborah further so said nothing. They went to sleep without another word.

Two more evenings passed with Deborah writing, tearing up pages, and writing again. She didn't talk with Miriam about the process, nor about what she was feeling or thinking. Finally, she produced a paper for Miriam to read.

"Are you sure you want me to read this? Are you ready to hear my response?"

"Yes," was all Deborah said, as she handed the paper to Miriam and left the bedroom so she could read it privately.

FRIENDSHIPS

What is it that matters to me in a friendship? What are the qualities which intrigue me? What captures my heart and makes my connection to another person special? There is no one answer but I can most easily talk about my love of my best friend. (That would be you, Miriam.)

You have touched me by being yourself. You are not like me, nor unlike me. I treasure your ability to stand strong in your own beliefs, despite being challenged. You know yourself better than I could ever dream to know myself, and I treasure you as a model of calm and acceptance. You see the best in each person and forgive them for their weaknesses. You are full of encouragement and you possess a charm which engages everyone, from best friend to stranger. You are wholly yourself.

It didn't matter this was not the story Deborah had set to write down. It was the story in her heart and Miriam greatly appreciated it. She was glad that Deborah understood that it was important that she bring emotions into her writing and she was especially glad to hear Deborah express something positive for a change.

"Billy Sunday Blizzard" in The Scranton Times

Purim Megillah scroll

CHAPTER NINETEEN

Overwhelmed

Mid-March, 1914

Their emotional discussions about writing having been resolved for now, the girls regained their equilibrium and invited Marilyn and Julie to their house one evening.

Following quick introductions, Mother took Sylvia upstairs for her bedtime rituals. Deborah noted how slowly Mother walked up the stairs and wondered whether Miriam noticed as well. Mother rarely stayed downstairs for the evening these days.

But Bubbie made sure to put out a full table of tasty treats.

"Bubbie. How sweet of you to make so many wonderful desserts for us," Miriam said as she brought the girls into the dining room.

After introductions Marilyn asked, "Can you tell me what these wonderful confections are? Both of our families are Spanish Jews, so we eat different foods than what you have served."

"Yu tell them, Miriam. Yu say words better."

"First are her famous *munn* cookies, which everyone is offered as they enter this house."

"Yes. I had some when I first came by, Julie. You should try one."

"These are cherry flavored *rugelach*, which Bubbie made from fruit she canned from our cherry tree," Miriam said, pointing to the small pastries with fruit oozing from all sides.

"And what's this?" Julie asked.

"*Babka*, the best coffee cake you'll ever eat, and another of her specialties."

Marilyn bit into the *babka* first, nodding her head in approval and announcing, "This is marvelous. I'd have a second piece, except I want to try everything Bubbie made."

Julie enthusiastically said, "This might be the best pastry I've ever had" as she licked her lips after her second *rugelach*. "It reminds me of something my grandmother used to make, only better."

While they ate, Deborah asked many questions of Marilyn and Julie of their Spanish ancestry. "I've not known Jews of Spanish origin. What do you know of your family's immigration to this country?"

Marilyn responded first. "Spanish Jews, or Sephardic Jews, as we're commonly called, have been coming to the States since the mid-1600s. The first Sephardic congregation was in Newport, Rhode Island, the Truro Synagogue."

"Did your family immigrate that long ago?" Miriam asked.

"No. My family arrived in the late 1800s following pressure to convert to Catholicism, something that had been happening for centuries. Their parents had been practicing their Judaism secretly, fearful of persecution. They heard of the Truro synagogue while they were still living in Spain and followed several other families from their village. My parents were both born in Newport, where they remained until after they were married."

"How fascinating," said Deborah. "And what about your family, Julie?"

"My family was originally from Portugal. They arrived in the United States, afraid to admit their religion to anyone. My grandfather was buried in a cemetery sponsored by the reformed temple, Ohabei Shalom. Until then, Jews had to be buried in New York or at the Truro Cemetery. They moved to Dorchester, where they were able to openly practice their Judaism, attending a small *shul* on Blue Hill Avenue. Now, they find comfort in being accepted at Mishkan Tefila, where your family attends services, despite being Sephardim."

The four girls drank tea and ate until they were bursting, enjoying their discussion of their family histories, excitedly talking over one another and laughing often.

The next week Deborah and Miriam received an invitation to Marilyn and Julie's house. On their way Miriam said, "Even though these girls live on their own like Abigail and Margaret, I'm certain their home will be more in keeping with our lifestyle."

As they walked into the small apartment in the West End of Boston and saw the tasteful furnishings, Deborah whispered, "You're correct." There were comfortable divans with lace antimacassars on the arms, a matching settee with an afghan draped over the back, a mahogany side-table with a decorative vase awaiting spring flowers and a bowl of Mary Jane candies, a new peanut butter and molasses confection made in Boston.

Marilyn and Julie were great hostesses. Julie served spicy ginger cookies and Tower Root Beer, made by another new company near Boston.

All four girls enjoyed the rich taste of the drink and Deborah said, "Delicious! This could be habit forming!"

"I'll buy more for the next time we get together," Julie said.

"Our house next week?" Miriam offered.

They had a delightful time, including a walk in their neighborhood. While they walked, Marilyn and Julie, who had only lived there a short time, told what they'd learned of the history of the West End.

"This neighborhood was built up in the early 1800s by a respected architect, Charles Bulfinch. He built homes for the wealthy, displacing the Irish people who lived here. Bulfinch also built Massachusetts General Hospital's domed granite building, which you can see to the left if you look out our front window," said Marilyn, pointing to the distant left.

"In the next block is the historic West End Market on the corner of Grove and Cambridge Streets," Julie said.

They passed the market, with chickens hanging in the windows and Hebrew lettering on the doors. Marilyn continued the monologue. "And when the wealthy moved to Beacon Hill, the area became an enclave of Africans, many of whom remain in the neighborhood. Then the Jews, fleeing persecution in Prussia and European countries, moved here. This neighborhood quickly filled with new immigrants."

"That's why we like it here," Julie said. "We feel comfortable as Jews, but we also find this a culturally rich area."

The conversation continued, with both Marilyn and Julie enthusiastic about the West End. Deborah and Miriam commented on the similarities of how this neighborhood and Denison House both honored multiethnic people. All agreed that they appreciated having the influence of folks from other cultures.

On their way home, Deborah said, "We've made some lovely new friends, with values similar to our own."

"I agree. Being isolated was one of our biggest challenges. And I suspect Marilyn and Julie will introduce us to others we will also like."

With a deep frown and furrowed brow Deborah said, "As long as we won't be anywhere where Sadie will show up."

Again, thought Miriam. She did not want to start another argument so she changed the subject. "I'm worried about Mother. I was thinking throughout the evening, about her taking care of Sylvia. I'm concerned about how she managed. I hope Sylvia went to bed without any problems so Mother could go to sleep early and not get up once she was in bed."

"Your mother seems to be slowing down, getting involved in fewer activities, taking more naps, and retiring to bed earlier."

"I noticed, too," Miriam said. "I offered to go to the doctor with her, but she refused. Mother seems to accept her lack of strength and vitality and never complains. I doubt I could be as accepting."

Deborah nodded. "She's a strong woman."

Back home, Miriam talked about Bubbie, too. "Have you noticed that Bubbie rarely leaves the house? I wonder whether this is due to her worry about my mother or her own failing abilities. She no longer goes to *shul*, and she's even been reluctant to visit her sick friends. When one of her closest companions died, she attended the funeral service, but didn't go to the cemetery to throw dirt on the grave. She's never done that before. It scares me that she's weakening."

"I'm worried, too."

The next day, their worries continued, adding Hannah to their concerns.

"Miriam, I'm sorry I wasn't able to come in this morning," Hannah said when her sister arrived at her home after work.

"We managed without you." It was a dishonest claim.

"I hope to work tomorrow, though the last few mornings have been very difficult," said Hannah.

"Do you think there's a problem?"

"I don't know. Mother told me I should feel better after the first three months, but I am already four months along and not much better. I hope my time isn't like Ruth's. She was sick for the whole nine months."

"I certainly hope you aren't! Would it help if William checked on you at lunchtime to see how you're doing?"

"The mere mention of lunch makes my stomach turn."

"Then it would be wise for him to take his meal at home with you to encourage you to eat. I hope your morning illness subsides soon."

"So do I. It came on suddenly. I hope it will stop just as quickly."

Hannah's illness didn't stop for the remainder of her fourth month. Bubbie made her chicken soup, which William delivered each day.

"Most days your soup was the only thing Hannah could eat," Miriam told Bubbie when she got home from her sister's one day.

"She be sick every day?" Bubbie asked.

"Yes. She spends much of her day navigating between the bed and the bathroom. Sometimes she can't even make it to the toilet, so William leaves a pail by her bed, which he cleans as soon as he gets home."

"He be good man."

"Yes, he is. I'm so glad she has him."

When Hannah's illness continued, William insisted she call the doctor. After coming to their house two times, but not being able to provide any relief to Hannah, he suggested she go to the local hospital, the New England Hospital for Women and Children on Dimock Street in Roxbury.

She fretted about getting there without vomiting all over herself and the car. William brought along several buckets and washcloths, and they made their way the short distance to the hospital.

Hannah disembarked from the car, nauseated, leaving a puddle of spit-up in nearby bushes before entering the large brick building. William guided his weakened wife down the halls, where she held the contents of her stomach throughout her appointment.

Their visit was somewhat successful. Hannah was given a few remedies: eating well, getting fresh air, and restrictions on wearing a corset. She thought the treatment suggestions ridiculously obvious, yet she was intrigued by the New England Hospital for Women and Children. She learned that it opened in the early 1800s, started by a German woman doctor who had been a professor of obstetrics at New England Female Medical College. She hired only female staff. The hospital hired the first woman doctor ever trained to be a surgeon and created the first nursing school in America. Hannah was convinced she'd be happy to give birth there should she not be able to deliver her child at home with a midwife. Actually, she hoped that would be the case.

After Hannah reached the milestone of five months, the nausea stopped suddenly, never to return. She doubted the corset restriction had any bearing on her renewed health. She came back to work, finding they were significantly behind on filling orders, so everyone was grateful for her arrival. Because her increased girth made her more awkward working the presses, she stuck to typesetting and translation duties.

In addition to worrying about Hannah and Mother, Deborah was also concerned about her own family. "My mother doesn't sound cheerful these days, and I haven't heard from my father, except that one telegram he sent saying he loves me. My mother rarely mentions him in her letters. I think something is wrong."

Miriam suggested, "I think you need to visit with them. That way you can see for yourself."

"But we're so busy …"

"No 'buts.'"

After conferring with the family, Deborah sent her parents a letter, suggesting they visit Boston. They would need to arrive before April 10, the beginning of Passover. She hoped the horrible weather wouldn't delay their trip. The papers continued to compare the heavy, wet snow to the Blizzard of 1888.

It was a couple of weeks before Deborah got a reply, and by then there were signs of Spring.

March 22, 1914

Dear Deborah,

I'll visit you next week. Father won't be with me. I'll send you details of my train schedule once I book my trip.

Mother

Deborah was disappointed that her reunion with her father wasn't to happen this trip.

One evening, well after dinner, when everyone was settled into their customary seats in the parlor, William burst through the door, long past the time he would usually come calling. "We are going to the hospital. Hannah is bleeding—down there."

"Oh, no," Miriam said with a flush across her face. "Do you want me to come with you?"

"No. I will stop by and tell you if she is all right."

"Even if it's the middle of the night?"

"Well, I guess that would not be good." William scowled.

"Please leave us a note under the door if everything is fine. We'll see it when we get up in the morning."

There was little sleep in the house. Miriam paced most of the night, awakening Deborah many times. Deborah held her tongue, never complaining. They didn't tell Mother about Hannah's condition, thinking there was nothing she could do anyway. They'd tell her in the morning, once they knew everything was fine.

There was no sign of William during the night and no note awaiting them in the morning. Deborah's first words, after she checked the doorsill for William's distinctive scrawl, were, "Get dressed, Miriam, and I'll drive you to the hospital."

Just then William pulled up in the car and Miriam ran outside with her coat thrown over her shoulders. She found a very pale William walking towards the house. "They think the baby is fine, and Hannah stopped bleeding. There may be nothing wrong, but they want her to stay in the hospital for another night. I'm going home to get her some bedclothes."

"Please stop by for me on your way back to the hospital," Miriam said shakily.

Deborah offered, "I can drive you."

"No. I'll go with William. You need to take care of Sylvia and then go to the shop. Without William, Hannah or me there today, it will be important for you to be there."

"Promise you will call to tell me how she is."

Miriam smiled weakly. "Everyone will know about Hannah being in the hospital if the nosy telephone operator listens to the call."

"I'm not worried about that. Let's hope Hannah and the baby are fine."

By mid-afternoon, there was still no call from Miriam. As Deborah was putting on her coat to go to the hospital, the telephone rang.

"Can you hear me?" Miriam shouted into the receiver, unused to using the telephone.

"Yes, Miriam," Deborah whispered. "Please talk softer or you'll hurt my ears."

"Sorry," she practically mouthed. "They've decided to keep Hannah one more night, but it's likely she'll come home tomorrow. They're suggesting she stay in bed and not go back to work."

"Not at all? Her baby isn't due for almost four months. How will we manage without her, especially when Yiddish speaking customers arrive?"

"William will help those who don't speak English. What's most important is that she take care of herself so she'll have a healthy baby," Miriam said disapprovingly.

Deborah hung up, concerned, thinking of ways they could distribute Hannah's work so no one person would be overwhelmed.

Deborah's Journal, March 16, 1914

So much is going on, and much of the worry seems to land on me. Sometimes they rely on me too heavily. I wish Miriam could take over more. After all, it's her family's business. I need to think of ways to get more help at the shop.

And now my mother is coming for a visit. What bad timing. I want to see her, but I'll not be able to take time away from the shop to visit with her. And why did my father refuse my invitation? I haven't heard from him in so long. I wonder if he continues to resent me for being with a girl. I miss having him in my life.

I hope Hannah is fine. Just one more worry.

Although already overwhelmed, Deborah agreed to write another article for the Denison House newsletter. She waited until after she and Miriam got to their bedroom one evening to tell Miriam about this since she was certain Miriam would be annoyed.

N.E. Hospital for Women and Children

"You'll need to spend many evenings working on this, but you're already exhausted," Miriam said, landing hard on the wing chair and shaking her head side to side. "Please tell them that you can't write this article."

"I told them no, but when I heard that Elizabeth, the 14-year-old girl whose story I'll tell, was the victim of a broken home because her mother is a suffragette, I couldn't resist."

"You have a family at home that needs you. I need you to watch Sylvia so I can spend more time with Mother, who is failing more each day. I also need to visit my sister since she's stuck at home on doctor's orders."

"Don't be so selfish. I need to do this for myself. You have Denison House, and I need to have something that interests me."

There was no persuading Deborah to give up this assignment. She had become fascinated with Elizabeth's story of being thrown out of their home by a father unwilling to support his wife's fight for women's right to vote. She felt badly for the girl, who had gone from a home of wealth and comfort to sleeping in a park with her sisters and mother, and then to the safety of

Elizabeth

Denison House. She'd never return to her previous life due to her mother's political convictions. Deborah wondered about her own convictions and how hard she'd fight for her own beliefs.

Deborah and Elizabeth met evening after evening until the article was complete. Once Miriam read the article, she understood Deborah's need to tell this story. She was pleased to get to know Elizabeth when Deborah invited her to dinner on several occasions once their task was complete.

(See Addendum for STORY: ELIZABETH: DAUGHTER OF A SUFFRAGETTE)

CHAPTER TWENTY

Breakdown

Late March, 1914

As Deborah helped her mother off the train and onto the crowded platform at South Station, she said "I'm glad you've come to Boston. I've looked forward to your visit. I've missed you."

"I'm glad to be here," Mrs. Levine said flatly, offering a small squeeze rather than the warm hug Deborah expected.

"I was hoping you and Father would both come. I've not seen him since he sent me that sweet telegram." But when she looked at her mother, Deborah could see something was wrong. "What is it, Mother? Is Father ill?"

"He's fine. But I've not been doing well. I've been worried about you."

"I'm doing fine. I sense better than you," Deborah said.

"I'll be fine now that I can see your face and see the happiness that was missing when you were in New York."

"I wasn't in good spirits during my last trip to New York. When Father rejected me from his life, I was lost. I'm so relieved that he's come to accept me as his daughter again."

Miriam, who had been standing off to the side of the platform, interrupted their conversation and greeted Deborah's mother warmly. Much to her surprise, she received a perfunctory kiss on the cheek. She also noticed Mrs. Levine seemed different.

During the day, Deborah's concern increased. She noticed her mother had grown thin and frail, no surprise since she hardly ate anything. Her skin was pale, and she didn't smile at all.

When they sat alone in the parlor on the second afternoon while Miriam was out for a walk with Sylvia, Deborah asked her mother, "Will you tell me what's wrong? Are you sick, Mother? Or is it something else? I've never seen you like this."

"I've been despondent lately. I've worried about you and also about your father. Since he dismissed you from our home, nothing has been the same. I felt forced to choose between loyalty to you and to my husband."

"I don't quite understand. Is there something I can do to help?"

Mrs. Levine broke into unexpected sobs and then became entirely unhinged, much like Deborah had been when her father had rejected her. Deborah put her arms around her mother to soothe her, but the crying continued until Mrs. Levine was gasping for breath. Deborah, who had never seen her mother cry like this, held her tightly.

As she ran out of tears, Mrs. Levine spoke softly into her daughter's neck. "I need to tell you the truth about that telegram. Do not be angry with me."

"Why would I be angry that he sent me such a sweet note?"

"He did not send it. You were so upset when your father rejected you, I felt I needed to do something to give you hope. I sent the telegram and signed his name."

"Mother, how could you do that? I've always trusted you to be honest with me." Deborah began to cry. "Does this mean he has not accepted me back into his life?"

"I'm afraid not."

Deborah's eyes bulged as her mind blurred. As she took in the news, tears formed in huge droplets. She clutched at her stomach and rocked back and forth.

Mrs. Levine managed a barely audible "I'm sorry" as her uncontrollable crying recurred. She could not seem to stop.

How could Deborah comfort the very same person with whom she was furious? Unable to reprimand her, given her fragile state, Deborah said nothing, but brought her mother close. Torn between her anger at her mother's deceit and her need to care for the woman whom she deeply loved, Deborah was lost. The two of them sat, their arms entangled and their hearts at the edge of breaking.

Feeling very alone, Deborah realized she didn't know the person who was sitting beside her. She was not the loving mother who had always comforted her. She was not the virtuous woman who had always shared openly and honestly. Her mother had taught her that telling the truth was of greatest importance, yet she'd lied.

When Miriam came home with Sylvia, she looked at the two tearful women sitting on the couch and wondered if someone had died. She took a deep breath, asking, "What's wrong?"

More tears followed, and finally Mrs. Levine said, "Deborah will explain." Then she looked away.

Deborah sat with her mother for quite a while but could not manage to say much of anything. Eventually, Miriam took Sylvia upstairs, and Mrs. Levine said to Deborah, "I'm going to rest. It was a long trip." She headed upstairs.

Deborah followed Miriam to their bedroom where they discussed the horrible situation.

With Deborah crying in deep, racking sobs, Miriam held her in the same way she did when Deborah's father had first rejected her and the same way Deborah had held Miriam following her own father's similar reaction. Miriam also wept, reliving her own experience once again. Once the tears stopped long enough for either of them to speak, they decided they needed to tell Mother and Bubbie. There would be no way to hide their emotions.

At dinner, after explaining what happened, there was little conversation. Mrs. Levine stared straight ahead for most of the meal, saying nothing. Deborah managed little other than, "Please pass the salt." After dinner, everyone headed to their own rooms.

In the morning, Deborah came downstairs to find her mother standing by her suitcase, though she wasn't due to leave for another week. Deborah took a deep breath and said, "No, Mother. You mustn't leave. I'm upset with you and distraught regarding Father, but I've learned that running away from difficult situations isn't the right way to behave. Miriam has taught me that."

No response.

"You must stay, and we must work this out. I'm disappointed in what you did, but I know you did it to protect my feelings. I love you."

Mrs. Levine stood still, showing no emotion. She didn't open her arms to Deborah, as she would have done any other time. She didn't cry. She just stared ahead silently.

"Mother. You're scaring me. You don't seem like yourself at all. I think you should sit down."

Mrs. Levine, still silent, did not move.

"Come with me. I'll put you to bed."

Deborah put her arm around her mother's waist and escorted her upstairs. She put her back to bed, fully clothed. It would be too intimate to undress her. Her mother said nothing at all, behaving like a small child needing to be cared for. Deborah was torn about what to do but left her alone and went to find Miriam.

"Miriam," Deborah said, entering their room. "I'm very worried about my mother. She's behaving very oddly. She's not talking and merely stares straight ahead. Do you think we should get the doctor?"

"Let's see how she is tomorrow. I'm sure she'll be fine."

She wasn't fine the next day, nor the day after, so Deborah reluctantly called the doctor.

The doctor's visit made everything even more frightening. "You need to send her to the asylum. She's had a breakdown and needs rest," he suggested. "There is a fairly new facility in Cambridge called the Boston Psychopathic Hospital, a department of Boston State Hospital. That would be a good place for her."

Deborah and Miriam looked at one another, stunned. Deborah said, "We'll decide by tomorrow morning whether to hospitalize her."

After the doctor left, Deborah, Miriam, and Mrs. Cohen sat in the parlor, discussing the situation. Sylvia sat quietly on Miriam's lap.

"I want to keep her here," Deborah said softly, the corners of her mouth turning downward.

Mrs. Cohen agreed. "We can take care of her. Love and rest will make her better."

"And Bubbie's good cooking will give her strength," Miriam added.

"I'll tell the doctor our decision," Deborah said shakily, "I'm really scared. She has never been like this before. And I feel awful that I caused her so much stress."

"It is not your fault," Miriam said, putting her arm on Deborah's shoulder. Mrs. Cohen nodded in agreement.

There was little change in Mrs. Levine's behavior. The next evening Mrs. Cohen brought some cookies upstairs to her. "I hope these raise your spirit." There was no response.

Deborah forced her mother to eat and brought her to the bathroom periodically since she didn't initiate any behavior. After two days, the day before her mother's scheduled departure, Deborah announced to everyone at dinner, "My mother certainly can't return to New York. I need to contact my father to let him know what's happening."

Miriam looked at Deborah with soft eyes and offered, "Do you want me to contact him?"

"No, she's my mother and I'll do it."

Mrs. Cohen said, "Please offer for him to come here. Maybe seeing him will help your mother."

Deborah nodded.

WESTERN UNION TELEGRAM COMPANY

To New York City, NY   March 22, 1914

Chaim Levine

Mother is unwell. Dr wanted her in asylum
but we can care for her here. Please come.

Deborah

Miriam stood by Deborah when she returned from sending the telegram and said, "Oh Deborah. How difficult this will be for you if your father comes. Will he be in the same room as you? Or even in the same house as you? Will he ignore you and pretend you aren't here?"

"I have no idea, but my mother needs him."

The next day, Deborah received the following Telegram:

WESTERN UNION TELEGRAM COMPANY

Received at Roxbury, Mass   March 23, 1914

Deborah Levine

Arriving on the 4:08 p.m. train today.

Father

"I'll ask William to drive me to South Station to pick up your father," Miriam said. "If you want to be elsewhere when he arrives, I'll make certain he's all right."

"I'll be here at my mother's side as I've been since she fell ill. If he chooses to ignore me, so be it. I'm here for my mother, not for him."

"You're a brave girl and I'll support you through this."

At South Station, Miriam waited on the platform, worrying. When she spotted Mr. Levine getting off the train, her heart thumped loudly. When she first tried to greet him, no words came. On her second attempt, she found courage. "Hello, Mr. Levine. I'm glad you have come. I'm certain Mrs. Levine will be glad to see you."

"I hope so," Mr. Levine said. The usually talkative man could muster no further comment, but his bloodshot eyes gave clues to his distress.

As they reached the waiting car, Mr. Levine nodded to William, who sat upright in the driver's seat. After a quick introduction, they climbed into the car and all remained silent during the ride home. Mr. Levine didn't comment on the sights of the city and Miriam explained nothing. As usual, William avoided small talk.

Mr. Levine thanked William for the ride, and followed Miriam into the house.

She offered, "Your wife is upstairs in bed, where she's been for the past week. Deborah's with her. I'll introduce you to my mother, grandmother, and Sylvia later. Right now, I'll take you to Mrs. Levine."

"Yes. Please do."

Mr. Levine and Miriam ascended the stairs silently, with his suitcase in tow. Miriam opened the door to the bedroom, let him inside, and stood in the doorway. Mr. Levine put his valise down and walked toward the bed. He nodded at Deborah, who was sitting in a chair holding her mother's hand, then glanced toward the diminished body of his wife. Deborah rose and Mr. Levine put a hand firmly on her shoulder as he turned his attention back to his wife. He looked directly into her eyes with a sorrowful look. Deborah backed away, saying nothing. He approached the bed and reached out to touch Mrs. Levine's arm, bending over to kiss her.

"Chaim. You're here," Mrs. Levine said softly, finally noticing her husband. These were the first words she'd uttered since climbing into the bed.

He reached down, putting his arms around her in the first hug Deborah ever saw between them. Deborah nodded to Miriam, heading to their room.

"How are you doing, honey, seeing your father for the first time in more than a year?"

"Anxious. Relieved. Sad. Overwhelmed. I don't really know what to feel. I was glad to see him, grateful he acknowledged me. But I'm so distraught about my mother it's hard to separate my feelings about him from my worry about her."

"I hope she'll come out of her sad state now that he's here with her," Miriam said. "Ruth said it was helpful when I sat with her while she was feeling blue. I hope your father's presence will be equally comforting for her. *Zal is zayn azoy*, may it be so."

After an hour or so, Miriam knocked on the door to announce dinner. Mr. Levine asked to stay in the room to eat with his wife. Miriam agreed to bring up the dinner tray.

After another hour Mr. Levine left the room, looking for the water closet. Deborah heard him and bravely went up the stairs. With her heart pounding loudly, she approached him before he returned to the bedroom.

"How is she, Father? Did she eat anything?"

"Yes. She ate most of the meal. She seemed very hungry."

"Thank G-d. She's hardly eaten during this past week. I'm so pleased your presence was what she needed."

"I'm glad I came."

"I'm pleased you're here," Deborah said, choking a bit on her words.

"I want to go back to her."

"I left a glass of water for you beside the bed. Is there anything else you need before you go to sleep?"

"No. I have everything."

"Good night, Father. Sleep well. See you in the morning," Deborah said in the same manner she used every night of her first twenty-one years.

"*Gay ga zinta hate*, go in good health." This was how he always responded to her and it made Deborah smile despite her anxiety.

She went back down the stairs where she knew Miriam was waiting anxiously. Miriam threw her arms around her, asking, "How did it go?"

"Better than I imagined. Father spoke with me as if we'd never stopped talking. Also, he said mother ate her whole meal as if she were desperately hungry, which I'm certain she was."

"Thank G-d. On both accounts."

"I think I'll sleep better tonight than I have since my mother took ill."

"And since your father rejected you. Let's head up to bed. Sylvia has been fast asleep for hours. I think it's time we join her."

"Did you have to remind me of Father's rejection?"

Miriam was surprised that now that the crisis was calming, Deborah was returning to her acerbic tone.

The next morning saw more improvement in Mrs. Levine. When Deborah brought breakfast upstairs, she found her mother sitting in a chair. She greeted Deborah with a barely audible "Good morning."

Deborah couldn't help releasing a large tear, which slipped down her face onto the tray. "Good morning, Mother. It's wonderful to see you sitting up. I hope you enjoy breakfast. Bubbie made your favorite—pancakes."

There was no response, and her mother seemed to slip momentarily back into a distant stare. When her father said, "It looks wonderful. I'm certain we'll enjoy it," her mother perked up and nodded.

"Maybe you'll feel well enough to come downstairs for lunch."

"We'll see," said her father.

At lunchtime, Mr. Levine requested the meal be brought to them, but mid-afternoon, when the house was quiet, he was able to entice his wife to come down the stairs. She was shaky on her feet so he held her tightly on the stairwell. As they sat, Bubbie came into the room, introduced herself, made a few comments in Yiddish, and handed the baby to Mrs. Levine as if that were the most natural thing to do. Mrs. Levine held Sylvia on her lap, stroking the child throughout the afternoon.

When the girls walked in the door after work, they found Deborah's parents and Mrs. Cohen sitting comfortably together in the parlor, with Sylvia taking a nap in Mrs. Levine's arms.

"What a wonderful sight," said Deborah with damp eyes, as she kissed her mother on the cheek.

Her mother kissed her back, and Deborah was certain the healing had begun, both in her mother's spirit and in her father's heart.

The next day, Deborah received a letter from Susan.

March 20, 1914

Dear Deborah,

I know you haven't been following the suffrage movement as you used to, but I thought you would want to know about the major event which happened yesterday. The U.S. Senate voted on women's right to vote, the first time there was such a vote since 1887. Unfortunately, the measure was defeated, but only by one vote. It makes me hopeful this will be voted on again, and we, as a country, will finally do what is right, to offer equality to women.

Fondly,
Susan

This note brought Deborah back to thoughts about the world outside her home. It reminded her that before this latest crisis, she and Miriam had intended to get re-involved with the suffrage movement, though neither had found the time nor focus to do so. She could hardly wait to tell Miriam the news. Maybe they'd get involved now after such an encouraging event. That is, thought Deborah, if Miriam wasn't focused on her new friend, Sadie. She could not shake that thought from her head.

Over the next few days, a pattern emerged. Deborah's parents got out of the house each day for a walk, and they all had dinner together, which was surprisingly comfortable. After Hannah's doctor released her from her bed restriction, she and William joined them. This newly conjoined family was quite at ease with one another.

There was no conversation between Deborah and her father about their long time apart, and initially they just talked about their patient's care. As Mr. Levine became more comfortable, he began asking questions, such as: "How does this city differ from New York?"

He gradually offered more personal queries. "Do you have nice neighbors?" "How does your *shul* differ from ours?" "Do you work long hours every day?" He included his wife in the conversation as much as possible and was even able to draw Hannah out of her shy silence on several occasions. He, as with most fathers, didn't pay much attention to Sylvia, though he was tolerant of everyone else's focus on her.

Gradually, and with great awareness, Deborah began to talk about her life in Boston. She was careful to avoid conversations alluding to the challenges which she and Miriam had faced at *shul*.

Deborah cautiously told her father about the publishing shop, and to her delight he seemed interested. He asked, "How do you prioritize which projects you work on first?"

"We complete things in the order they come in," Deborah said, wondering why her father had questioned this.

"You might try looking at all your work every few days and make decisions about which jobs to complete ahead of the others. You can prioritize by many other criteria, not just by the order they came in."

"I never thought of that, Father. What a great idea."

"And once you have a plan, you can tell people when their order might be ready, based on your present workload. People will then have a realistic idea of what to expect."

"And I can give my important clients priority so they don't have to wait for their job to be next," Deborah said, taking his suggestion seriously and realizing the positive ramifications this change might bring them.

After her father smiled and nodded in approval, Deborah asked, "Father, would you be willing to come to the shop and see how it works? I'd welcome other suggestions."

"Certainly, Deborah, but your mother is my priority."

"What if you both come?"

The next day Mr. and Mrs. Levine accepted a ride downtown from their daughter, and he complimented her on her driving skills. And when they reached the office, he seemed impressed with everything, especially with the number of jobs they were completing each week. He commented repeatedly on Deborah's business acumen. Mrs. Levine said little, yet seemed interested.

When they got home, the conversation between Deborah and her father was extremely animated as they discussed the publishing business. He suggested they hire more staff to keep up with the current workload and allow them to take on more. Deborah was thrilled with his involvement, adding a new dimension to their relationship and helping speed their healing process.

After business talk, they moved seamlessly to a discussion of their Boston *shul* and later to Sylvia. Mrs. Levine offered a few comments regarding their child, which pleased them all.

Mr. Levine also brought up the case of Leo Frank, the Jewish factory supervisor for the National Pencil Company in Atlanta, Georgia, who was tried for murdering his fourteen-year-old employee, Mary Phagan.

"Have you heard of this case?" Mr. Levine asked.

"No. Tell us about it," Miriam said.

"Leo Frank was president of the local B'nai B'rith chapter. Many Jews feel antisemitism was to blame for the authorities targeting him. Back in August Mr. Frank was accused of raping and murdering a young girl who worked for him. Public outrage regarding her murder reached a fever pitch, and the factory watchman, a black man named Conley, and three others were arrested in the case. Later, Conley and the others were released, and Mr. Frank was convicted of murder. Many Jewish groups took up his case, thinking the conviction was based on his religion."

"Oh no!" Deborah said, wide eyed.

"The situation was worse than could be imagined. Mr. Frank's throat was slashed by another inmate while he was in jail, but he survived. He was found guilty, and within weeks of the trial friends of Frank sought assistance from northern Jews. He has already been through an appeal, though his sentence was not commuted and another appeal was set."

"I wish there was something we could do," said Miriam.

"You need to leave it to us lawyers right now," said Mr. Levine. "I'll keep you informed about whether his conviction is overturned."

"Please do."

Mrs. Levine continued to improve, coming downstairs for each meal on the arm of her husband. She was a mere outline of her former self, but she was making significant progress.

Deborah's father decided his wife was doing well enough to go to temple for Shabbos. The previous weekend, with Mrs. Levine's situation so critical, they'd all ignored the Sabbath.

"What a lovely service and such a beautiful *shul*," Mrs. Levine said after the prayers ended, displaying a bit of her old enthusiasm.

Leo Frank

"I'm so glad you enjoyed it," Miriam said. "If you feel up to it, I'd love to introduce you to some of our friends. We meet for a short while after services. They've heard much about you I'm certain they'd be happy to make your acquaintance."

With a deep breath and a sideward glance toward her husband, Mrs. Levine said softly, "But I'm not myself. I would not make a good impression."

"We don't need to do this," Miriam said hesitantly.

"She'll do fine," Deborah gave Miriam a critical look, as she placed a hand on her mother's shoulder. "We'll stay just long enough for introductions."

Mrs. Levine agreed, and they headed to the spot where Deborah and Miriam's friends met. Marjorie was the first to approach and, as usual, she was delightfully warm. After a few more introductions, they bid good-bye with Deborah wanting to protect her mother.

On Shabbos afternoon, the four of them took Sylvia to the nearby Arnold Arboretum. Since the stroller was difficult to fit into the car, they took turns carrying her.

Miriam offered a travelogue in the same manner both her mother and Mrs. Levine had done in other locations. "The Arboretum was founded more than forty years ago by Harvard University as part of the Emerald Necklace, a chain of parks around Boston. Frederick Law Olmsted, a brilliant and talented man, designed this, calling it a 'great country park.' It connected Boston Common to Franklin Park, stretching around the city for over seven miles."

"We know of Olmsted," Mrs. Levine said. "He designed Central Park in Manhattan."

Miriam grinned. "How silly of me to forget."

It was a pleasant day, though Mrs. Levine was still weak and needed to rest frequently. Both Deborah and Miriam returned to work on Monday.

By midweek, Mr. Levine said to his wife, "I think we should return to New York. What do you think about that?"

Mrs. Levine smiled.

That evening Deborah and Miriam talked. "I think I should go with them, Miriam. What do you think?"

"I agree that you should go, but I don't feel I can leave at the same time. I can't leave Sylvia or the publishing shop, but mostly I need to be with my family for Passover."

"I understand," said Deborah. "Mother and Bubbie would be lost without you for the holiday, and Sylvia would do better keeping to her regular routine. Maybe it would be good for us to each spend the holiday with our own family."

Miriam wondered whether Deborah really needed to go, or whether she was looking for an excuse to get away.

The next morning, Deborah spoke with her father. "I'll travel to New York with you to watch over Mother when you return to work."

"What a good plan," said Mr. Levine. "I was worried about leaving her alone all day. I don't think she's quite ready for that, though she's certainly much improved."

As Deborah packed her bags, her stomach was sour. She turned to her journal for comfort.

Deborah's Journal, March 30, 1914

It's worrisome to think I'm about to be my mother's sole caretaker, without Miriam, Mother, or Bubbie for support. What if she gets worse again? Also, I'm concerned that my father and I will have a great deal of uninterrupted time together. Will that be awkward? Will he ask questions I would rather not answer?

I'm also worried about leaving the shop. It will be a terrible burden for everyone since I don't know how long I'll be needed in New York. The office will be closed for the first two and last two days of Passover, but there are many workdays when I'll be absent. How will they manage without me?

In addition, I'm worried about leaving Miriam. I'm aware Miriam will be free to see Sadie all she wants during my absence. I'm not certain if this is a realistic concern, but I can't put this thought out of my mind.

Arnold Arboretum

CHAPTER TWENTY-ONE

Separation

Early April, 1914

An hour into their six-hour train ride to New York, Deborah looked to the row on her left. Her parents had drifted off to sleep, lulled by the train's rhythmic sounds. Did her mother have wrinkles across her forehead before? Was the graying at her father's temple new? Were they holding hands? Maybe this crisis brought them closer to one another.

Deborah looked around at the well-appointed car. The rich mahogany ceiling and walls, velvet maroon drapes, and plush seats created a comfortable atmosphere, but Deborah could not relax. She decided to write to calm herself.

Deborah's Journal, April 7, 1914

In addition to worries about providing adequate care for my mother, I'm also concerned about what I'll say to my brother and sister when we get to New York. They've been left in the care of staff people for the past couple of weeks, which I'm certain was uncomfortable for them. Father called them a few times, but they were out of touch with Mother the whole time. They must be concerned and confused.

Also, I'm acutely aware of the discord between Miriam and me. I'm worried this time apart could accentuate our troubles. I feel insecure, not certain our love is strong enough for us to survive this period of strain. Is Sadie an actual threat to our relationship or is the problem between us bigger than my jealousy? Why has this happened? Am I at fault, with my disagreeable nature? Or is there really reason to be concerned? I wish I knew the answer. It's hard to trust we'll survive our emotional distance intact.

Writing only made Deborah more anxious, so she put away her journal and closed her eyes. It was quite a while before she drifted off to sleep. Finally, like her parents, she was rocked to sleep by the train's motion and the constant hum of the locomotive. She didn't awake until the conductor announced, "Grand Central Station."

Once home, Deborah's mother was more expressive of her needs though often inaudible. She seemed to have few emotions other than sadness, but being home added some comfort. Deborah made a sincere effort to make everything seem normal, but nothing was.

Deborah found her siblings distant. They didn't know how to behave with their ill mother. Milton's typical humor was absent, and Anna wasn't her chatty self. Deborah knew she needed to carve out some time to talk with each of them individually.

Worry about Mrs. Levine permeated the whole house. Deborah sat with her during the daytime, prompting her to conversation and some minimal activity such as needlework.

Deborah called home every few days, a huge extravagance. She told Miriam, "I miss you, but I am glad I am here to monitor my mother. I've encouraged Mrs. B. to visit her, and now she's making daily visits."

"I miss you also. Mrs. B. always knows just what to say," Miriam said.

"She certainly does. She's engaging my mother, getting her to talk more. While this has been going on, I've noticed a change in my relationship with Mrs. B. She's beginning to feel more like a friend, rather than the adult who saved us from disaster."

"I know what you mean. Although she's ten years our senior, we're now parents and part-owners of a successful business, which makes her feel more our equal."

Deborah hesitated a moment. "We've matured more in the past two years than I imagined possible."

"Some days I feel very old."

As Deborah planned, one of her first tasks after she arrived in New York City was to get the house ready for Passover, which was only a few days away.

Mrs. Levine said, "It's time to clean the kitchen of *chametz*, anything not *kosher for Passover*. And I'll tell the kitchen staff which holiday foods to buy. My list includes *matzoh*, *matzoh farfel*, *matzoh* meal, and *kosher for Passover* wines. Is there anything missing?"

"Eggs! Bubbie gets 12 dozen eggs for the holiday!" Deborah said with a smile.

"We won't need that many. Our Passover will be simpler. I'll also remind them to remove all wheat, rice, and other grains from the house."

"And don't forget to tell them no corn, beans, lentils, or other legumes."

Deborah and her mother guided their two kitchen staff to switch to the Passover dishes, pots, and utensils, which were stored in a back closet to be retrieved for this eight-day holiday.

"I'll have the cook change the dish drainers and dishcloths. That's the one thing they forget to do each year," Mrs. Levine said.

Deborah talked of Passover as if it were any other year, though the pared-down guest list included just the immediate family, plus Mr. Levine's aunt, uncle, and two cousins. Mrs. Levine supervised the preparation of the traditional foods, including *charoses*, *gefilte fish*, chicken soup with *knaidel*, brisket, and potato *kugel*.

At the *Seder*, Milton, as the youngest boy, would be responsible for asking the Four Questions. "Do I need to do this again? Can we invite some younger boy to join us for the holiday so this isn't my responsibility?"

"You always enjoyed your part before," Mrs. Levine said.

"But Mother! Now I'm seventeen, not a child."

"You're still the youngest boy at the table, so the responsibility is still yours."

When Passover arrived, familiar smells permeated the dining room. Deborah looked at the *Seder* plate and watched the meal served on the same platters used during her whole childhood. She became nostalgic, thinking back to both her grandmothers sitting at their Passover table. She also reflected on Miriam's *Seder*, missing her and Bubbie's special kitchen talents.

Milton not only fulfilled his responsibility with the Four Questions, but he helped his father tell the story of the exodus of the Jews from Egypt. As he chanted in Hebrew, Deborah noticed that his voice had changed to a lower register. Milton and Anna added levity to the first *Seder*, with his jokes and her tales of adolescent drama. Mr. Levine focused on the service, Mrs. Levine on the food, and Deborah on her parents.

The second *Seder* was an even smaller group, without any invited guests. Both days were a huge change from tradition when a roomful of people typically gathered for the service and meal, but the holiday was a good step in getting back to normal life.

The day after the second *Seder*, Deborah spent time with each of her siblings, something she'd rarely done since Miriam entered her life.

"Come sit with me on the couch, Milton. We never get any time together, and we're finally alone for a while. I want to hear what's going on in your life," Deborah said to her brother, who obediently sat down.

"Going on in my life? Nothing much."

"Now that can't be true. I know what it's like to be seventeen. School is full of challenges and friendships are complicated too," Deborah said, enticing him to say more.

"I guess so."

"Let's start by talking about what's going on with Mother. There's been much commotion, and I've no idea what anyone has said to you about her. I worry Father told you very little."

"No one talks to me. It's as if I'm not a real person."

"You're old enough to know the whole story."

"No one thinks I know anything. They treat me like I'm stupid or I'm the same as Anna. She's just a childish girl who only cares about getting her own way."

"It certainly sounds like you've not been treated like the smart young man I know you to be. We can talk about Anna later, but right now I want to concentrate on Mother."

Milton had figured out she had had a breakdown and he was very worried about her.

"Yes, when she was visiting with us, she was very distraught. She was not talking and barely eating. We called for a doctor, who thought she belonged in a hospital. Did you ever see signs that she was becoming ill?"

"She's been acting strange ever since you were here last time. I know Father stopped talking to you, but no one would tell me why. Mother tried to explain why he was angry, but she did a really bad job of making an excuse. I think he's angry because of Miriam. Because of you and Miriam."

Deborah gulped. "So why do you think he's angry with the two of us?"

"Deborah. I'm not ignorant. I know you two sleep in the same bed. I've known for a long time that you're together—sort of like being married, but not exactly."

"You're right, Milton. I'm very sorry I never respected you enough to talk with you about this. I guess you were still young when this started, and I never seemed to find the right time or way to tell you."

"Well, you moved in together. My friends called it a Boston Marriage. Do you call it that? And then you took Sylvia to live with you, so how come you never thought I understood?"

"I guess I was too caught in my own worries to think about you. I've been as bad as Mother and Father, leaving you out of adult conversations. But now you're almost as old as I was when I fell in love with Miriam." Then, with a lump in her throat and an awareness she was going to say this out loud, she said, "Yes, we're in love."

"Thank you for finally telling me. I had figured it out so it made me angry that no one said anything to me."

"Well, it's about time I treated you as an equal, not as a young boy."

"I'm not that young. Now I'm almost old enough to join the army."

"Oh, Milton. Are you thinking of joining?"

"I am. As soon as I'm old enough, on my next birthday, I plan to do just that. And I've already signed up to go to boot camp this summer in Gettysburg, Pennsylvania. Several of my friends have also signed up."

"Tell me about boot camp."

"Everyone agrees a great war is going to happen. They set up two military instruction camps for college students. I'm eligible because I've been accepted at Columbia University for the fall. They'll teach us the skills necessary in warfare."

"Does anyone else in the family know about your plans?"

"No. They wouldn't care."

"I disagree. They love you very much. I think they've been overwhelmed with all the problems I've caused."

Milton smiled. "You've certainly done that."

Deborah explained a little more about Father's rejection and admitted he'd not talked to her at all during her last trip to New York. She told him that when Father came to Boston they had to talk about Mother and that broke the silence between them. Deborah became tearful while explaining about their reunion, and Milton reached out and held her hand.

"Thank you for your support. I'm so glad we had this time to talk, Milton," Deborah said, regaining her composure.

"I am too. You feel like my sister again, not merely some stranger who upsets my parents."

"I'll do my best to cause less friction in the family, though my life may always be a problem for the rest of you. But I'm glad to have you back in my life. We grew far apart, even though I always loved you a great deal."

"I love you too."

The next day, Deborah sat down with her sister, Anna, to see if she could improve their connection as well. It did not start off well.

"I'm offended."

"I'm sorry if I've said anything to upset you, Anna," Deborah said with concern.

Anna sat down hard on the divan to get Deborah's attention. "You're just like the rest of them. Everyone treats me like a child. You don't understand that a fourteen-year-old has feelings and even intelligence."

"I know you're bright, and I certainly didn't mean to ignore your feelings."

"Everyone does. You do, too."

"Let's see if we can change that. I'm here to listen. Please tell me what's going on in your life."

"Ever since Mother got sick, everyone avoids telling me what's going on. She gets all the attention, and no one cares about me anymore."

"Certainly we care about you. I'm happy to explain everything to you and answer any questions you have. First, please tell me what you have figured out."

Anna took a deep breath and began, "Mother is insane. She hardly talks, has to be reminded to eat, and rarely leaves her bedroom unless someone tells her to do something. She's not said much of anything to me. That seems like madness to me."

"Anna, Mother had a mental collapse. We're trying to help without sending her to a hospital."

"A hospital for lunatics? Would she have to stay there?"

"We're trying very hard to avoid that. With all the attention everyone is giving her, she's improving."

"Improving? She certainly doesn't seem improved to me," Anna said with a snicker.

"Yes. She's doing much better than she was when she was in Boston. She's eating better now that she's with her family. We're making her stronger."

"Why did this happen, Deborah? Is this something I can catch from her?"

"No, sweetie. You can't catch it."

"There you go again, calling me sweetie. I have a name. You can call me Anna, not one of those silly names you called me when I was a child."

"I'm sorry. This may take some practice. I need to remember you have grown up and need to be treated differently."

The discussion went along in this manner, with Anna being more concerned with her own needs than her mother's, typical of a fourteen-year-old's view. Deborah did her best to explain their mother's condition, but Anna wasn't really interested. She just wanted to know when her mother would return to her old behavior, a question Deborah wished she could answer.

Before long, Anna changed the subject to talk about a new boy at school who she liked a lot. She had wanted to tell her mother about this, as would have been the case before their mother's collapse. Deborah listened and must have said the right things because Anna seemed pleased to once again be the focus of conversation.

Back in Boston, Passover, which began on April 10, was unlike any Miriam had ever experienced.

"Marjorie, it was very sweet of your parents to invite my family to join you for the holidays," said Miriam.

"I knew things wouldn't be the same without your father to lead the services, and the strain of cooking would be hard on Bubbie."

"You're right. Bubbie is not up to the task this year, and Mother is also weak. I worry about her a great deal too. She's refused to go to the doctor, even though I asked her several times."

"I know how you fret about them both. I am sorry that your Mother won't get medical advice. I hope it will help to make things easier for you to be at our home for Passover."

"I was looking at this holiday with dread, and now you've helped me look forward to it fondly as I always have. And I know Hannah and William are pleased also."

"Your family has always felt like part of my own family, so we are thrilled to include you," Marjorie said with a warm smile. Then she added, "I'll also help you ready your home for the holiday. It's too much for Bubbie and you to do, and I doubt Hannah is feeling up to helping this year."

"You're a true friend."

Marjorie helped Miriam bring all the Passover dishes up from the basement and gather all the *chametz*, the foods not blessed for the Passover holiday.

"I'd like to send our *chametz* to Denison House, where people will appreciate our foods," said Miriam.

"That's a wonderful plan. We usually sell ours to a non-Jewish neighbor for a penny, but I'll be glad to gather my food to send along, too."

"I'll ask William to take care of the delivery."

"Or I could ask my boyfriend, Micah, to do this," Marjorie said blushing. "He's planning to spend most of the holiday with my family."

Miriam smiled. "This is a sure sign that your relationship is serious. He would never have left his own family's holiday table unless he was feeling very attached to you. Maybe it will soon be time for a wedding."

Marjorie's face turned a deeper red. "Miriam!"

William and Hannah picked up Miriam, Sylvia, Mother, and Bubbie and drove them to Marjorie's home for both nights of Passover. The *Seder*, the combined service and meal, was equally lovely each night, with a room full of welcoming guests. The table was set with delicate pink-flowered Passover dishes only brought out for this holiday. The table linens, embroidered by Marjorie's grandmother, were a reminder of the lovely lady who had passed away last year but was still present in everyone's mind.

Of the cousins present, it was the youngest who was most excited, as evidenced by his repeatedly asking whether it was time yet for the *Ma Nishtana*. He was finally old enough to recite The Four Questions. Though he had practiced for weeks, he needed a little help from his older brother, who sweetly whispered the next line when he got stuck.

The adolescent cousins giggled as they drank their second tiny glass of Manischewitz wine, the sweet *kosher for Passover* wine enjoyed at most American *Seders*. Their parents reminded them to be careful not to drip the red, syrupy wine on the special table linens, but they always seemed to add at least one bright red spot to the cloth.

The service went on for several hours. Mrs. Cohen tired, as did Bubbie and Sylvia, who became a little fussy. William noticed their fatigue, as evidenced by Mrs. Cohen's slumped position and Bubbie's occasional closed eyes. He whispered to his mother-in-law, "I will drive you home as soon as the meal is done."

Hannah, who was now in her sixth month said, "The baby in my belly wants to leave, not me." Everyone giggled.

None of them stayed for the conclusion of the service and the eating of the *afikomen*, the *matzoh* saved for the end of the meal. They also missed the tradition of two more glasses of wine.

That night, when Miriam headed to bed, she thought about other Passovers with Father reading the entire service in such quick Hebrew that no one could follow, Mother setting a beautiful table, and Bubbie cooking the traditional meal. That was never to be again, which made her sad. She also missed Deborah being by her side. She fell asleep with tears in her eyes.

CHAPTER TWENTY-TWO

Temptation

Late April, 1914

After the eight days of Passover ended, Miriam found herself returning to her pattern of fixing her hair carefully when getting ready for Denison House and choosing her favorite dress (the one with the slight plunge to the neckline). She looked herself over in the mirror approvingly, grinning at her image. But thoughts of what she was doing panged her, and her grin turned to a pout. She knew her behavior was dangerous.

Miriam noticed Sadie had recently been paying more attention to her own appearance than when they first met. Although there had been no improprieties between them, the air felt charged whenever they sat together in the back room chatting after their shifts ended. Miriam felt the calmness and lightness of Sadie pulling her.

When Miriam arrived at Denison House the first week after Deborah left for New York, Sadie commented on how nice Miriam looked. Miriam blushed. "Thank you, Sadie," was all she said, thinking about how to tell Sadie that Deborah was out of town. Each went to her regular shift with school-aged children and after the tutoring ended, they both hurried to their usual meeting spot.

"Deborah went to New York to be with her mother," Miriam blurted out as soon as they were alone, barely able to keep this news quiet another moment.

"How long will she be gone?"

"At least another week."

"Well, that's really good timing," said Sadie as a tinge of red covered her cheeks. "My family has gone to visit relatives who weren't able to come during Passover. I chose not to join them because I didn't want to miss coming here. They worried I might be lonely but maybe we could get together."

"I'd like that," Miriam said quietly, her heart was beating wildly in her chest.

"Would you be free to come to my house tomorrow evening?"

Miriam explained she'd need to arrange for Bubbie to watch the baby as Mother wasn't feeling up to watching Sylvia for long periods. She also told

Sadie that Bubbie went to bed early, necessitating only a short visit. But they excitedly made arrangements.

The next day, Miriam could hardly concentrate at work. She was distracted by thoughts of her evening alone with Sadie. Marjorie noticed her distraction, assuming it was because Deborah was gone.

Work ended and dinner was quick. Bubbie, as usual, ate earlier in the kitchen. Miriam fibbed a little, telling Mother and Bubbie, "Some of the girls from Denison House are getting together for the evening. Would you care for Sylvia so I could join them?"

It wasn't a real lie since Sadie was a girl from Denison House, though it just was the two of them and not a group as she'd implied. Miriam handed the baby to Bubbie, promising to come home in a few hours.

As Miriam walked the several blocks to Sadie's home, she couldn't wash the smile off her face. She worried neighbors might ask why she was so gleeful. Then she worried others might see her walking by herself or going into a stranger's house alone. *Am I doing something wrong?*

As she turned onto Sadie's street and she saw the house where she met Sadie many volunteer nights when they traveled to the train station together, she got excited. As she headed up the walkway, guilt took over and she considered turning around and going back home. Just then the door squeaked open and Sadie stood there. She'd obviously been watching through the window.

"Welcome to my home," Sadie said with a huge grin. "I'll show you around since you have never been inside. Give me your hat and shawl first."

Sadie helped Miriam off with her shawl, caressing Miriam's shoulder slightly while doing so. The touch made Miriam shiver involuntarily. As Miriam handed her hat to Sadie, their fingers lightly brushed, and all Miriam's attention turned to that touch.

Walking through the first floor, Miriam noticed that Sadie's house was similar to her own with a lovely double parlor decorated in varied shades of blue, Miriam's favorite color. The kitchen was the mirror image of her own, and there was a pantry and storage room in the spot where Bubbie's room was located.

When Sadie offered to show Miriam the upstairs, Miriam's breath caught. She remembered taking Deborah upstairs to her bedroom when they first met. This felt too personal and she refused the offer.

Miriam sat in the formal parlor while Sadie readied a pot of tea and a plate of cookies she'd prepared in advance. When she arrived with the treats, Miriam looked at her, really looked at her. Her features were pleasant, with small eyes the shade of a bluebird. Her nose was delicate, but it was her mouth that was most distinct. Her lips were large, full, and pouty. They were often slightly parted, especially when she was concentrating on something as mundane as pouring a drink. Sadie's full head of hair was light brown and fell in unruly puffs around her face. Miriam imagined running her fingers through the soft-as-air strands, then stopped herself as Sadie handed her a cup.

At first, their conversation was a bit stiff, both of them feeling awkward with the potential of intimacy. But by the time they'd each consumed her first cup of tea, they relaxed and began chatting naturally as they usually did at Denison House. Miriam felt her shoulders relax, and she sat comfortably in the overstuffed parlor chair as Sadie talked of her long-term friendships with girls from her *shul*. Miriam talked about her friend Marjorie, then Ruth. They found themselves laughing and enjoying the silly tales Miriam wove about Ruth's prancing around in her bathing costume for all the boys. When the conversation turned to the story of Ruth giving birth and not caring for her own baby, the talk became more serious. Sadie had not known the details of how Miriam became a mother. Sadie asked many questions, never being invasive, but expressing interest in Miriam's life.

Soon, the time came for Miriam to return home to relieve Bubbie of her child care duties. When Sadie retrieved her shawl, she wrapped it around Miriam's shoulders rather than handing it to her. Miriam was aware of a spark when she was touched. Sadie must have felt it too because she put her arms around Miriam, holding her a bit too tightly for a good-bye hug. They stayed in this position for several seconds, much longer than was necessary. Miriam felt the pull of Sadie's body and wanted to stay like this, but her mind took over and she pulled away. As she did so, she felt Sadie's lips brush her cheeks lightly. Now Miriam was certain Sadie was feeling the same way she was and that was frightening.

"Thank you for coming," Sadie said as Miriam created more space between them. "Would you like to come again another evening?"

"Maybe," said Miriam, torn between her increasing desire and her awareness that this was becoming risky. She found herself saying, "You could stop by the shop one day and we can go out for lunch." This felt a safer way to be together.

"I plan to be downtown tomorrow, and I'll not be far from Newspaper Row. Shall I stop by then?"

"Fine. See you tomorrow at noon."

Miriam departed with both excitement and fear.

The next day, Miriam talked with Marjorie and Hannah.

"I have a friend from my volunteer job stopping by for lunch." Miriam deliberately avoided mentioning Sadie's name lest she blush. Additionally, she didn't want either of them to repeat the name to Deborah.

Hannah scrunched her cheeks and asked, "Lunch? Where can you go for a *kosher* meal?"

"We'll go to the small *kosher* bakery a few blocks from the shop. That's the only place I can think to go downtown."

Miriam headed out the door just before noon, waiting on the side of the front entrance to meet Sadie when she arrived so they wouldn't be seen. The two of them greeted each other with a perfunctory hug, neither wanting to pull attention in their direction. They walked arm in arm as was the custom for two young women walking down the street, though Miriam noticed Sadie held her arm more tightly than any of her other friends. She assumed no one else would notice.

When they arrived at the bakery, the girls' glances fell on the tall pile of *challah* and the parade of people picking up their bread for Friday night Sabbath. They sat at one of the three tiny tables in the corner after ordering bagels, lox, and cream cheese at the counter. They ate slowly, enjoying the food and especially their time together. The smells of the freshly baking bread and pastries were too much to resist, so once done with their bagels each ordered a raspberry *rugelach*. They sipped tea with the mouthwatering treats, thoroughly licking their lips with each bite. Miriam wondered whether Sadie really had planned to be downtown today since she had no satchels to tell of her errands.

During their short lunch, Sadie asked, "Is there another time that we can get together?"

Miriam, leery of asking to leave the house another time, was unsure what to say. She didn't want Sadie coming to their house and risk Deborah being told of their meeting. Instead, they arranged to meet the next day to attend Sadie's temple, Avath Achim Anshe.

Miriam wasn't used to going to a different *shul*. But because Hannah attended *shul* with William, and neither Mother nor Bubbie was likely to go, only Marjorie would be aware of her absence. Well, maybe their other friends too, but Miriam hoped no one would mention this to Deborah.

Saturday morning arrived and Miriam began the walk towards the temple. Sadie met her at the appointed meeting spot and suggested something very bold—that they skip *shul* entirely.

"I've never missed attending services in Boston, only in Western Massachusetts where there was no *shul* to attend." Miriam said. And, as she worried about spending an entire day alone with Sadie, she refused the tempting suggestion.

After services, which Miriam found delightful, they left immediately rather than staying for the traditional luncheon. Instead, they headed to Sadie's house, walking at a rapid clip. There they feasted on a meal that Sadie had prepared before Sabbath. They had no plans following lunch, which made Miriam anxious.

Sadie sat on the couch in the parlor and invited Miriam to sit next to her. As soon as Miriam sat down, Sadie took Miriam's hand in hers and began gently rubbing it. Miriam bristled. This was quite bold and unexpected. Miriam withdrew her hand, and Sadie's features dropped.

"What's the problem?" Sadie asked, tilting her head forward and opening her eyes widely.

"I can't do this."

"Do what?" asked Sadie with a cockeyed smile, trying to lighten the mood.

"You know," said Miriam. "Just because Deborah is out of town, I can't pretend she doesn't exist."

"I don't want you to feel uncomfortable," Sadie said, but there was disappointment in her voice.

Miriam looked directly into Sadie's sad eyes and said, "I think I should leave." And she did.

Two evenings later, after Miriam put Sylvia down for the night and Bubbie and Mother had both gone to bed, Miriam went to the parlor with a book. As she settled into a comfortable chair, she heard a quiet knock at the door. Startled to hear a knock so late, she asked who was there, listening behind the door.

"It's Sadie. May I talk with you?"

Miriam opened the door to Sadie and said, "Come in."

Sadie looked around and asked, "Has everyone gone to bed?"

Sadie

"Yes. I just placed Sylvia in her crib, and Mother and Bubbie have already gone to their bedrooms."

As Miriam turned to lead Sadie into the parlor, Sadie reached for Miriam's shoulders, turning her around to face her. She moved in very close and sweetly placed a gentle kiss directly on Miriam's lips. Stunned, Miriam pulled away and stared at Sadie.

"I've been wanting to do that for a very long time," whispered Sadie as she assertively pulled Miriam into a deep embrace and kissed her more firmly. Miriam tried to move away, but Sadie placed more pressure on her lips and ran her fingers through Miriam's hair. She moved as close as she could to Miriam's body.

They stood in the doorway, kissing with such passion they became lost. Their tongues glided into each other's mouths and their hands explored each other's bodies. Miriam's heart beat wildly and a soft moan escaped her. As Sadie's hands vigorously massaged her breasts, Miriam heard a door upstairs open, and both girls froze.

She heard a faint call. "Miriam, could you get me some water? I forgot to bring a cup to bed with me."

Miriam, rattled, called back, "Certainly, Mother."

She straightened her clothing and headed to the kitchen to get a glass of water for her mother, whispering to Sadie, "I'll be right back."

When she returned just a moment later, Sadie was sitting on the couch, awaiting her with open arms.

"No. No more," Miriam told Sadie. "This cannot be. You must leave. We can't continue with such behavior, no matter how much we both want it."

"I'll leave, but I must tell you I'm encouraged that you wanted those kisses as much as I did. I'm relieved I didn't read you wrong."

"You did not. But it can't happen again. Never."

"Then I will love you from afar."

Miriam saw to it that Sadie left the house instantly and closed the door behind her with both relief and fear.

Miriam didn't see Sadie again during Deborah's absence, but that didn't stop Miriam from reliving their kisses over and over in her mind.

Miriam's Diary, April 21, 1914

How wonderful it was to give in to Sadie's insistent lips. They were as soft and full as they appeared. Her kisses were so different than Deborah's,

more sensual and sweet, although equally insistent. I know she cares
deeply for me, but how do I feel about her? Is it Sadie whom I desire, or
just an escape from this terrible time of disappointment in my relationship?

I'm overwrought with such terrible guilt. Why did I let Sadie kiss me?
It's a horrible thing I've done, exactly what Deborah feared I would do.
Will I ever forgive myself? If Deborah ever found out, I'm certain she'd
never forgive me.

After writing this down, Miriam realized she couldn't risk Deborah ever seeing these words. She ripped the page carefully out of her diary and tore it to shreds, throwing it in the fireplace, to burn all evidence of her betrayal.

After two weeks in New York, Deborah decided her mother was stable enough for her to leave. She missed not only Miriam and Sylvia, but also her working and writing life. She knew the business was suffering in her absence, and she missed the responsibility that sat happily on her shoulders. Deborah hoped she was missed at home as well. She nervously scheduled a train trip, not certain if things had changed at home. Was Miriam relieved to have her gone? Had she been seeing Sadie? She sent a telegram to Miriam, notifying her that she was to return.

CHAPTER TWENTY-THREE

Discord

Early May, 1914

On the train ride home, Deborah read the newspaper to take her mind off her mother, Miriam, the business, and everything else that was troubling her. To her astonishment, on the front page she learned about the huge suffrage parade in Boston on May 2, National Woman's Suffrage Day. How could she and Miriam have been unaware of this? Had Susan mentioned something about this in one of her letters? Nine thousand suffragists had marched through the Boston streets past thousands of onlookers. The papers said it was the greatest parade of women in the history of New England and similar to previous parades in Washington and New York. Yet she had missed it.

Deborah took out letter-writing paper, and wrote a note to Susan, re-dedicating herself to this movement.

May 3, 1914

Dear Susan,

So much has been happening for me. I'll catch you up with the most important issues. It would take a book to tell you everything!

Most significant in my life right now is that my mother had a mental breakdown. She lied to me, pretending my father had forgiven me, yet she was torn apart by her own dishonesty. My father and I have reconciled, which has assisted in her recovery and has calmed my nerves.

At the same time, we're worried about Miriam's mother, who seems to get weaker every day, though she'll not tell us what's wrong. Hannah is pregnant, which is wonderful, but her morning illness causes her to miss a great deal of work. We're constantly getting more projects to complete and every day we seem further behind.

I've been tending to my mother in New York for two weeks, and I'm writing you from the train as I journey back to Boston. While traveling, I just read in the newspaper about the huge suffrage parade, which took place yesterday in my very own city! I'm ashamed I missed National Woman's Suffrage Day completely. It pains me to think I've been so caught up in my own life that I was blind to such significant progress. I plan to renew my dedication to the cause.

The final issue, and the one of greatest significance, is that Miriam and I are having a difficult time in our relationship. I've been jealous of a young woman with whom she volunteers. I don't know whether there is truth to my concerns, but my fear of their possible intimacies has made me ill-tempered.

I'm sorry this letter tells only of problems, but that's all that surrounds me these days. I hope your life has taken some wonderful turns and that you can cheer me with some good news.

Fondly,
Deborah

As Deborah's train traveled toward Massachusetts, Miriam's anxiety increased. She knew she needed to behave as though nothing had changed, though she was wracked with guilt over her behavior with Sadie. When she heard William pull up outside in the car, Miriam stiffened and put on a false smile.

"I'm so glad to be home," Deborah said, walking into the parlor and throwing her arms around Miriam, hoping all was well.

Miriam hugged her somewhat stiffly and said, "Tell me how your mother is doing." She tried to look into Deborah's eyes to welcome her home yet found it difficult.

"Much improved. She isn't quite like herself, but she's more conversant and eating more regularly. As usual, Mrs. B. was the key to the changes. She came every day to add cheer."

"That woman has saved us so many times. First it was you and me, and now your mother. We're so fortunate to have her in our lives."

Deborah shrugged her shoulders. "We certainly are. I wish there was some way we could show our appreciation."

"I don't think she's looking for thanks. She's a naturally caring person, wise in the ways she provides support."

"Miriam, before we talk any further and you tell me how everything is at home, I want to say hello to Bubbie and Mother and to see Sylvia. Is she napping?"

"Mother and Sylvia are both napping, but I know where we can find Bubbie."

"Yu welcome home," said Bubbie, as they entered the kitchen. She greeted Deborah with a warm, wet hug, and with smells and grease soaking her apron.

"It's wonderful to be home, Bubbie. I'm glad to report my mother's doing better. I think your cooking helped with the healing."

"I glad she like my food. Everybody like my food."

"They certainly do. You're an excellent cook."

After a bit more chatter, Deborah and Miriam headed back into the parlor. As they sat, Deborah asked, "Is Sylvia doing well? And the business? And how's your mother's health? And Hannah? Tell me all."

There was lots to discuss as they caught up on their two weeks apart, which was a relief to Miriam. She worried that her conflicted thoughts would somehow show on her face. It did not seem to be the case.

Rising off the couch, Miriam said, "I hear the baby. I'll get her and bring her down. She'll be excited to see you."

The two girls spent time with Sylvia, pleased their child was especially cuddly with Deborah. They deduced she'd missed her other mother.

The rest of the day and evening went well. They talked of the National Women's Suffrage Day, which Miriam had also heard about after the parade had taken place. The two of them dreamed of fitting meetings into their already busy lives. During the evening, Miriam relaxed and didn't think about Sadie at all. But when the house was quiet and they headed to bed, Miriam became anxious.

As Deborah put her arms around Miriam and stroked her hair, Miriam was brought right back to her moments with Sadie. Deborah was so excited to be back home that she didn't notice the shift in Miriam's attitude at first. But when Miriam pulled away when Deborah tried to kiss her intimately, Deborah questioned what was wrong.

Miriam was torn. What she'd done was wrong, but not telling Deborah was also wrong. They shared everything, and having a conflict that was hers alone felt awful. Miriam had no excuse for her distance.

"What's the problem?" asked Deborah again.

"Nothing," said Miriam, though her hesitance said more than her words.

"Something is wrong. I can sense it. Are you glad to have me home?"

"Very glad. I missed you terribly."

"Does your anxiety have anything to do with that girl?"

As Miriam began to cry, there was no hiding her feelings from Deborah.

"Were you with Sadie while I was gone?"

"No. I, well yes. But it was all wrong."

"What happened in my absence? Tell me all."

"Oh, Deborah. Nothing happened. Well, nothing much. I saw Sadie a couple of times and she tried to get too friendly. It scared me."

"Scared because you wanted her?"

"No. Scared because I don't want to lose you, and I worry you think she's coming between us."

"What exactly did she do?"

"She tried to kiss me. I almost got pulled into it but then I thought of you and how much I love you and I pulled away. I told her to leave, and I didn't see her again while you were gone."

"You told her to leave? Was she here? Was she kissing you right here in our own house?"

"She surprised me by stopping by one evening. I did not invite her."

"And you let her in? Into our house? With your mother and grandmother and our baby here? How could you?"

"I stopped her. And I didn't see her again. I love only you, Deborah."

"Now you're talking of love. Do you love her? Or maybe she loves you." Deborah stepped back, taking air into her lungs and holding it a long time. "Do you love her more than you love me?"

"No! Deborah, I don't want her to come between us. I won't see her anymore. I'll stop working at Denison House if you need me to." Tears flooded Miriam's face as she said these words.

"Don't be ridiculous. Denison House is important to you. But I don't want you to see her there—or anywhere. I'm not happy that you and she have been getting closer. You know I've been worried about her right from the beginning."

Miriam sobbed. "Yes, you were. And I should've listened to you. Sadie isn't good for me or for our relationship. I'll ask to have my assignment changed to another night."

"I'm glad to hear you say that. But I'm upset about what already happened. You were kissed by another girl and I feel so hurt. How can I trust you?"

"Deborah. It won't happen again."

"I certainly hope not. If it does, that's the end of us."

This comment stopped the conversation. They looked into each other's eyes.

"I promise it won't happen. Please trust me," Miriam said after a minute, her eyes pleading with Deborah.

"I hope you speak the truth. I love you, Miriam, and I don't want to lose you."

"It will never happen again. I promise. I love you."

There was no loving that night nor any night that week. There was a chilly distance between Deborah and Miriam as they both contemplated what had happened. Sadie had caused a rift that might be difficult to mend.

Entrance to Forest Hills Cemetery

CHAPTER TWENTY-FOUR

Forgiveness?

Mid-May, 1914

Deborah and Miriam tried to go on with their lives as if nothing had happened. They took another trip to the zoo, again with Rachel, as they'd been promising to do since their short winter jaunt. The zoo, which had been open to the public for under two years, was delightful. Frederick Law Olmsted, the same landscape designer who created the Arboretum and Central Park, had envisioned this part of the Emerald Necklace as a zoological garden, a naturalistic area for native animals, rather than a traditional zoo.

They spent about an hour walking around, not getting too far because Sylvia wanted to stay with each animal they visited. Rachel was able to entice her to move on to the next animal without tears by walking ahead and calling back, "Come see what I found, Sylvia." By now she was able to say the sounds of several of the animals, no longer repeating "woof" for each animal sound. She and Rachel had obviously been practicing. By the time they left, they all agreed to be regular visitors to this wonderful place, barely half a mile from their home.

Miriam changed her volunteer night to Thursdays, which helped Deborah's mood slightly. Though they didn't argue as much, there was sadness and hesitancy between them. When they received a letter from Susan, they read it separately and each wrote her own letter back. Previously, they'd have talked about this and signed a joint letter.

Marilyn and Julie invited them to their house as they'd done on several other occasions, but Deborah couldn't rouse herself to go.

"I don't want to socialize. Please tell them we're not able to visit at this time," Deborah said.

"They've invited us at least three times, and we always make an excuse. I'm afraid they'll think we're disinterested," Miriam said, her voice shaking.

"I'm sorry. You'll have to come up with an explanation."

Miriam wasn't able to think up an adequate reason for refusing again so she feared this might be the end of their new friendship.

Deborah spent many evenings upstairs, writing. She didn't share her writing with Miriam, which did not go unnoticed. This writing would never be published.

FORGIVENESS

I want badly to forgive, yet I cannot forget. I want to find compassion in my heart to soothe the bitterness. I need to relinquish my grudges, yet my head screams "betrayal" so loudly that the soft words of love are hardly heard.

Was this my fault? Was I so difficult to live with that I caused distance between us? Had I been more loving and more compassionate, would she have strayed? Had I understood her needs, would she have turned to me instead?

Miriam spent her evenings downstairs—doing chores, reading, worrying. There were no evening walks, as they'd been prone to, especially in the nice weather. Miriam penned letters to Mrs. B. and to Helen, never discussing the tension in their home, nor the reason for it. She even turned to needlework, a certain sign things weren't well, since this had never been a favorite activity.

Miriam's Diary, May 14, 1914

How did I get myself in such a predicament? I can hardly believe I was tempted by Sadie. My thoughts of her are no longer of longing; they've turned to sadness and sometimes distaste since our short dalliance has caused so much pain.

Deborah's foul mood might have been partially at fault, though sometimes I think I was just curious about what it would be like to be with someone else. Hopefully, I'll never be tempted again.

During the daytime, the girls managed adequately. They were fine at work, at meals, with the family, and in their role as parents so their rift was not obvious to the others.

One evening Miriam called out, "Come look at Sylvia. She's walking so steadily." Miriam said it with a smile after dinner one evening.

"I think she grew up while I was gone," Deborah said, minus the smile she found difficult these days.

"She's doing so well, standing up while holding on tightly to the chair. And she's understanding more and more of what we say to her."

"She certainly understands when we tell her NOT to do something. Most of the time she listens to our requests, though sometimes she gets very stubborn. She's really strong-minded when we take away one of her toys."

"I try hard not to grin when she gets that determined look on her face. I know she's upset, but she looks so cute when she gets mad," Miriam said, imitating Sylvia.

Deborah grinned momentarily at Miriam's contorted face, but then her lips tightened. "My greatest worry right now is about her eating. She doesn't chew her food before she swallows."

"That's why I asked Bubbie to mash everything she eats."

"But Bubbie won't mash her *munn* cookies. She has too much pride to turn them to mush."

Deborah and Miriam continued talking about Sylvia's accomplishments, taking great pride in her growth. Hearing their voices, Bubbie came into the dining room. Sylvia, as usual, was mute.

"I talk with yu, Miriam, Devorah." This was the name that Bubbie had recently been calling Deborah.

"Why do you call me that?" Deborah asked.

"Be name my cousin. You be like my cousin," said Bubbie.

"You can call me whatever you want. What is your cousin like?"

"She be my favorite cousin," Bubbie said, looking away. "She very strong, like you."

"I'll take that as a compliment. Thank you, Bubbie."

Bubbie changed the subject. "Sylvia be two, 16 April. What cake you want for birthday?" Bubbie asked.

"I love chocolate," said Miriam. "I hope she takes after me."

"I do too," said Deborah, "but maybe we should stick with vanilla."

"Why? Just because she has difficulties swallowing doesn't mean that she would like vanilla better. I think we should teach her to like what we like."

"My concern is that she'll like it too much. She's already getting a little plump, and I don't want her to be fat."

"She be perfect," interrupted Bubbie. "My *shaina meidel*, my pretty girl."

"Yes, she is," Miriam responded. "You decide, Bubbie. Just make sure it has lots of frosting so she'll swallow it more easily. And make certain the frosting is chocolate."

"You're incorrigible." Deborah smiled.

"I not know what you mean. I make chocolate frosting. Ice cream?"

"Certainly. Sylvia loves it when you make ice cream. I'll help you," said Deborah. "If you make vanilla ice cream, I'll cut up pieces of chocolate to put in."

"I'm glad you have come around to my thinking," Miriam said with a full grin. "Chocolate in the ice cream and chocolate frosting. I'll concede my need for chocolate cake!"

"Somehow you always get your way," Deborah snorted, not unkindly.

Sylvia's birthday party was delightful. William assisted Hannah into the house, as she now waddled awkwardly with her huge belly. Hannah called it her watermelon, which made them all laugh.

Leah, the neighborhood girl who could not walk, attended. William, pleased to have a role, carried her into the house, leaving her wheelchair outside. Leah had written a birthday song, and everyone sang along with the chorus, "Sylvia is a big girl now." They all made a huge fuss.

After everyone left, Mother, saying she'd filled up on cake, excused herself and the rest of them had a light dinner of soup and rye bread. Then Deborah and Miriam headed upstairs with Sylvia to put her to bed. As they sang their little girl to sleep, Miriam reached over lovingly to Deborah. Deborah didn't stiffen as she'd been doing, which made Miriam feel brave.

"I'd like us to talk. To really talk. My heart is breaking as we go through each day with no joy being together. Please help me figure out how to make things better. I'd do anything to have things back to the way they used to be." Miriam's eyes moistened as she spoke.

Deborah took Miriam's hands in hers and squeezed hard. She sat on a wing chair and motioned for Miriam to sit in the other one. "I agree we need to talk. It has been painful to feel the distance between us. We've been like strangers occupying the same space."

"I don't want things to continue this way," Miriam said. "I want to be excited every time I look at you."

"I want that, too. I want us to go back to our innocent loving, to the blind trust that we had for each other. But I don't think we can go backward," Deborah said. "Too much has happened, and we aren't as innocent and naïve as when we met. Our relationship has weathered illness and death, and our family's lack of acceptance of us. I moved to Boston, and we took over parenting Sylvia. And now there is this Sadie problem. All of it has made us different people."

"Maybe we can start over. We can have a new beginning."

"Oh, Miriam. I wish I could tell you that all is forgiven and I'll completely trust you from now on. I want to believe those words, but I'm having a difficult time. I think you believe you'll never turn to another girl again. But you would never have thought it possible that someone could tempt you as Sadie did. What promise could you make that it would never happen again?"

"I promise. I promise. I love you. I always loved you," Miriam gasped, tears flooding her face.

"And I love you."

"Let's remember to love each other every day," Miriam said between sobs. "I understand better now that there will be temptations, but I value our relationship. That's what's most important to me."

"I'll make my best effort," Deborah promised, getting out of her chair and approaching Miriam.

Miriam rose too and they embraced, holding each other so tight they could hardly breathe.

"I will try," Deborah said.

Over the next week, they both attempted to reconnect, though at first it seemed forced. They both felt fragile as the tie between them was frayed. By the end of the week they had an evening of physical, but hesitant, intimacy. There was release with mixed emotions, with both of them attempting to bridge the unspoken chasm between them. There were many quiet tears and many sweet words of hope.

In an effort towards healing, Miriam suggested a trip to Forest Hills Cemetery, as they'd planned during the winter.

"What a lovely idea," said Deborah, pleased that Miriam had remembered her earlier request.

"But I don't think Mother could manage, even though she asked to accompany us. Do you think we should invite her?"

"Definitely. Let's make it her choice," said Deborah.

To their surprise, Mother accepted their invitation, though Bubbie declined when they invited her too. The next Sunday afternoon, despite it being May, they bundled Mother in blankets, since she often got chilled with the slightest breeze. They snuggled Sylvia in the car next to her grandmother and headed the short distance to Jamaica Plain.

They followed a horse and buggy into the magnificent park, through the huge sandstone gothic arches flanked by two pedestrian gates and two square gatehouses. There was a map of the more than 275 acres, and they realized they'd better follow it or they might be lost for days.

They drove the windy paths, marveling at the natural beauty of the well-maintained gardens and picturesque views. The dramatic crypts fascinated them, each more ornate than the last, so very different than the simplistic gravestones they were used to in Jewish cemeteries. When they reached Lake Hibiscus, Deborah and Miriam disembarked as Mother chose to stay seated, with a sleeping Sylvia leaning against her leg.

"I'm so impressed," Deborah said. "And to think this is under a mile from our home."

"Thank you so much for suggesting this. It's wonderful to have this treasure so close by."

Just then a tall man with a clerical collar walked by. They suddenly felt a bit out of place, remembering this was a Christian cemetery. They'd seen crosses on some of the tombstones, but most of the graves were adorned with

Lucy Stone Blackwell's urn

striking sculptures or ornate carvings so they'd been overlooking the religious aspect of this park. When this man tipped his hat toward them, they felt an odd mixture of acceptance and dissonance. When he gestured toward the middle of the lake, Miriam wondered if he was pointing to a religious icon, and Deborah questioned whether they were doing something improper. At second glance, they saw him gesturing to a huge bird perched on a rock on the edge of a tiny island in the middle of the lake. The bird stood perfectly still, and they both wondered if it was a statue.

"That's our resident great blue heron," the man announced. "He spends many hours sitting there for our viewing pleasure."

"Thank you so much for pointing him out," Miriam said. "I'm so glad that we didn't miss seeing him."

The man, or priest, or whomever he was, took this as an invitation to engage them in conversation and began telling them all about this extraordinary place. The girls listened, fascinated by his extensive knowledge, though they didn't know the names he listed of famous people buried here. That is, until he mentioned Lucy Stone.

"Lucy Stone?! The suffragist?" Deborah asked, louder than she intended.

"Yes. The very same. I can't show you her grave because she was cremated. She was actually the first person ever cremated here. But I can show you her urn. It says 'Blackwell', her married name."

"No," Miriam said, reacting quite strongly since cremation wasn't acceptable to Jews.

They thanked him politely for sharing so much with them and headed back to the car. They could hardly wait to get home, to write to Susan and Helen about how close they were to Lucy Stone's resting place.

One more healing moment for their relationship came in the form of yet another story that Deborah was asked to write for the Denison House newsletter.

Deborah met with Yuan, a pale-faced sixteen-year-old girl with diminutive stature and almond-shaped eyes who was, at first, hesitant to talk. Deborah calmed her by asking, "Tell me about the place you called home in China."

"I come from traditional family. Many generations in Hunan Province," Yuan began softly.

"Who was most important to you growing up?"

"Father most honored, but also respect grandmother, called White Peony."

"Tell me about your grandmother," Deborah said.

"Matchmaker give grandmother a *laotong*, a girl bonded to her when she seven years old. White Peony and her *laotong*, Waning Moon, have contract together for whole life. More important than marriage. They always be with each other, for foot-binding, for marriage, for old age."

"Was her husband jealous of the bond she had with this girl?"

"No. She did "bed business" with him, so he fine."

"What type of contract did they have?"

"Special papers in *nu shu*, language for women."

"A woman's language?"

"Yes. Only women write it, talk it. Men not to see it. Cannot touch paper with *nu shu*."

"That sounds fascinating. Would it please you to tell the story of your grandmother? You can tell me about her and I will write it all down."

"Oh, yes. To honor her memory."

That night, Deborah told Miriam of Yuan's grandmother's relationship with her *laotong* girlfriend. She told Miriam of the closeness these girls had, participating with each other in all life's major events and how they shared their everyday lives. Deborah and Miriam talked of how they hoped to re-create that intense intimacy again for themselves.

(See Addendum: YUAN'S STORY OF HER GRANDMOTHER, WHITE PEONY)

Yuan

CHAPTER TWENTY-FIVE

Solutions

Late May, 1914

The repair in Deborah and Miriam's relationship came none too soon as they both needed to shift all of their focus to the publishing shop. Work was becoming more and more challenging as new business arrived practically every day. Mr. Levine's idea of prioritizing was helpful, but it looked as if they'd never catch up.

When a second customer left in frustration because his booklet couldn't be started for two weeks, Deborah said out loud, "We need a plan to change things."

She looked around at the messy piles of unfinished projects all over the office and felt overwhelmed.

Deborah called Miriam into the front office and cleared a space for her to sit down. "Something needs to be done. We're starting to lose business because we can't keep up. With Hannah out most of the time, things are worse than usual. And before long she'll have her baby and be unable to come in at all. And then William will be distracted even more than he is now."

"What can we do?" asked Miriam, not expecting an answer. She should have known better.

"We need more staff, as my father suggested. I have an exciting idea that I think you will like."

"Anything to relieve the stress and help the business would be wonderful."

Deborah looked intently into Miriam's eyes. "I think we should employ Susan and Helen to help us."

Standing up, Miriam said, "What an incredible idea. In our most recent letters from each of them, they were frustrated that neither had found jobs after graduation. They both have skills that would suit the business."

"They don't know Yiddish since neither is Jewish, but they both write extremely well and are very bright. It would be wonderful to work with them."

"And if they both came to Boston, they could be together. Right now, they hardly get to see each other," Miriam said excitedly.

Miriam, sitting back down, wore a wide grin until her face slackened and she asked, "But where would they live? We can't pay them enough to afford an apartment."

"With us. At least until they can afford a place of their own. Sylvia could stay in our room, like when Ruth visited, and they could have their own room."

Miriam thought about the idea for a moment. "I wonder how Mother would deal with having another couple like us in her home."

"She's adapted very well to having the two of us. I'm certain she'd like both Susan and Helen a great deal. I think having a houseful of young women would be pleasant for her. Bubbie would not mind having two more mouths to feed, a benefit, since lots of food is going to waste. She still cooks the same amount she always did even though she no longer has Father or Hannah to feed. I think it might be so good for both of them they may never want Susan and Helen to leave."

Miriam thought about this idea for a minute. "But this is a difficult family situation. Mother is ill, Bubbie is old, Hannah is pregnant, our baby has many needs, and the business is overwhelming. Do you think Susan and Helen would really want to take on our family issues?"

Susan and Helen

"My guess is that it would be worth dealing with everything for the opportunity for them to live together. Think back to what it was like before the Berkowitzes provided us a way to be together."

Miriam smiled. "You're taking on the role I usually take—skipping ahead four steps. Let's think this through very carefully before we offer them jobs."

Deborah did not smile. Instead, her mouth turned downward into a pout, and she said, "Mention of the Berkowitzes reminds me that as summer approaches they're all gathered in the Berkshires. I hoped we could visit my family at Stonegate, but that doesn't seem possible this year."

"Certainly not right now. That's more motivation to hire enough staff so the shop can run smoothly without us for a couple days," Miriam said.

"And so it runs smoothly with us here too."

First, they talked with William, as part-owner in the business. They called him into the office where he stood between the large paper piles, having nowhere to sit.

"What a wonderful idea," said William. "We can use some help. But would you expect me to train them?"

"You did a wonderful job training Hannah and then the two of us," Miriam reminded him.

He blushed from the compliment. "I would rather have you train them. They are your friends."

As soon as they arrived home Deborah and Miriam brought Mother and Bubbie together in the parlor, and when they were all seated, they explained the plan.

As expected, Mother said, "It would be lovely to have your friends live here and help you in the shop."

"I feed them good. They like *kosher* food?" Bubbie smiled.

"Neither of them is Jewish. Will that matter to you?" Miriam asked.

"Be fine." But Miriam noticed the inadvertent widening of Bubbie's eyes as she spoke.

Hannah liked the idea, feeling guilty that she had not been doing her share lately and anticipating that with her baby's arrival she'd be even less available. To Deborah and Miriam's surprise, not one of their family members voiced any concern that they were inviting another couple like them into their home.

The final step was to approach Susan and Helen, assuming they would love the plan. Deborah and Miriam sat in the dining room with writing paper and a pen as they discussed the letters they were about to send. They decided to offer each $5 per week, which came to $260 per year, less than they were worth, but as much as the business could afford for now.

"I hope that with their help, we'll be able to increase our profits and pay them more in the future. And it does include room and board," Deborah said.

"I don't think we should tell either of them that the offer is for both of them," Miriam said with a twinkling in her eyes. "I think we should keep it a surprise. Do you think that would work?"

Deborah agreed, and Miriam wrote the letter to Susan first. They had little apprehension about Susan's acceptance of their proposal so they were surprised when she expressed concerns.

May 18, 1914

Dear Deborah and Miriam,

What a wonderful job offer! There is no one I'd rather work for, yet I'm concerned that moving to Boston will take me away from my family. I went to college nearby so I could see them often, and I assumed I'd be settling near them. I've never considered moving away.

I also have another worry. Being further from Helen would make it even more difficult for us to see one another. Helen is from upstate New York, a distance that's already too far, yet Boston would be even farther.

I'll think seriously about this since I don't want to disappoint you, yet I'm not certain if I can get past my concerns.

Fondly,
Susan

After receiving the letter with Susan's worries, Deborah suggested she make a telephone call. They arranged a time, and Susan was waiting by the phone at her aunt's house when the call was connected.

"Susan, it's lovely to hear your voice," Deborah said loudly, yelling from state to state, as she stood in the corner of the kitchen where the telephone had been installed.

"I agree," Susan said, modulating her voice so Deborah would understand that she didn't need to shout.

Due to the cost of this call, which she knew would be over one dollar for three minutes, Deborah got right to the point. "We really want you to come to Boston to work with us. I understand your concerns, but I think we've an answer for one of them."

"My parents …"

"No. Not that one," Deborah said with a slight giggle. "We can't solve that. But we can solve the distance from Helen."

"What do you mean?"

"We want both of you to work with us. You could live together in our home."

Susan burst into tears. Deborah, slightly choked up herself, tried to calm her to hasten the call and agreed to write all the details in a letter. They ended the call with Susan still weepy from happiness.

After hanging up the phone receiver, Deborah joined Miriam in the parlor where they wrote a letter detailing their excitement.

Once Susan agreed to this plan, they plotted to keep the full arrangement from Helen, telling her only that she was being invited for this job.

May 23, 1914

Dear Deborah and Miriam,

I could hardly believe my good fortune. Getting a job offer from you was the best thing that has ever happened to me. (Other than meeting Susan!) Finances are very tight for my family, and I feared that I'd continue to be a strain because I couldn't find employment.

I've been desperately lonely for Susan. Even though we'll be farther apart when I'm in Boston, this is too wonderful an opportunity to pass up.

I happily accept your offer of employment, and I'll be in Boston as soon as you like. Thank you so much for your generosity.

Helen

Deborah and Miriam repeatedly pictured the moment when Helen discovered she was to share her new life and her bedroom with her girlfriend. "Imagine the glee on each girl's face," said Miriam.

"I'm glad to be part of this," Deborah said, visualizing the scene.

Within the month Deborah and Miriam moved Sylvia into their room, and they converted her nursery to a bedroom for their friends.

Miriam commented, as they looked upon the newly decorated space, "This room again resembles Hannah's old bedroom."

"It does. There have been so many changes since I met you. First it was Hannah's, then Sylvia's, and now it will house our two wonderful friends."

"It's a room of happiness."

❦

Susan arrived first. The girls traveled together to pick her up at South Station, and their reunion was joyous. After warm hugs, the three of them carried Susan's suitcases to the waiting car. They talked nonstop all the way home, barely showing Susan the sights along the way. There would be lots of time for tours of her new city.

After greeting Susan at the door, Mrs. Cohen flopped down in a chair in the parlor, completely out of energy. Susan was surprised by how sickly she looked, even though Miriam had written about her illness. Her eyes were sunken and her skin had an unhealthy hue. Susan pulled her glance from Mrs. Cohen to look around the welcoming parlor, and she could smell dinner cooking.

Miriam left the room to get Bubbie, who walked in with Sylvia in her arms. Their child wore a fluffy pink dress, carefully chosen to impress their guest. Susan reached out for the baby, making a fuss about her, and bringing a smile to everyone. Bubbie held out a plate of *munn* cookies, and Susan took one while holding Sylvia's squirming body.

As usual, the sweets were appreciated. Mother and Bubbie asked about Susan's food choices to make certain she'd feel at home. Susan described foods such as meat and potatoes, and not pork or shellfish, as Miriam and Deborah had spoken to her about living in a *kosher* household. Mother was pleased to hear her choices.

Deborah led Susan upstairs to her bedroom where Susan was delighted with the accommodations, commenting about Miriam's lovely taste in furnishings. After she put all her belongings away, the three plotted the surprise for Helen. Susan had not written back to Helen, who excitedly wrote of her job offer, so Helen had no idea about the situation.

The next day, Deborah and Miriam picked up Helen at South Station, leaving Susan at home for the reunion.

"How wonderful to see you!" Helen said, greeting Deborah and Miriam with warm hugs.

"It's wonderful to have you here," Miriam said.

As they walked to the car Helen said, "I was surprised and thrilled to get your job offer. I wrote to Susan about it, but I have yet to hear from her. I know she will be happy for me even though we are further away from each other."

"We're glad to have you join us. We're desperate for assistance, and we thought that your artistic skills would add additional talent to our work."

"So that's why you chose me instead of Susan? After all, you were her friend first."

Deborah placed Helen's suitcase in the car, then opened the door for her. "We did consider Susan first, but she was very hesitant to leave her family."

"Yes, I know how closely she's tied to them. I hope she can visit us here in Boston. Would that be possible? Oh, how impolite of me to ask before I've even gotten to your house. You're already offering me so much."

"It would be our pleasure to have Susan here," said Deborah, looking away, lest her smile give away the secret.

On the way to their home, Helen asked whether they had heard from Susan recently and strangely, Deborah said, "Yes," and Miriam said, "No." Helen wondered about their conflicting answers, but just then they saw a beautiful automobile go by and remarked on it.

At home, Helen met Mother and Bubbie, and most importantly, Sylvia. Helen was very comfortable with young children, having several younger siblings and many little cousins. She looked around the parlor as Susan had, and commented on the gallery of family portraits.

After Helen was given a description of every family member pictured, she ate two cookies with her tea and was then led by Miriam upstairs to her new bedroom. Miriam hesitated outside the door, stepping aside so Helen could enter first.

When she heard the delighted scream, she quietly closed the door so her friends could have a private reunion.

Inside the room, the girlfriends hugged and cried as Helen asked, "How long can you stay?"

"Forever, if they'll have us," responded Susan. "I'll be working beside you at the shop every day, and I can sleep next to you every night."

More kisses and tears followed.

When Deborah and Miriam reached the parlor, Miriam turned to her mother and said, "Thank you for agreeing to this arrangement, Mother. There are two very happy girls upstairs."

"And two very happy girls right here, too," said Deborah. "It's wonderful for us to have our good friends with us, and it will be great to have their help at the shop."

"They seem like nice girls." Mrs. Cohen smiled a weak smile, pleased that this would be a good situation for all of them.

The four girls found themselves in deep conversations, which they all craved. Although Deborah and Miriam had new acquaintances, there was nothing like having old friends. They spent their first evening in the parlor, their animated chatter lasting for hours.

While gathered together, Susan explained, "Life at Barnard College became challenging for us once we realized we were a couple. As we spent more time together, sneaking off every chance we got, our friends felt slighted and invited us for fewer gatherings."

"Initially," Helen continued, looking over at Susan, "this pleased us, since it gave us more time alone, but gradually we realized we were becoming isolated."

"Also, we were uncomfortable, worrying how others would react if they found out the nature of our relationship," Susan said. "Graduation was a sad day for both of us since we returned home without each other. It was wonderful to be back with my family, but I missed Helen terribly."

Helen continued. "We visited each other only once in the past year because both our families discouraged us from seeing each other."

"For us, as educated women, graduation was a sad ending and not the beginning of a new life. As with your families, I'm certain, we were expected to go home to find husbands, rather than jobs. Neither of us was interested in marriage, and we were denied visits with one another so life was difficult and without much joy—until now. You have saved us!"

There was no time to be wasted. The day after Helen arrived, Deborah said to Susan and Helen, "We'll show you the sights of Boston another time, but first we need our new employees to learn about the publishing shop."

They all piled into the car together for their first day at work. Miriam hoped Hannah would come to the shop for their orientation, but she wasn't feeling up to it, as she was due any day.

When Helen and Susan walked into the shop, their noses twitched from the strong smell of the ink. Deborah and Miriam no longer even noticed it. They were also assaulted by the noise of the presses, again something that neither Deborah nor Miriam paid attention to anymore.

After a quick introduction to William, who was always limited in conversation, and a warmer introduction to Marjorie, who was glad to finally meet them, Deborah and Miriam showed their new employees around. Miriam pointed out all the machinery, most of which was unfamiliar, and Deborah explained a great deal about the workings of the publishing shop. Both trainees were wide-eyed all day, trying to take in an enormous amount of information all at once. By the end of the day, they were exhausted.

They climbed into the car, with Susan and Helen in the front seat so they could observe the neighborhoods, and Miriam by herself in the back seat. On the way home, Susan turned her bleary eyes to Miriam and said, "I hope you two haven't made a mistake by asking us to help you. I'm not certain that I'll be able to learn everything."

"I feel the same way," Helen said nervously, with a tear falling onto her cheek. She turned away from Deborah, the driver, since she didn't want to distract her, but Miriam caught sight of it. "Learning the publishing business is going to be tough, and not knowing Yiddish will limit what we can do. Are you sure you want us to try?"

"I'm sorry we overwhelmed you today," Deborah said quickly. "It wasn't my intention to scare you. I only wanted to teach you as much as I could about how the business operates."

"It's Deborah's style to pack everything she can into each minute. Maybe I should take over the instructions," called Miriam from the back seat.

"No. I want to teach them," Deborah said, slightly raising her voice.

"We can discuss this when we get home and figure out a way to make this easier. I don't think we gave enough thought to this training. We will have to do better."

"I've given it a great deal of thought, though obviously my way didn't work."

Susan and Helen looked at each other, a bit shocked. They were unused to hearing their friends argue, and this added to their worry that it was a bad idea to come here.

When they got home, Deborah was quite distraught, feeling like she'd failed her friends. Then it struck her that she knew someone who could assist her. After the dishes had been cleaned from dinner, she went into the kitchen and sat at the telephone table to call her father. When he got the call, he thought something was wrong, but he was pleased to learn Deborah had turned to him for advice. By the end of the conversation he'd been a valuable support for his upset daughter, and he'd imparted a new plan for the training to her.

Thanks to Mr. Levine's advice, Deborah and Miriam sat in their bedroom and had a civilized discussion about how to proceed. "So," Miriam began, "Susan will follow you for a few days, and you'll explain what you're doing and why. You will answer questions, but not expect Susan to do any actual work. Likewise, Helen will follow me, to learn more of the backroom activities."

"Yes. And when they feel ready, they'll switch off and learn the other half of the business."

"Will they both need to learn everything?" asked Miriam.

"They need to get the whole picture so we can figure out where each of them might be of most assistance. We can choose, based on their skills and their interests."

"What if they both want to do the same thing?"

"I don't think we should worry about that right now."

Deborah and Miriam conceded that it was unfair to expect help this first week as both had anticipated. Instead, they'd spend the first days acquainting the girls with the business practices. Susan and Helen would be productive the following week. This would also give the new employees time to learn how to deal with William, not a difficult chore, but one that required patience and understanding.

The most difficult adjustment for their guests wasn't to their work, but to the emotional tension in the house. Helen, sitting on the small chair in their room, said to Susan, "Deborah and Miriam seem to disagree on many things. Have you noticed how they respond differently to Mrs. Cohen's illness?"

"Yes. Deborah expects a lot of Mother, but Miriam protects her, not letting her strain herself," Susan responded.

Helen took in a deep breath. "Another issue of discord seems to be regarding Sylvia. Again, Deborah wants their child to do everything on her own, even if she fails repeatedly."

"And Miriam shields Sylvia from feeling frustrated. She abandons tasks that are difficult for her."

"I don't think we should get in the way of these issues," Susan said.

After dinner on their third day, Susan and Helen excused themselves for the evening, saying they were both tired. In their own space, Susan turned to Helen and said softly, "Do you think we'll ever adjust to living here?"

Helen sat on the bed, letting out a deep sigh. "I'm not sure. What did you expect it to be like?"

"Not like this," Susan said. "Deborah and Miriam had both written to me about their challenges with Mrs. Cohen's illness, Bubbie's frailty, and Sylvia's limited development, but I hadn't thought about how these problems would affect them as a couple."

"They told me in a letter that they were facing difficulties in their relationship," said Helen, "but I never expected they'd turn on one another. They're both so irritable."

Susan, with a sideways glance, said, "I'm worried about whether we can live in a house filled with this much tension."

"And the jobs that they expect us to do are challenging."

"But we must remember," Susan said with a wink, "that we get to live together if we stay here."

"It's worth a lot of stress to be with you, so we should try our best to make it work."

"Agreed."

Deborah and Miriam, leaving Sylvia at home under Mother's watchful eyes, wanted their friends to enjoy their new city. On Sunday, after Susan and Helen returned from church and they'd all eaten dinner, they went downtown to see the Boston Public Gardens. They rode on the Swan Boats and walked along the beautiful flower paths, noting the pansies in multiple colors, tall purple irises, and huge pink peonies, Helen's favorite flowers. They watched children delightfully splashing in Frog Pond as people had been doing for centuries.

"This is the oldest city park in United States. It was originally a cow pasture," began Miriam. "Then it was used as a British encampment during the American Revolution. After it became a public park, the wonderful water feature was added in 1848 to commemorate the country's first public water supply."

Frog Pond on Boston Common

"How did it get its name?" asked Susan, looking around to see if there were any frogs.

"Not clear," said Deborah, who had been reading up on Boston history since arriving in this city. "Legend has it that the Frog Pond earned its name from the soldiers of the Revolutionary War who hunted its amphibians for food. At that time there were three ponds on Boston Common, and probably lots of frogs. I think the young boys who sailed their toy boats along the shore saw frogs, but I've yet to see one!"

Susan and Helen enjoyed their afternoon learning of Boston's history and, more importantly, having a lovely day with Deborah and Miriam.

But when they got home, Deborah was irritable. It seemed to come from nowhere. She yelled at Miriam in front of Susan and Helen.

"It was a lovely day today," Deborah said calmly, "but if we want to take Susan and Helen to see other sights, I always need to drive." Quite loudly she said, "I can't believe that you won't drive. One small incident, and you have refused to get behind the wheel again. No one got hurt. Why can't you get over it?"

"I don't know why. But I am scared," said Miriam timidly.

"I wonder if you would be scared if Sadie asked you to drive."

Susan and Helen looked on in shock, wondering what caused Deborah to suddenly turn.

"Deborah, stop it," Miriam said firmly.

"I'm sorry," Deborah said, as she walked away.

Helen put her arms around Miriam, who burst into tears.

"I don't know why she is so jealous. We had such a nice day together, and I have no idea why she got so upset. Just when I think that everything is going so well, she turns on me."

Susan put her arm on Miriam's shoulder, offering support, but also not wanting to take sides. Once Miriam left, Susan and Helen looked at one another and shook their heads.

Once upstairs, Deborah approached Miriam with further apologies. Miriam did not want to set Deborah off, but it was difficult for her to forgive Deborah. In addition to being upset about Deborah's jealousy, she was embarrassed by Deborah's display of emotions in front of their friends. Miriam let Deborah hug her, but in her heart she remained distant.

CHAPTER TWENTY-SIX

Baby Sarah

Early June, 1914

Just after dinner on June 3rd, William arrived at the Cohen house. "Miriam, come quick! The baby is coming!" William yelled, flinging open the door.

"How exciting, William," Deborah said. "I'll get Miriam. She's upstairs, changing Sylvia."

"She needs to come right away. I don't want to leave Hannah alone." He turned toward the door, but Deborah stopped him.

"Wait here for a moment while I fetch her. I'll make certain she's quick. It will be faster if you drive her."

"Oh yes. I forgot she does not drive. But hurry."

During the three minutes it took for Miriam to get ready and hand Sylvia to Deborah, William paced. He tripped as he headed to the car with Miriam just behind him. She caught his arm and steadied him.

"You must calm down, William. It's unsafe for you to drive when you're so worked up. If you want me to ride with you, you need to steady yourself. Also, if you're frantic, it will make it harder on Hannah. You must be calm, providing her with comfort and support."

William took a few deep breaths and seemed in better control so they took off.

"When I got home from work, she was on the couch, writhing in pain," he said while looking straight ahead to the road. "It was awful. Then it stopped and she was fine. The midwife said it could be like this for a long time and not to go for her immediately. But it kept happening. She had horrible pain and was drenched in sweat; then she would be exhausted."

"That's how it's supposed to be," Miriam said steadily. "How long has she been having the pains?"

"She said they started this afternoon, but they were not so bad. All of a sudden, just before I got home, they became much worse."

"Has her water broken?"

"She did not tell me."

"You would know if it had. We probably don't have to worry that she'll give birth soon if that didn't happen yet. I'll ask a neighbor to send for the midwife."

They arrived at the house to find Hannah on the floor in the parlor, surrounded by a small pool of liquid tinged with blood. Hannah was crying, and it was unclear whether it was from pain or embarrassment she'd wet the floor.

As Miriam cleaned the floor, William ran to help her into a straight-backed wooden chair, not wanting to wet an upholstered cushion. Once she was seated and William had wiped away her tears, her face contorted with the onset of a new cramp. She moaned and clutched the bottom of her enormous belly. William ran to her and pushed her hair off her face as she clenched her teeth while a wave of pain shot through her.

Just then a loud knock at the door momentarily startled everyone. Miriam welcomed the midwife, a relaxed middle-aged lady who had probably delivered many babies, and escorted her to the patient. She took a quick look at Hannah sitting on the chair and said, "Please get her to the bed. As soon as the next contraction passes, I want her husband to take her there, even if he has to carry her."

William stood up to his full height, ready to take on his assignment. Miriam cleared a path to the bedroom, knowing William would never think of doing this.

A few minutes later another contraction, the strongest thus far, racked Hannah's swollen body. William tried to comfort his wife. When the pain subsided, Miriam quietly reminded him he was to help her to the bed, which he did in a loving manner.

As soon as he placed Hannah on the bed, she screamed, "The baby is coming. I want to push it out."

"Go boil some water," the midwife suggested to William, not knowing this simple request was something William had never done before.

William blanched and headed to the kitchen. Miriam sidled up to the midwife, awaiting instructions. At the next contraction, the midwife handed a cloth to Miriam, suggesting she let Hannah bite on it when the pain got bad. She instructed Hannah to push when the next cramp started. It was time to birth this child.

The pain was intense as Hannah's belly convulsed. She gritted her teeth, biting so hard on the cloth that Miriam thought she'd bite right through. Miriam waited anxiously for the newborn to fall into the midwife's waiting hands, but that didn't happen. Instead, the contraction passed and there was no infant. This happened several more times.

"Let's hope this baby isn't breech," said the midwife. Miriam had had the same thought. She'd heard of some women having difficulty birthing because the infant was upside down, which she knew was what the midwife meant.

During a momentary period of calm, Miriam wiped the sweat from her sister's brow and offered words of comfort. "You're doing fine, Hannah. You can do this."

"I don't know if I am strong enough," Hannah said weakly to her sister.

"You are, Hannah. Just push that baby into the world."

Another pain, another push, but no child.

After things continued in this manner, the midwife, with a stern expression on her face, reached down to Hannah's swollen belly, felt around the entire orb, and suddenly grabbed the mass of flesh in her two strong hands and seemed to rotate it. Hannah called out in pain, but when the next contraction came the top of the baby's head appeared. Everyone took a deep breath.

After two more contractions the infant's body emerged and the midwife announced, "It's a girl."

Miriam cried out, "*Mazel tov!* Congratulations! Sylvia has a little cousin," and then headed out the door to get William. She found him standing with a pot of hot water, which he had tried to boil for a very long time. He had waited impatiently, never figuring out that he should put a top on the pot and turn up the heat.

Miriam knew the hot water was a potential hazard, so she took the pot from him before announcing, "*Mazel tov.* You have a daughter!"

William burst into tears and practically ran into their bedroom where he found Hannah lying quietly with a tiny bundle at her breast.

"Come meet your little girl," said a sweaty but smiling Hannah.

Miriam joined them as they completed the ritual of washing their hands and reciting the *Shehechiyanu* (*Baruch atah Adonai, Elohenu melekh ha'olam, shehecheyanu vekiymanu vehigi'anu lazman hazeh.* Blessed are You G-d, L-rd of the Universe, Who has kept me alive, and sustained me, and made me arrive at this day), the prayer said for every new blessed event.

Miriam left the room to give the couple a moment together with their new infant.

After about ten minutes Hannah had some mild contractions, which confused William. The midwife asked him to leave the room, but he initially resisted, with panic in his eyes. As Hannah's face contorted from another pain, the midwife insisted William depart and told him this was normal. William stood outside the door, wringing his hands and pacing, wondering if there was to be a twin. After the midwife expertly delivered the afterbirth, she told William he could return. He found things as he had left them, with one baby.

The midwife was aware that William was too emotional to retain instructions so she asked Miriam to join them in the kitchen. She told them what to expect, both for Hannah and the infant. She told them to call for the doctor if anything seemed abnormal, such as excessive bleeding or a high fever, or if the baby had any difficulties at all. Miriam repeated this information to William before they both left the house.

Once at home, Miriam went directly to Mother's room to tell her the good news.

"You're a grandmother. Hannah had a little girl. She is perfect."

"How exciting! I was worried when you did not come back quickly."

"It wasn't an easy birth, but Hannah is fine. The baby is adorable."

"I want to go see the new baby."

"Can you wait a couple of days? Once Hannah has recovered, we can bring the infant here."

"I don't want to wait. I'll go tomorrow. I'm sure Bubbie will want to go, too."

"I need to tell Bubbie the news. She'll be excited to have a second great-granddaughter. You go back to sleep while I run downstairs to tell her."

First thing the next morning Deborah and Miriam rushed down the block to see how Hannah was doing. They were pleased to find her tired but feeling better. She was anxious to show off her new baby to her mother and Bubbie so Deborah picked them up at lunchtime to meet the new infant. It was a short visit. Mother seemed surprised Hannah and William named the baby Sarah, after William's grandmother, Suri, rather than after Hannah's great-grandmother, Samara. But since the two names started with the same letter, the Hebrew name would be the same for both. Mother and Bubbie would always think that Sarah was named for their own beloved relative even if she wasn't.

Miriam spent as much time with the newborn and new parents as she could over the first few days. Deborah was very understanding, suggesting that Miriam leave the shop midday to check on the new family, even though they were desperately behind with orders. If it weren't for Susan and Helen, she couldn't have been so generous.

"Hannah," said Miriam to her sister, "You're so natural at being a parent. It's as if this were your fourth child, not your first."

"It's easy to figure out what Sarah needs. It's either a diaper change or another feeding."

Miriam smiled, taking the infant from Hannah's arms, pleased with the baby smells as she held the newborn next to her. She resisted putting the baby into her cradle. "It's such a pleasure to spend time with this child. You need to treasure every moment."

"Do you ever wish that you could have a baby of your own?" Hannah asked softly.

"I wished to have several children of my own, but I've been blessed with Sylvia and now Sarah. They fill my heart."

"And you fill their lives with love."

Baby Sarah

Sarah's cradle

William's new car

CHAPTER TWENTY-SEVEN

Honest Reflections

Mid-June, 1914

Hannah and William's first anniversary was a time of quiet celebration since they were all exhausted. The whole family had dinner together, including Mrs. Cohen, who rarely made it to meals these days. Bubbie made a tall, luscious lemon cake with a tart icing, Hannah's favorite, and Mrs. Cohen had a second piece. This pleased them all since her appetite had been waning.

The greatest excitement was when Mrs. Cohen offered Hannah and William an extravagant anniversary gift. "Here are the keys to your new car, William."

He rushed outside to see the shiny new vehicle that he had eyed in front of the house next door. After a quick inspection, he rushed back inside to thank her repeatedly. They all assumed the car was in case there was another catastrophe, as they all feared the known and unknown troubles ahead.

For Hannah, birthing Sarah was easy in comparison with parenting an infant. Her initial ease evaporated after the first week. Every time the baby cried, Hannah panicked, thinking she should know what to do. Hannah was at a loss when neither food nor a diaper change was enough. She cried right along with the newborn.

Deborah and Miriam wanted to help, and Deborah envisioned a solution. She called Miriam and William into the office to explain. "What if we hire a nurse during the daytime to help Hannah learn how to care for the baby? Miriam and I have only minimal experience with newborns, so this woman may have better ideas than us."

"Wonderful idea," said Miriam. "I'm also hopeful this woman could help Hannah get some sleep. She looks exhausted, and I think that being tired makes parenting harder."

"We should use some of our business profits to hire this woman so we can all come to work," said Deborah. Miriam nodded approval.

William was very touched by their support, as evidenced by the moisture in his eyes as he said, "Thank you."

Miriam felt it necessary to provide even more assistance to her anxious sister, offering to come over daily after the baby-nurse left. She'd stay overnight until Hannah was comfortable with her responsibilities. She shortened her work hours, coming to the shop when William returned after his midday visit with Hannah and his newborn daughter.

Each evening at eight o'clock, Deborah drove Miriam to Hannah and William's apartment. This was Deborah's first experience with nighttime driving and not one she appreciated. She was challenged by the acetylene lamp on the running board, which required her to open each of the lens covers once the generator had been started. It took her a few tries to get the lights working. Gaslights were only on the main streets, so she was very glad to have good vision. Luckily, she did not again bring up thoughts about Miriam driving.

The evening duties weren't easy for Miriam. She got up each time she heard the baby wake, giving Hannah tips how to comfort her child. Hannah was tremendously appreciative.

The nights while Miriam was gone and Deborah was alone, Deborah had time to reflect on their relationship. Evening after evening she sat at her desk, penning her deepest thoughts.

ANGER

My trust in Miriam has been shattered. She promised me over and over that she does not want a relationship with Sadie, but it is hard to trust her words. I do not think she knows what she wants.

Now, while she is gone, I must think through the life I have chosen and decide if this is the life for me. I need to figure out if there is a way to mend our relationship—and whether I want to do that ...

SWEETNESS

If I think back to the beginning of our relationship, I remember what attracted me to Miriam. It was her sweetness, her innocence, her appreciation of the goodness in the world, and her love.

I need to remember the calm Miriam has brought to my life. She is one of the kindest people I have ever met. She takes care of Sylvia, Leah, and the children at Denison House with an endless capacity for love.

I know she loves me. I have never questioned that. I am certain she wants to have me in her life, despite the terrible ways I have treated her lately. She has endless patience and she cares for me despite all my faults...

TIMING

This is such a poor time to be questioning our relationship. Susan and Helen have recently moved in with us. Hannah just had her baby. Mother is getting sicker every day, and Bubbie worries us with her declining strength. Miriam and I need each other during this difficult period yet I find it hard to turn to her for support. I do not want to share my feelings with her because I will hurt her with my anxiety...

RETALIATION

How would Miriam react if the situation were reversed? What would she do if I were to behave in the same way? What if I were to kiss Chava? Or to have daydreams about her? Would Miriam tolerate this? I suspect she would not.

I do not know how long I will feel compelled to punish Miriam for her behavior. Part of me wants to act in a despicable way just to hurt her as she has hurt me. It only seems fair that she suffer, as I have...

After two weeks, Miriam believed Hannah was able to care for her infant at night on her own, with the nurse continuing daytime hours. The first day Miriam was to return to her regular work hours, Sylvia had a slight cold so she remained home all day.

After work, Deborah came upstairs quietly and found Miriam sitting at their desk, with page after page of Deborah's writing in front of her. Deborah had foolishly left her journal open on their desk when she left for the shop in the morning, and Miriam had obviously read her recent pages. Miriam was sitting in a puddle of tears, reading and rereading every word.

"Now I know how you feel," Miriam said, weeping into her handkerchief. "You're seriously questioning our relationship, despite saying you would try to make things work."

"I am trying. And I am questioning."

"Do you think there's any hope for us? Or have I ruined everything? Have I destroyed our relationship?"

"I wish I had an answer. I'm trying hard to understand my feelings and my reactions. I want to return to trusting you but I'm finding that very hard to do."

Miriam turned and stared at Deborah. "What do you want from me?"

"I don't know, but I don't want to give up on us. I want to figure out what part of our collapse was my fault. Had I been kinder to you, more patient, more loving, you might never have sought companionship with Sadie."

"I agree that your attitude and your behavior made it easier for me to turn away, but I wasn't seeking a new relationship. It was Sadie pursuing me and I was weak. I was troubled by your anger and constant frustration with me, which made me more vulnerable to her advances. Now I'm troubled by your distance, Deborah. I don't want Sadie or anyone else. I only want you."

Deborah looked directly into Miriam's eyes and reached for her hands. "And I want you so badly I hardly know what to do. I want to forget everything that has happened and go back to our loving relationship. But I don't know how."

They both stood, tears running down their faces.

Deborah said, "I think writing everything down helped me a bit. I'm sorry you saw it all, my anger, my fears, and my hopes. But maybe it's good that it's all out in the open, rather than having those atrocious thoughts running through my head. I couldn't share my feelings with you, but now my papers have done just that. Now you understand my pain better than I could speak it. I don't want to blame you anymore. I want to admit I'm partially at fault. I wasn't treating you well. All the stresses of Sylvia, Mother, Hannah, and the shop were a burden. I'm afraid I took it out on you."

"Please. Let's try again. Don't run away from me or punish me further for what I've done. If I could do it all over again, things would be so different. I'd talk with you of my discontent, rather than remain quiet and have my head turned by solace elsewhere."

"And I'd look to you for support, Miriam, rather than approaching you with blame."

"Do you think we can try again? Can we return to loving each other completely?"

Deborah sighed and withdrew her hands. "I'm unsure. We're no longer foolish young girls together. We've become the young women we never imagined being."

They stood, looking at each other with tear-stained faces, neither knowing what to say next. After several awkward minutes, Miriam headed to the bed, crying endless tears. Deborah went downstairs to the parlor. At dinnertime, Deborah made excuses, saying Miriam had a headache. Deborah stayed downstairs on the divan, sleeping separate from Miriam for the first time since they'd moved into this house together.

In the morning, long before it was time to get ready for work, Deborah quietly entered the room with Miriam and Sylvia. Miriam was sitting on the bed, cradling their daughter.

"We need each other right now and always. I love you, Miriam, and I want to try to make things right between us."

"I love you too," Miriam said through a face wet with tears. She put down the baby and stood, facing Deborah.

There was less than a second of hesitancy before Deborah reached out her arms and lovingly brought Miriam into her embrace.

"I don't want us to ever sleep apart again," Deborah said. "We must fight through our anger and our frustrations."

They cried together, holding each other tightly.

No one commented when they arrived at breakfast with bloodshot eyes.

Throughout the day they checked on one another frequently. There was no conversation of the day before. They touched one another more often than usual, rubbing a shoulder or placing a hand on an arm. Marjorie watched them quietly, hopeful that this tiny new intimacy was the beginning of a change for her friends.

They loved each other with a new openness that evening. Having all their fears and worries laid out in front of them allowed them to be honest with one another. They both felt hope. The two of them stayed up much of the night, talking in a manner they'd not been able to do since Miriam's betrayal. They discussed everything Deborah had written and also everything Miriam had been feeling and thinking. They aired it all, hoping the openness would lead them on a new path.

After hours of talking, Miriam had an idea. "Deborah, I don't want us to do this healing alone. I think we need support from those around us. Typically, we turn to Mrs. B. for her wisdom, but now we have a new opportunity with Susan and Helen here. I think we should tell them what's going on between us."

"I'm not used to sharing my most sensitive feelings with anyone except you and Mrs. B., but I think your idea's a good one. We have wonderful friends right here in the house with us, and I think they'd appreciate our sharing."

"I'm certain they've seen the tension between us. How could they not?" Miriam said, rubbing her hands over Deborah's back.

"Let's talk with them and tell them the whole story. I hope it doesn't shock them or turn them against us."

"If they're true friends, they'll be our support, our guides, and maybe they'll keep us on track if they see us stray."

Deborah shook her head. "I don't want to give them any responsibility to keep us together. It's not up to them. But I think that by sharing it will strengthen our friendship and help to make us all a family."

"Then it's decided. We'll talk with them. But right now, I think we need to go to sleep or we will be dozing off at work tomorrow. My boss won't like that."

"Before we go to sleep, I think we need to share our hearts by having some intimate time together."

"Oh, Deborah. I want that badly. Just promise you'll not be angry if I fall asleep in the middle. It's very late and I'm exhausted."

"A few soft caresses will do for tonight. But tomorrow, I plan to head to bed very early and to show you all the love I'm feeling."

"It's a date," Miriam said through her yawn.

After some sweet loving, they fell asleep in each other's arms.

❦

The next day, as planned, they talked with Susan and Helen. As they sat around the dining room table after dinner, Susan spoke first. "I'm so relieved you shared your situation with us. Now I understand the tension I've felt between you two, and I trust you will work this out."

"And I feel honored," Helen interrupted, "that you shared this with us. I know it couldn't have been easy."

"It was easier than I expected," Deborah said. "Now that Miriam saw everything I wrote, I feel better about sharing my feelings."

"And I feel comforted you're being more open." Turning to Susan and Helen, Miriam said, "I'm glad you're our friends. Thank you for being supportive."

They all agreed it was wonderful to have real friends, with shared values and an increased openness.

When they went to bed later in the evening, Miriam initiated a return to the intimacy they had the night before. "Last night you promised to show me how much you love me."

"I certainly will. I'm glad you remembered," Deborah said with a smile.

"How could I forget?"

Miriam began to caress Deborah slowly, but Deborah took over, ready to fulfill her promise. After removing all of Miriam's clothing and her own, Deborah began kissing her breasts. Once they were thoroughly stimulated, she moved lower, kissing and licking her tiny belly. Miriam moaned with pleasure. Deborah moved lower. She nuzzled in Miriam's nether region, then used her tongue to caress everywhere near Miriam's sweet spot. Miriam squirmed and directed Deborah's tongue to the area that was wet and waiting. Miriam's gasps were loud so Deborah pulled away momentarily and put a finger on her own lips, reminding Miriam that others might hear such sounds and know what they were doing. And they did not want to wake Sylvia.

As Miriam writhed in pleasure, Deborah moved around in the bed, offering her own excited private area to Miriam while maintaining her contact with Miriam's excited body. Miriam caressed Deborah with her fingers first, then directed her tongue to the exact spot where Deborah would have the most pleasure. It didn't take long for both of them to be excited beyond control, and they simultaneously arched and moaned rhythmically as they reached the pinnacle of pleasure. Miriam lay back on the bed. Deborah moved her body back toward the top of the bed so she was aligned with Miriam's. They looked at each other with wide grins and then embraced in a loving hug. After kisses and statements of love, they started all over.

Anger

My trust in Miriam has been shattered. She promised me over and over that she does not want a relationship with Sadie, but it is hard to trust her words. I do not think she knows what she wants.

Sweetness

If I think back to the beginning of our relationship, I remember what attracted me to Miriam. It was her sweetness, her innocence, her appreciation of the goodness in the world, and her love.

I need to remember the calm Miriam has brought to my life. She is one of the kindest people I have ever met. She takes care of Sylvia, Leah, and the children at Denison House with an endless capacity for love.

Deborah's note

CHAPTER TWENTY-EIGHT

More Tsoris (heartache)

Late June, 1914

As their relationship troubles reached a sweet end, their other worries continued to mount. About a week after her reconciliation with Deborah, Miriam awoke with a start. She felt her heart racing from a dream in which her mother's body was shriveling. In her dream, she gave Mother some of Sylvia's extracts in hopes they'd improve her health.

Upon waking, Miriam said, "Deborah, I'm more worried than ever about Mother. I had a bad dream about her. She's getting extremely weak, and she sometimes clenches her teeth from pain. I fear there are many days she hasn't left her bedroom all day."

"I'm worried too."

"I think we should bring the doctor here, whether or not she wants to see him," Miriam said.

"You know she won't see him, but you should talk with her about what's wrong."

Miriam agreed to ask her mother again about the true nature of her obvious decline.

"Mother," Miriam said when they were alone for a few minutes while cleaning up from breakfast. "I'm worried about you. You're not like yourself these days. Is there something you aren't telling me?"

Miriam's mother stared at her daughter and broke down in a flood of tears. Mrs. Cohen held Miriam's hand and led her to a chair. They sat close together, still holding hands.

"You are a smart girl, Miriam. Yes, there is pain in my heart and in my body. You see, the day you caught me crying and I told you about Mrs. Shulman being sick, I was not truthful. That was the day the doctor told me the news I attributed to my friend. I am the one who is ill."

"Oh, Mother. This is what I feared. What sickness do you have?" said Miriam, her voice raspy, with tears streaming down her face.

"He claims not to know what is wrong but…," and changing to a hushed tone she whispered, "I think it is cancer." She said the dreaded word so softly that it was barely audible.

"Is there anything the doctor can do for you? Is there some treatment? We will take you anywhere."

"He says there is nothing to be done."

The two of them burst into wails, bringing Deborah scurrying with half-dressed Sylvia in her arms. "What's wrong?"

"Mother thinks she has cancer. She saw a doctor, and he told her to get her affairs in order."

Then Deborah burst into tears. She put the baby down, and the three women stood in the dining room, holding each other, trying to bring peace to one another. The word "death" wasn't mentioned, but the unspoken word was on all their minds.

Once they all regained composure, Deborah picked up Sylvia.

Mrs. Cohen questioned, "What do I say to Hannah and to Bubbie?"

"They should be told right away," Miriam said, as both Deborah and Mother agreed.

"I'll talk with Bubbie this afternoon, and to Hannah when she and William come to dinner tonight," Mother said, looking down, shoulders slumped.

Later in the afternoon, when the girls heard sobbing in the kitchen, they were certain Bubbie had learned the sad news.

When Hannah and William heard the truth, Hannah encouraged Mother to see other doctors.

"I don't want to be subjected to tests and treatments. I will let nature run its course."

"I'm saddened by your decision," said Miriam.

"Is there anything I can do to persuade you to change your mind?" asked Hannah.

"No. Please let me make my own choices."

They all sadly acquiesced.

Miriam watched her mother fail more each day. "I don't think Mother should be alone while we're at work. I know Bubbie is home, but her focus is on Sylvia."

"Mother would be upset if we were to stay home with her, but I think one of us needs to check on her during the workday."

Miriam thought for a moment, finally saying, "William goes home midday to see Hannah and Sarah. Maybe he could swing by our house on his way, drop me off for a while, and pick me up when he heads back to the office."

"Good idea. And, if you feel it necessary, you can stay home, sweetie," said Deborah. "We should also talk with Bubbie, to hear her thoughts." Miriam offered to speak with her.

"I'm worried about Mother being alone during the day," Miriam said to Bubbie in the kitchen as they were drying the dishes from dinner.

"She fine," was the response.

"She's not fine. I can see she's in pain, and she's spending lots of time in her room lately. I've come to ask you if she's experiencing many bad spells during the daytime."

Bubbie turned away, averting her eyes from Miriam. "All good."

"Bubbie, you're not telling me the truth. I know it. Did mother ask you to tell me everything is fine?"

When Bubbie remained silent, Miriam moved around so she could see Bubbie's face and found tears streaming down her cheeks.

"Oh, Bubbie," said Miriam as she embraced her grandmother. "Obviously Mother has sworn you to secrecy, but I want to know if things get worse. I can stop working and spend more time with her."

"No. You no do. You Ema afraid yu do dat."

"Now I understand. Mother knows I'd choose to care for her rather than work and she's right. But I don't want her to be mad at you for letting me know. I'll keep your secret for now, as long as you promise to tell me if things get any worse."

"That be fine."

But all was not fine. Mrs. Cohen's health failed so quickly it wasn't necessary for Bubbie to admit this to anyone because it soon became too obvious to hide. Mother admitted to Miriam she'd been feeling badly for a long time but had not wanted to upset anyone. Miriam was extremely concerned and talked with Deborah about approaching the rabbi so they could let people at the *shul* know what was happening.

The same posse of women from the Temple Sisterhood who had come to chastise her daughter now came to check on her welfare. They sat in the parlor in the very same chairs they'd chosen the last time they were there although this time they came in support of the family. They were shocked by Mrs. Cohen's sickly appearance and kindly offered to help, despite this being the home with questionable morals. After asking about the family's challenges, they agreed to pick up groceries and to spend time at the house while Deborah and Miriam were at work. The girls were grateful for the assistance and even more appreciative that Mother's old friends would be there for her when she needed them.

"Mother is getting worse," Miriam said, returning to her bedroom one evening.

Deborah agreed, wondering if Miriam was finally coming to terms with her mother's dramatic decline.

"I'm afraid she's dying. I know I have been denying this to myself, but Deborah, I'm so afraid," Miriam said, breaking into tears.

In a calm manner, which she hoped didn't give away her own panic, Deborah said, "I'm worried about that too."

Miriam was too tired to shed any more tears.

Bubbie, the primary care provider for Mrs. Cohen, and also the cook and the child minder, was exhausted by the end of each day. The Sisterhood women helped as did Susan and Helen. The greatest challenge became evenings and overnight. Deborah and Miriam took turns so neither was unduly overwhelmed with the nighttime care. Whoever cared for Mother overnight took the next day off from work.

Miriam called for the doctor on multiple occasions, sometimes late at night, which was when Mother seemed the worst. He often gave her a tincture to ease her pain and allow her to sleep, which seemed to be the only relief she got. The doctor rarely had words of encouragement.

Hannah spent as much time with her mother as possible, though caring for a newborn left her exhausted. Several evenings, she came to give Deborah and Miriam a break. She'd leave Sarah downstairs with the rest of the household to fuss over the baby while she visited with Mother. Hannah often fell asleep in the chair in her mother's bedroom. She'd awaken when William arrived to take her home. Miriam felt badly Hannah didn't have much waking time with their mother since one or both of them slept through much of their time together.

CHAPTER TWENTY-NINE

Loss

Late July, 1914

As Miriam was about to leave for her volunteer job on Wednesday evening, she said to Deborah, "I don't think I should go to Denison House today. Mother has been doing so poorly, that I want to spend time with her instead."

"You have been spending every evening with her. I think you should go to your volunteer work, as you planned, so you can spend a little while thinking of something other than your worries."

"But I've a really bad feeling tonight. I fear I won't have many more evenings to spend with her."

"I'm afraid you're right. But I also think getting away from the anxiety and sickness you face every evening would be good for you."

"I'll go today since they're expecting me. But I'll tell everyone this will be my last evening for the foreseeable future." She put on her coat and readied herself for the trip.

"That sounds like a good plan," Deborah said with a sigh, comforted Miriam was being realistic.

Miriam went to Denison House, telling those she was closest with and the person in charge that she wouldn't be coming back for a while. Everyone expressed sadness, understanding that she needed to be home with her ailing mother.

When Miriam headed to the back room to collect her things at the end of her shift, she thought of all the wonderful evenings she and Sadie had spent in this small space, talking over the plight of the world and sharing their personal stories with each other. As she opened the door, she had quite a shock. There stood Sadie.

"Sadie. What are you doing here?" Miriam asked anxiously.

"I need to see you. You left your shift on Wednesday nights suddenly, and I've missed you terribly," Sadie said with sad, lonely eyes fixed on Miriam.

"But Sadie, I left because I couldn't see you anymore. Deborah became very jealous and I was unhappy with my behavior."

Sadie came closer, approaching Miriam as if she was about to hold her or kiss her or maybe attack her. As Miriam pulled back, repeating Sadie's name several times, the door flew open. Who should be standing there, but Deborah, with a look as shocked as Hannah's when she came upon them in bed that fateful day.

"Deborah! Why are you here? Is Mother all right?"

Deborah glanced at the unfamiliar girl, then turned right back to Miriam. "No, she isn't. She's taken a very bad turn. Her breathing has changed, and I fear the end may be near. I need to take you to her right now."

Both girls looked toward Sadie, who was standing by herself, with empty, stricken eyes. Neither said anything to her, as they dashed out the door.

"How could you?" was all Deborah said.

"She surprised me by showing up just now. I did not know she was coming here. She is the last person I wanted to see." Miriam wondered, "Does Deborah believe me?"

"We'll discuss this later, but right now you need to get home quickly to be with your mother."

"Is she dying, Deborah?"

"I think so."

They left silently, rushed to the car, and did not talk all the way home.

Deborah dropped Miriam off at the house and went immediately to get Hannah. Miriam walked in the room to find Mother lying on her bed, taking in air in periodic gasps. Her skin was gray and her hair matted to her head. Bubbie sat at the corner of the bed, holding Mother's hand. Miriam sat down quietly on her other side, providing comfort, yet crying inside.

When Hannah arrived a short time later, the three of them surrounded Mother, and she roused for a moment, looking intensely at each of them. She was past words, but she showed her love for each of them through her eyes.

They were at her side as her breathing rattled. Both her daughters held her hands and sang familiar Hebrew songs to her. As her breath faltered for the final time, the girls and Bubbie recited the *Shema*, the prayer said at the time of death. All three of them made a small tear in their clothing, as was the custom. She died on July 27, just a year after her husband's passing.

Deborah had taken Sylvia and Sarah into the parlor and put them to sleep on opposite sides of the couch. She was sitting in the middle of the babies, with her outstretched hands rubbing their little bodies, when Miriam came downstairs with tears in her eyes. Deborah wasn't surprised when Miriam softly said, "Mother has passed away." Deborah patted each of the children and stood to hold Miriam. They embraced tightly, both whimpering.

William arrived a few minutes later, having gone to get the rabbi. The rabbi greeted Miriam and Hannah with, *Barukh atah Adonai Eloheinu melekh ha'olam, dayan ha-emet.* (Blessed are You, Lord, our G-d, King of the Universe, the Judge of Truth.)

Then to all of them he said, "May her memory be a blessing."

Once everyone was upstairs, including the babies and William, the rabbi led them in prayers over the still warm body.

Bubbie, as she had when Mr. Cohen died, insisted she sit vigil over the body. "I be wit her." She insisted she be the one to follow Jewish custom of *shemira*, guarding the body until burial as the soul hovers overhead. Bubbie, as expected, recited the psalms while sitting with Mother.

Although Miriam, Deborah, Hannah, and William each offered to relieve her, she said, "I stay with her. I protect her." Miriam found it very sweet that she felt the same compassion toward her daughter-in-law as she had towards her own son.

As is tradition, the very next day was the funeral, which was held at the cemetery with many temple members in attendance. At the graveside, the family wept as Mother was lowered into the ground. The *Mourner's Kaddish* and the *El Maleh Rachamim*, a prayer for the rest of the departed, were both recited. Each chose a small stone to throw into the grave. They had postponed the unveiling of Father's headstone on the one-year anniversary of his death the week before, due to Mother's ill health. The draped headstone next to Mother's newly dug grave was a reminder of the full extent of the loss they had faced over the past year.

After the ceremony, the mourners returned to the house to begin the *shiva* period. As was customary all mirrors in the house were covered and the mourners sat on low chairs. They wore their torn clothing throughout the *shiva* and William didn't shave his beard. The rabbi arrived in the evening, as he would do each of the seven days, gathering ten men to form a *minyan*, the number required to recite the *Mourner's Kaddish*, the Jewish prayer for the dead.

As they headed to bed after the first day of mourning, Miriam said, "I was told by many people today that my mother taught them about acceptance. They were touched by her loving embrace of us."

"I was surprised and amazed myself." Reaching out her hand to stroke Miriam's face, Deborah said, "I'm pleased that what we feared would lead to ostracism instead led to admiration by some for her bravery in the face of what most would have felt as shame."

"She really loved and respected you. She saw your goodness, and she trusted that you're good for me."

"She also saw my stubborn side and my impulsivity and, as she'd have done if I were her daughter, she accepted me with all my faults."

"Your strengths far outweigh your weaknesses. She knew that. And she knew that I love you with all my heart."

During the second night of *Shiva*, Marilyn and Julie arrived. Miriam motioned them into the back hall to talk with them privately. "I really appreciate you coming today, especially since we haven't been good at maintaining our friendship with you."

"It's all right," Marilyn said.

"No, it isn't," Miriam said with a deep sigh. "I want to tell you, Deborah and I like you both a great deal, but there has been too much going on for us lately to follow through on your generous offers of companionship."

"That's nice of you to say," Julie said.

"I mean it sincerely. Both Deborah and I were thrilled to meet you, and we really wanted to develop our friendship with you. But then many things began going badly for us and we couldn't manage getting together. We weren't trying to put you off as it must have appeared to you."

"I appreciate your honesty," said Marilyn. "What if we try again once things calm down for you?"

"I'd like that a lot, and I'm certain Deborah will too. I'm genuinely pleased there will be another opportunity for us. Once things have settled, we'll invite you to our home. Our two wonderful friends, Susan and Helen, are living here and working with us, and I'm certain you'll like them too. Come with me now and I'll introduce you."

They found Susan and Helen in the back corner of the parlor. The two newly introduced couples spent the evening talking. Once they'd greeted most of the mourners and many of the guests had left, Miriam and Deborah made their way to where the four were still chatting. After a short exchange, it was clear this group of six would have many more conversations. Deborah and Miriam had found a group of like-minded friends, fulfilling the goals they had ever since they were first together.

In the weeks after Mother's death, Miriam and Bubbie both shed tears freely as they talked of being glad Mother was no longer suffering. Bubbie cooked enough food for each meal to feed Hannah and William, should they decide to join them. This happened with great regularity, both because Hannah was too tired to prepare a meal and because she needed to spend as many hours with her sister and grandmother as possible.

Hannah and Miriam sometimes spent a few minutes alone after dinner each evening, sitting with babies on their laps, reflecting on their mother's goodness and also on their fears about Bubbie. She'd outlived her husband, son, and daughter-in-law. Miriam wondered how she'd weathered all this loss and still projected such a loving heart.

After Mother's death the house would have been eerily quiet except for the addition of Susan and Helen. Their presence added warmth and companionship at what would have been an especially lonely time. They helped Miriam sort her mother's belongings, a difficult task. They all held their breath as Miriam opened the door to the chifforobe, and Mother's smell wafted toward each of them. After selecting a few treasures for herself, Miriam packed everything else into satchels she'd readied, planning to bring it all to Denison House. Miriam knew it would be touching to see the women dressed in her mother's clothing. In a small way, it would serve to keep Mother's memory alive.

After Mrs. Cohen's clothing had been distributed, Deborah and Miriam cleaned out Mother's room. Gradually, they moved all their things in, giving Sylvia a room of her own again. It was helpful to have their own private space, though Deborah and Miriam on lonely nights sometimes fell asleep in the small bed next to their baby. They always returned to their own bed sometime during the night.

Cohen burial plot

Stonegate

CHAPTER THIRTY

Healing at Stonegate

Early August, 1914

Not only was the world at Homestead Street, Roxbury shifting, but the larger world was changing too. On July 29, the newspapers announced the beginning of the Great War all had feared for a long time. Conflict had begun in Europe and everyone worried about the impact this war would have on the rest of the world. Deborah and Miriam hardly noticed this dramatic event, in light of Mother's passing, but after the *shiva* was over, Susan and Helen brought up the topic over dinner one night.

The girls worried about whether the war would come to the United States and about the men in their lives: Mr. Levine, Mr. Berkowitz, and William. Then they worried about the younger males: Deborah's brother, Milton; Marjorie's boyfriend, Micah; and Ruth's brother, David. Which of them would be called for service? Milton had already pledged himself to train in warfare at the upcoming Boot Camp. Susan and Helen feared for their relatives and friends, too.

Susan sat next to Deborah and said, "I know you're especially worried about your brother, Milton, who leaves in just a few weeks for his military training. I think you should travel to the Berkshires to spend time with him and the rest of your family. I know you still have concerns about your mother's welfare and you and Miriam would benefit from some time to yourselves after what you have been through."

"But …" Deborah began to say before being interrupted by Helen.

"You need your family right now. You have just lost Mrs. Cohen, and we know how difficult that was for both of you. You should take a few days to heal."

Miriam's face lightened as she said, "They're right, Deborah. It would be helpful for us to get away. This has been a difficult time with my mother's illness and death. I agree you need to visit with your brother before he leaves. And your father always has wonderful ideas for our business so maybe you can justify this trip as business."

They all laughed softly and Deborah conceded. "It would be healing to be with my family, and they haven't seen Sylvia in a long time. I want to check on my mother and see if she's doing as well as she claims."

"Enough reasons," Miriam said. Turning to Helen and Susan she said, "Thank you. I know it will be difficult at the shop when we're gone so we'll just go for just a few days. We'll spend Shabbos with Deborah's family and then come back quickly."

"You've taught us enough that I'm certain we can manage," Susan said.

Deborah added, "You have learned so much in such a short period. I know you'll do fine. And William is quite capable."

"Also, we'll enjoy having some time with Bubbie," Helen said.

Before Deborah and Miriam left for Great Barrington, Marjorie greeted them at work with a grin spread across her whole face. In light of the frightening news of warfare, smiles were rare on anyone.

Miriam asked, "What is it, Marjorie, that has you so cheerful this morning?"

"Micah and I had a long talk last night about his impending involvement in the war, which he believes will need him. He wanted to make certain I'd be waiting for him, so he's asked me to marry him."

"Oh Marjorie! What exciting news, though I'm not surprised."

"I was.! He had this all planned out. We were sitting in our favorite spot, along the Neponset River, and he casually pulled this ring out of his pocket."

"Let's see," Miriam said with wide eyes and an upbeat lilt to her voice as she moved closer to examine the small ring on Marjorie's finger. "It's beautiful."

"I know it's a tiny diamond, but it's all he could afford right now. He promised he'd buy me a bigger ring when the war is over."

"But it sparkles. You can look at it while he's gone and remember how much he loves you."

"I can't take my eyes off of it. I'm so happy!"

"I'm extremely thrilled for you. But now please let me into the shop so I can put down my packages."

"Sorry," said Marjorie, with a huge grin.

Deborah and Miriam left the next Thursday, taking the morning train to Great Barrington. They were greeted by a new staff member sent from Stonegate and were in the driveway of the stately home within five minutes.

When they arrived, Deborah waved to her mother, who was on the porch sipping lemonade as she had the first day Miriam came to their house. It was wonderful that she was acting like her old self, smiling at both of them, hugging them enthusiastically, and taking a sleepy Sylvia into her arms.

"I'm so glad to be here, Mother," Deborah said.

"I'm thrilled to have you here. I know your visit will be short so I want to spend every minute with you."

"Sorry, but we need to fit in a lot during our quick stay. I want to spend time with Milton and Anna, and Mrs. Berkowitz has said she and her husband will drive down from Lenox with the girls on Sunday."

"Let me change my statement. We'll make certain you do everything you want, but I look forward to every moment I can spend with you."

"I'm so pleased to see you looking so well," Miriam added.

"I'm relieved to feel like myself again. That was a very difficult time for me, when I was in Boston."

"It's a great relief to see you've recovered, Mother. We were all very worried about you."

"No need to fuss about me anymore. Now that my family is back together, I'm fine. Speaking of all being back together, your father will arrive tomorrow for the weekend. He'll be glad to see you."

Indeed, Mr. Levine was very pleased to have his family together. As he entered the front door, he greeted Deborah with his usual hug and then turned to Miriam for a hug too. Miriam squeezed him, smiling. When he reached out for Sylvia, they knew things would be fine.

During the weekend, Deborah made certain to have some time alone with each of her siblings. Milton was especially pleased. He and Deborah took a walk down West Street to have time alone. He was enthusiastic about boot camp, which would begin in less than two weeks, and they spoke about the Great War.

Later in the afternoon, after Sylvia woke up from her nap, Deborah brought her to the parlor where she found Anna sitting in a comfortable chair reading a book. Deborah was pleased; this was a perfect way to spend some time with her younger sister.

Anna spoke first, "This isn't the book Mother wanted me to read, so I hope you'll not tell."

"Your secret's safe with me. I know how Mother insists you read the same books during the summer that her mother forced on her."

"I wish she'd let me read what I want. After all, I'm fifteen."

"It looks like you have a found a way to read both. You're smart, Anna. Now show me what you have chosen to read."

"It's *Dracula* by Bram Stoker. My friend lent it to me."

"I read that last year and loved it."

"Don't tell me what happens. I'm only halfway through."

"I'll keep that a secret, too. But please tell me when you're finished so we can discuss the ending."

"Sure."

Anna was happy to have attention focused on her. She put down her book and talked nonstop to Deborah about the other adolescent girls living in Great Barrington and about all the attractive boys she'd met. Deborah was happy to be included in Anna's confidences.

Another visit, which Deborah and Miriam felt was necessary was a trip to the ice cream parlor to see Ruth. When they got there, it felt very different from before. Miriam noticed the walls had been painted a cotton-candy pink, and the noisy group in the corner was made up of fresh-faced youngsters much younger than Miriam and Deborah. They thought back to their times at the ice cream parlor and realized they were younger, too, when they used to gather in those seats. There were only a few people they knew, since many of their friends had gotten married and were no longer in Great Barrington for the summer. Or maybe everyone had tired of Ruth.

"How nice to see you," Ruth called out as they entered the shop. She rose to greet them, hugging them both with enthusiasm. Miriam tried her best to be cordial. Ruth prattled on about her summer and, true to her pattern, never asked them anything about their lives. She never noticed that Deborah and Miriam had no real interest in what she was talking about. Luckily, she did have the decency to offer condolences for their loss or they would never have forgiven her. They stayed long enough for each to have a soda and then to falsely claim they were sorry to leave so soon. Ruth never even mentioned Sylvia.

The most entertaining part of the weekend was the arrival of the Berkowitz family. The young girls ran into the house ahead of their parents, excited to see Sylvia. Before long, they smelled cookies baking and left in search of a treat. After they left, Miriam noted, "Fannie seems more sociable than during their last visit."

"I wonder if she was putting on a show of good behavior for us," Deborah said, scrunching her eyebrows and heaving a sigh.

Miriam shushed her, saying, "I think she's better. Maybe her adolescent anger has relaxed." Deborah was unconvinced, though she was pleased Fannie's behavior had improved, no matter what the reason.

Their greatest pleasure was the time they spent with Mrs. B. They took a long walk with her, telling her all about their recent relationship challenge on the terrible night Deborah walked into Denison House and found Sadie with Miriam. As they walked, Mrs. B. expressed great relief they were doing better. "You're learning about the ups and downs of relationships. Nothing of value is perfect all the time. Sometimes the way you resolve conflicts strengthens your ties to one another. You're learning to be honest and trusting, even when it's tough."

Miriam said, "You're right Mrs. B. I feel our relationship is stronger since we dealt with our problems."

Deborah took a deep breath. "Our conflicts tested our relationship, yet we have mended it."

Mrs. B., pointing to a stone wall for them to sit on, asked, "Do you feel stronger?"

"Yes. My anger was terrible when I walked into Denison House and found Sadie there, but Miriam assured me she didn't initiate or want the rendezvous, that Sadie's visit was unplanned," said Deborah as she sat on the wall.

"As I've told you repeatedly, I was shocked to find her there, and I was busy telling her to go away when you walked in."

"Do you believe her, Deborah?" Mrs. B. asked.

"Yes, but it opened my old wounds when I had to face that girl."

"You need to heal those wounds for good, Deborah," Miriam said. "I need you to trust me. I love you, and I'd never intentionally do anything to hurt you again. I never meant to hurt you in the first place."

Mrs. B. got up and walked over to Deborah, put her hands on her shoulders, and looked into her eyes. "You need to trust Miriam."

"I'm trying my best."

"Should she trust you, Miriam?"

"Absolutely."

"Then you need to put the incident behind you, Deborah."

"I'm doing my best. I will try. I really will."

Yiddish books

CHAPTER THIRTY-ONE

Moving On

Mid-August, 1914

This shrinking family was changing faster than anyone expected, but happily there was youth to replace the older generation. Deborah and Miriam wished Bubbie a long life. They weren't ready to be the family elders at ages 21 and 22. But within a month of Mrs. Cohen's funeral Bubbie passed away quietly in her sleep.

Death brings out the best or worst in people. For Deborah and Miriam this was a time of deep bonding. They mourned the passing of Mother and Bubbie together. Miriam said, "Deborah, you seem as deeply affected by their passing as I am. Occasionally, I forget you only knew them a short while."

"Sometimes," Deborah said, smiling warmly, "It seems we've always been together, sharing touching moments, difficult decisions, love, and *munn* cookies."

"How sweet of you to say."

Bubbie's room was harder to clean out. "Her only real valuables were her Yiddish books," Miriam said.

"It would be important to her that they go to people who appreciate them," Deborah said.

"I gave several to Micah, but because many of Bubbie's friends passed away before her, we have to search for someone who would want the rest."

In an odd coincidence, it was suggested they give the books to a lovely elder who lived nearby. It turned out she was Sadie's grandmother. Neither girl could face delivering the parcel there, so they let the members of the Sisterhood take the neat packages they bundled together to anyone of their choosing.

Once Bubbie's room was emptied of her belongings, they converted the space into a playroom for Sylvia and Sarah during the daytime and a den where Susan and Helen could spend time by themselves in the evening. The home had become a comfortable place for all.

Deborah and Miriam, along with Hannah, William, Susan and Helen, spent many evenings engaged in enriching conversation filled with loving stories. The new family they created was one of respect, admiration, joy, and ease.

Deborah and Miriam began inviting Marilyn and Julie to their home with great regularity and they fit in comfortably. Not only did they befriend Susan and Helen, but somehow they were able to bring out Hannah's sense of humor. Even William was surprisingly talkative on the evenings they visited.

Susan and Helen attended suffrage meetings regularly. After missing several meetings, Deborah explained, "Neither Miriam nor I feel we have enough time in our week so we've decided to stay home rather than get involved in the movement again, despite our pledge to do so."

"We understand," Susan said.

"But please keep us abreast of the suffrage activities and accomplishments. And we'll gladly assist with any projects we can accomplish from home, such as folding flyers or putting together packets to be distributed," Miriam said.

"We can also volunteer our presses for any materials that need to be printed," Deborah added.

"That will be extremely helpful to the cause," Helen said.

Each evening, after they returned from a meeting, Susan and Helen shared descriptions of what had been discussed.

And as life continued, what of the anxiety that had threatened Deborah and Miriam's relationship? Much of it melted away. As they mourned the loving women who had tied the family together, their problems seemed less significant. Deborah remembered to love the wonderful girl sleeping by her side each night—and to trust her.

It also helped when a note written in a delicate hand appeared in the mail one day.

August 24, 1914

Dear Deborah,

My name is Sadie. I was a dear friend of Miriam this past year. She and I got to know each other when we were volunteering at Denison House on Wednesday evenings. I was encouraged to find another girl like me. I mistook my excitement for infatuation. I was too bold in expressing myself, and I scared Miriam and pushed her away.

After Miriam changed her volunteer night, I missed her companionship and wished to apologize for my inappropriate behavior. I surprised her one evening at Denison House, invading her privacy. Within the first minute after I revealed myself, you walked in the door, probably mistaking our being together as her choice. I apologize to you, and to her, for any misunderstandings you may have about my sudden reappearance in her life. She was just expressing shock at my presence as you walked in. She had no part in my bold intrusion in her life. I hope it did her no harm.

I never wanted to come between you. I know how much she loves you. Please accept my sincerest apologies and my hopes your relationship has not been affected by my presence. I wish nothing but happiness for the two of you.

Sadie

Deborah shared the letter with Miriam, and they both agreed that it put a fine ending to the incident with Sadie.

Deborah and Miriam were now, at their young ages, the matriarchs of a new and wonderful family of their choosing, a unique blend of loving people. They became the cornerstone of a new type of family, one built on love and support. They hired Rachel, the Lowell Mill Girl from Denison House, to care for the two babies, and they hired Rachel's mother to cook for them when they were weary after a long day at the publishing shop. Deborah and Miriam filled their home with entertainment and caring. It was a modern family, one that would enter 1915 with a new vision of love and a resolve to be together, facing the coming strife and sacrifice sure to affect them in the Great War.

The End

Munn cookies

Addendum

Bubbie's Munn Cookies

- About 3 cups flour
- 1/2 of a cup of poppy seeds
- 1-1/2 small spoons baking powder
- 1/4 spoon salt
- 1 cup soft butter
- About 2/3 of cup white sugar
- 1 egg (separate the white and the yellow parts)
- 2 big spoons lemon zest
- Juice from a lemon

1. Preheat oven to 350 degrees.

2. Cover baking sheets with a little butter.

3. Stir together the flour, poppy seeds, baking powder, and salt.

4. Mix the butter and sugar together. Beat until light; beat in the egg yolk, lemon zest, and lemon juice. Add the flour mixture and mix well.

5. Divide dough in half and roll each half out on a board coated with flour. Make 1/8 to 1/4 inch thick. Cut with cookie cutters and place cookies on the baking sheet. Brush tops of cookies with beaten egg white and sprinkle with white sugar.

6. Bake at 350 degrees for 12 to 15 minutes or until the edges are light brown.

Astrological Signs: Deborah and Miriam

Although Deborah and Miriam are fictional characters, with fictional birthdates, the astrological descriptions for their birthdates are surprisingly accurate descriptions of them.

Deborah (Scorpio)

Scorpios are intense, with a heart like a live volcano. They have a powerfully frank, piercing style. They value honesty above all else and detest hypocrisy. They refuse to operate on a dual standard.

Miriam (Virgo)

Virgos are Earth mothers, who prefer not to be in the spotlight. They provide essential support while others take the bows. They are often drawn to rash but inspired individuals. They have an impeccable eye for detail and a strong sense of duty.

Historical Background: 1913–1914

THE GREAT WAR/BOOT CAMP

One extremely important concern of this time period was significant worries about impending war, which Europe entered in 1914. It was on the minds of everyone in the United States and affected many decisions, especially for young men. Officially, no one could join the military until age 18 and could not be sent overseas until age 19, yet there were thousands of underage enlistees who lied about their age in order to serve their country. Also, war created worry among the women, who feared that their menfolk would soon be abandoning them.

The Preparedness Campaign (Boot Camp) was responsible for the creation of two experimental military instruction camps for college students to attend during their summer vacations. Known as the "Plattsburg Idea," these boot camps trained young men who were later commissioned as officers in the war.

IMMIGRATION OF JEWS

The number of Eastern European Jews immigrating to Boston increased significantly in the late 1800s to early 1900s, therefore broadening the number of people who needed a Yiddish publishing service. The increase in the Jewish population was due in part to the persecution of Jews in the Russian empire and to an ethnic cleansing in Prussia, a predominantly German state extending through territories that are now Poland, Lithuania, and Russia. Many Jews escaped to the United States, looking for religious freedom and economic stability. Jews, with an entrepreneurial culture and an ethic of self-support, became financially secure more quickly than the other immigrant groups. In 1875, the Jewish population of Boston was estimated to number only 3,000, but by 1900 it had reached 40,000. By 1913, over 80,000 Jews lived in the city. No wonder their business was having difficulty keeping up!

SETTLEMENT HOUSES

Settlement houses were created to bring poor and rich folks together by making daycare, education, and healthcare available to all. By 1913, there were 413 settlement houses in 32 states.

The first settlement houses:

1889, Hull House, Chicago

1892, Denison House, Boston

1893, Henry Street Settlement House, New York City

SUFFRAGE

Of great importance during this time period were the changes in the suffrage movement. Nine states had ratified women's right to vote by 1914. Although Deborah and Miriam remained only minimally involved, this was an important period in the changing status of women. Massachusetts was a hotbed of political activity, beginning with Lucy Stone (a Boston native), Elizabeth Cady Stanton, Lucretia Mott, and Susan B. Anthony stirring suffrage activity in 1850 at the First National Women's Rights Convention which convened in Worcester, Massachusetts.

Massachusetts males voted on women's suffrage as an amendment to the United States Constitution in 1895. The referendum was defeated by over 65 percent, with only the town of Tewksbury voting in favor of suffrage. Four states in the east—Massachusetts, New Jersey, Pennsylvania, and New York—were still against full suffrage for women during the time of this book.

LESBIAN LIFE

Also happening during this era was the increasing lesbian community in Boston. A society began to develop, thanks to some female Wellesley College professors who began gathering the lesbian elite of the area. They opened a settlement house, Denison House, in the West End of Boston, the same place where Miriam volunteered. In the 1910s, several lesbian couples, notably Emily Greene Balch and Mabel Cummings, Agnes Perkins and Etta Herr, and Katherine Coman and Vida Scudder became supporters of Denison House. They began gathering women like themselves, much in the manner of Gertrude Stein and Alice B. Toklas in Paris some years later. Deborah and Miriam were fortunate to fall into this emerging Boston lesbian community.

ILLNESSES

The illnesses of the characters in this book were accurate for the times. Although most deaths in this era were attributed to communicable diseases, Deborah and Miriam's middle-class status would likely have kept their families out of harm's way. Their connection at Denison House with immigrants and those previously living in poverty would have increased their chances of contracting some of these diseases.

Although never labeled as such in the book, I will share the diagnosis of other characters. Hannah and William would both currently be labeled as having Asperger's syndrome, and Leah's inability to walk would be called cerebral palsy. Cancer, unlabeled for Mother until late in the book, was diagnosed as such as early as the 1700s but would have probably been a speculation of the medical doctor, and not screened or treated during this time. Diagnoses of most disorders would generally not have been shared with the patients or their families.

One of the characters (I will not spoil your read by telling you who) has a situational mental breakdown with a temporary catatonic-like state. Several 2019 therapists determined her current diagnostic category would be a "Brief Reactive Depressive Disorder."

DOWN SYNDROME/MONGOLOID IDIOT

Another tremendous stress for Deborah and Miriam was parenting a child with special needs. Though Sylvia, who would then be called a Mongoloid idiot, brought Deborah and Miriam a great deal of pleasure, caring for her was challenging. Most children with disabilities were placed in institutions, which were considered by popular belief to be a better place to serve them. The Experimental School for Feeble-Minded Children, one of the oldest institutions in the United States to deal with the disabled, was later named the Walter E. Fernald State School. It existed as a state institution until 2014, one hundred years after Sylvia was evaluated there. The photograph in the book is a current view of the main building of the now-closed institution.

Mongoloidism, now termed "Down Syndrome" was named after the English Dr. John Langdon-Down, the doctor mentioned in the book. He and his physician sons developed theories about the educability of these children, believing the popular belief in eugenics wrong. Eugenics was a scientific belief and practice of controlled breeding to eliminate all imperfect human traits. (Later, this was the doctrine adopted by Adolf Hitler and the Nazis.) Winston Churchill commissioned a study resulting in the British "Mental Deficiency Act of 1913," denouncing state-sanctioned sterilization of the mentally deficient, the general course of ridding the world of these "undesirables." In the United States, there was no protection, so anyone trying to raise an "imperfect" child would have faced scrutiny.

Experimental School for Feeble-Minded Children

Early History

- In 1848, Dr. Samuel Gridley Howe, director of the Perkins School for the Blind, established The Massachusetts School for Idiotic and Feeble-Minded Youth, an experimental boarding school for children with intellectual deficiencies

- The school was viewed as a model educational facility in the field of mental retardation

- 72 buildings were built to house, feed, and teach the residents

1898

- There were 109 children in teachable classes, 176 in kindergarten and practical classes

- Most children were in physical, sense training, manual and industrial classes

- Dr. Fernald hired his first assistant physician, who had been the head farmer until he completed medical school

1909

- 113 males and 30 females were discharged to hospitals for the insane, proving the difficulty of diagnosing imbecility from adolescent mental disease

- Female attendants' salary increased from $20 to $25 per month

1912

- Dr. Fernald celebrates his 25th anniversary as superintendent of the school

- 555 applications for admission, mostly pathological people and helpless idiots

- Horrible overcrowding, with up to 60 individuals sleeping on mattresses on the floor

- Maria Montessori's book on child-centered education increases the number of visitors

- Massachusetts pioneers in care of feeble-minded and imbeciles

1913

- All residents are given psychological testing and Binet-Simon tests
- Of 1665 residents, 559 have mental age of under 5, 810 5 to 8 years, and 296 at 9 to 11

1915

- Urged by State Board of Insanity to open outpatient clinics
- Two outbreaks of diphtheria with 3 deaths; 6 cases of typhoid; 3 cases of pellagra

Later History

- In 1925 school renamed in of honor Water E. Fernald, an advocate of eugenics
- From 1946 to 1953, The Fernald School was the site of the joint experiments by Harvard University and MIT that exposed young male children to radioactive isotopes
- During the 1970s, a class action suit was filed to upgrade conditions at Fernald, and in 1993 the school guaranteed a level of care to compensate for neglect and abuse
- In 2003 it was determined that the facility would be closed and the land sold by 2007
- Presently it remains vacant

Experimental School for Feeble-Minded Children

1910 Census

When the Census was taken in 1910, the Experimental School at 200 Trapelo Rd, Waltham, Massacusetts was completely left out. There was no one listed at that location, though there were 1665 residents in 1913, as noted above. The residents of the school were not counted as Massachusetts citizens, nor citizens at all.

1910 Census ledger page

Rachel: The Lowell Mill Girl

When I was sixteen, I was living in a small town outside Boston with my parents, three sisters, and a thirteen-year-old brother, but suddenly everything changed. My father, Abba, (Hebrew for father) had learned his trade at a sweatshop in the Lower East Side, New York, when he and his family emigrated from Russia. He became ill and could not work consistently. His work in textiles suffered as he became weaker; he could no longer carry the large bolts of fabric that he was expected to bring to the seamstresses.

Abba lost his job, and Ema (Hebrew for mother) was having trouble taking care of him and my sisters and brother while trying to make ends meet. I offered to find a job, but it was difficult for a girl to find work.

One day I saw an advertisement for a job as a Lowell Mill Girl in the textile industry, and I rushed to the meeting where they promised good wages, plentiful food, and a nice boarding house. What I did not tell my parents was that their way of assuring their girl's good moral character was to require every girl to attend the local Episcopal church. This would be unacceptable for a nice Jewish girl like me, but I had no choice. One less mouth to feed would help put more food on the table for the rest of my family, and I would have a little money to send to them.

I packed my belongings in a small trunk and took the long trolley ride to the town of Lowell. I was welcomed into the mill-owned house by the boardinghouse keeper, Mrs. Becker. She showed me the dining room, with the attractive mahogany furniture and matching china she had brought with

Lowell Mills worker

her from Boston, which made me feel at home. When shown to my bedroom, one of over a dozen such rooms I was soon to learn, my worries began. I had not expected I would be sharing my bed with a perfect stranger. Edna, a girl from a farm in Vermont, had a skin rash that scared me, and I was afraid to sleep on the same sheets as her. I was careful never to roll to her side of the bed. Our bedroom was small, with just enough room for our two small trunks.

On my first day, they woke us at 4:45 a.m. for a 6:15 a.m. breakfast, as I soon learned was the custom. This gave all the girls time to do their morning chores. As the newest girl, I was assigned to the worst job: cleaning the chimney. I arrived at the meal with soot in my hair, under my fingernails, and coating my eyelids. Everyone giggled at me. I was looking forward to someone newer than me arriving so I could give up this horrible task. Sadly, I was stuck with this job for over a month.

At breakfast, my plate was piled high with more food than I usually ate in a day, and more than I ate during some whole weeks since Abba was laid

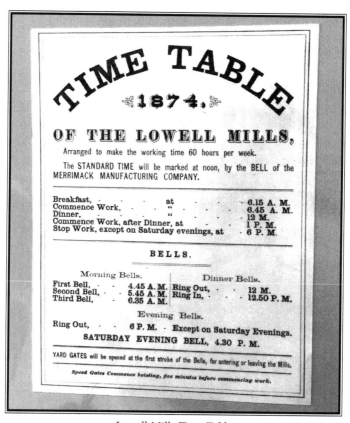

Lowell Mills Time Table

off. I ate a small bit and was chastised by Mrs. Becker for not cleaning my plate. She told me I would need to fill my belly to get me through the hard work I was about to face, but I could not consume another mouthful of the wonderful breakfast she had cooked.

After helping with the rest of the morning chores, I followed the other girls across the canal to the textile mills where I would work from 6:45 a.m. until 6:00 p.m., five days per week, and from 6:45 a.m until 4:30 p.m. on Saturday. While climbing the circular staircase to the floor where cotton was made into usable fabric, I was warned to be careful not to step on my long dress, causing me to trip and bring several other girls down with me. When upstairs, I was first assaulted by the noise. The eighty-six belt-driven weaving machines on our floor created quite a racket, which had worn away the hearing of many of the girls who had worked there for a long time. I was also overwhelmed with the smell, which I attributed to the sweaty men running the machines, who clearly did not bathe often.

I was assigned to be a threader. I was told my small hands would help me to run individual threads through the reeds and into each tiny hole in the heddles, which were loops of wire on the looms. My job was not an easy one. I was given repeated warnings not to catch my fingers in the fast-moving shuttles, which contained the bobbins of thread, or my clothing in the belts that powered the machines. If a thread broke, the machine was shut down and I was to quickly replace it so progress could continue. Every second lost was costly. We produced large quantities of material, which would later be made into dishcloths.

At noon, I was led back to the boardinghouse where I was expected to consume an even larger meal. Again, I was a disappointment to Mrs. Becker. After 6:00 p.m. that first day, I returned to my new home and was expected to eat a third meal. I hurried to my bed, ashamed and feeling terribly lonely for my family. I cried myself to sleep that night and many nights to come.

On Sunday, I followed the other girls to the nearby church to participate in the required service. I worried some would know I was Jewish because of my name, and others would figure it out when I knew nothing of their religious practice. I wanted to hide my religion for fear I would be fired. Luckily, there were many other girls who were unused to the Episcopal service so I did not stand out.

The work was hard and the conditions difficult, especially in the hot summer months when sweat poured down my face, making it difficult to see, and in the cold winter season when frozen fingers made threading difficult. There were many times I was scolded for the extra time it took me to accomplish my tedious task. After just one year, I was called into the overseer's office and told I had made too many mistakes and I was too slow. I was to leave at the end of the day and collect my wages for the week. I should pack my bags and be ready for the first trolley in the morning to take me back to my family. Although I would miss the income, I was relieved that this chapter of my life was over.

Ema was thrilled when I walked in the door, rushing to me with open arms and huge tears falling down her face. It had been a difficult year for all of us. First, my Abba had become even weaker and eventually succumbed to his illness. Soon after his death my little brother got dysentery and he also died. Ema and I cried together, and she told me she could no longer manage. She was grateful I had arrived that day because in just two days the whole family would be moving to Denison House. This would be a place where she could ensure we would all have food and shelter. That is how I got here.

Mildred's Trip on an Orphan Train

Last year was the worst year of my life. Everything changed all at once when I came home from school one day to find my neighbor waiting for me on my doorstep. She was crying so hard she could hardly tell me the news that my parents were in a buggy accident and they were both killed.

I was stunned. Suddenly, at eight-years-old, I had no one to take care of me. My neighbor took me in for three days but then explained I could not stay with her, nor could I go home. She said I was very lucky we lived in New York because I would be able to get help from the Children's Aid Society. She helped me to pack a bag with some clothing and took me to their offices. A nice lady named Lucy promised they would find me a new family. My neighbor left me in the care of this stranger. I was petrified.

Lucy told me that as soon as she had thirty orphans, we would be taking a train to Missouri to find new parents for all the children. I had to ask her the meaning of the word "orphan," a word that later moved me to tears each time I heard it. I did not know anything about Missouri, not expecting it was a three-day trip from New York, the only place I had ever been. I had no choices.

Lucy showed me to a cot in a huge room at the back of the Society. She gave me a toothbrush and an extra pair of scratchy panties. I was the only child there, and I was very lonely that first night. During the next two weeks, new children arrived every day until all the rows of beds were filled. We were fed apples, bread, and soup, which made me long for my mother's wonderful meals. All of us were upset about losing our families, so there was little joy.

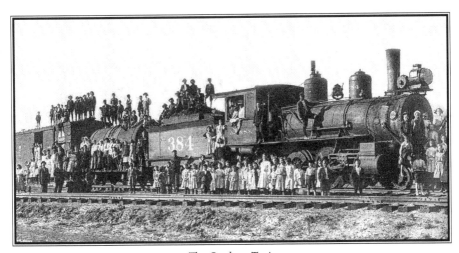

The Orphan Train

The smells became almost unbearable when little children who had soiled their clothing had no way to bathe or change.

Finally, the day came to get on the Orphan Train. They brought each of us outdoors, through the back door of the Society, made us strip down, and cleaned us with buckets of soapy water so we would not smell any more. They gave us each a new set of clothing, which we had to change into right outside. Lucy and some other women combed each girl's hair and gave each of us a colorful hair ribbon to match our new dresses, and everyone got a Bible. The boys went out a separate door, and from what I could tell they did not get anything special except soap and Bibles.

Lucy tried to comfort everyone by telling us what would happen next. First, she promised she would stay with us until every last child had a new family, which I hoped was true. Next, she explained the train would make three stops. At each station there would be a group of people from the town who came to select a child. Some of them had been unable to have children of their own, and others wanted to add another child to their family. We were to be friendly so that we would be selected. The children whispered to one another that they heard the families were more interested in someone to help on their farm than a child to love. I knew nothing about working on a farm and I was not strong, so I wondered if anyone would choose me.

At the first stop, we were walked from the train depot to a local playhouse. They paraded us onto the stage and told us to sit in the chairs they had lined up facing the audience. All the potential parents were watching our every move and pointed to the children as they talked to each other. There was a small band playing cheerful music, and when everyone was seated there were speeches by Lucy and the local pastor. When they told us we were to each have a turn to say our name or sing a song, I had to work very hard not to cry. After everyone had their frightening minute to sell themselves, they brought us into a large room where we had to be with all the families. It was awful. They looked at our teeth, and I saw them feeling the muscles of the boys, making me believe they were looking for farmhands.

By the end of the evening, fourteen families had chosen their children. Most of the tallest and strongest children had been selected, along with some pretty little girls. Those of us who had not found parents were silently walked back to the train. We all felt awful. That same night we headed toward the next town. At the second stop, after another performance, though this time at the train station, I was chosen by a young couple to be their child. They seemed okay. Lucy had them fill out some paperwork, and she sent me off with these strangers.

On the way back to their farm, Eugene and Dorothy told me they had been unable to have children of their own so they were pleased to have a girl like me. But neither understood what it was like to be a parent. They worked me hard from morning to night, fed me very little food, and rarely talked with me. I was very lonely and unhappy there. When Lucy came to check on me after six months, as she said she would, she was surprised how thin I was. I told her I did not want to stay. She let me come back to New York on the train with her. After a few days back on the cot, she sent me to Boston to Denison House, explaining the staff there would take good care of me. That is how I got here. I have been well cared for, and I have lots of new friends. I am very grateful.

Orphan Train flyer

Elizabeth: Daughter of a Suffragette

My family was destroyed by the Suffrage Movement. If my mother was a suffragist, a member of the nonmilitant wing of the movement to gain the right for women to vote, things might have been different. But my mama is a full-blown suffragette, a woman who believes their motto, "Deeds not Words," and is willing to fight for the rights of all women. She follows the doctrine of Emmeline Pankhurst, the British woman who has been campaigning for equality for women in the English government since the turn of the century. Since I was ten, her name was as common out of my mother's mouth as the name of G-d.

My father, on the other hand, is opposed to the entire suffrage movement, believing strongly that women should not be involved in politics. He thinks a woman's place is in the home, and he thinks it should be enough that he grants mother freedom with the family. Luckily, he is not one of those men who believes that women are not smart enough to have political opinions, but he has always wanted my mother to stay home to darn socks and cook meals. When my mother got involved in the movement, she no longer focused her life on making our home a perfect showplace of domestic life. This irritated him on a daily basis, and our home became a battleground.

When my mama stood firm on her beliefs and marched in parades, my father threatened her. He feared that she was going to chain herself to buildings and destroy works of art, as the English suffragettes had done. He said that if she did not desist from her activities, he would cut off her access to money. That did not work since she had hidden away some money to feed us. Next, he said he would throw her out onto the streets if she did not stop. That is exactly what happened.

This autumn, my sisters, our mother, and I spent several nights sleeping on the ground in a park in town. Mother did not dare to ask her friends to take us in, afraid their husbands would follow suit and throw them out of their homes, too. On our third night outdoors, a policeman discovered us huddled together on the ground, clutching at our satchels of precious belongings. A kind man, he brought us to Denison House instead of the police station. We were grateful to be taken in and given shelter and food.

Since at Denison House, my mama has been calm, though she tells us she feels defeated. She is not willing to go back to our father and the secure life we led. My sisters and I try not to resent her for pulling our family apart and making it necessary that we accept the kindness of strangers to exist. Since Mama has no way to support us, I think we will be living here for a long time, maybe forever.

THE SUFFRAGIST   THE SUFFRAGETTE.

Contemporary political cartoon

Yuan's Grandmother, White Peony

I am telling you the story that was passed down to me from my mother, in a tender tale that she was afraid to say out loud. We begged her to tell us about the elderly woman whom she worshiped as the strongest influence of her childhood. I am sorry Grandmother did not live long enough for me to sit near her, to take in the essence of power that filled the air around her.

Grandmother, called White Peony, was born in 1842, a year of the Black Water Tiger in the Republic of China. The story she told was a secret, written in a special language created by women for women, which I learned is the only such language anywhere. Men are not allowed to learn the characters nor touch the words, whether they were written on rice paper or on a delicate fan. This secret code was called "*nu shu*", whose name itself brings tingles to my spine.

Grandmother was third daughter, a position of minimal worth in the family. She pledged her allegiance to her own father, and later to the family of her husband, but I am rushing ahead.

White Peony had to endure the painful experience of foot binding in order to have tiny feet that would be beautiful enough to win her a valued marriage. After picking the most auspicious day when she was seven years old

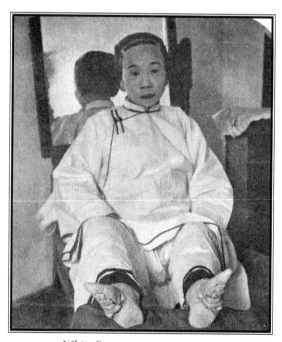

White Peony as a young woman

to begin the binding of the feet, her mother wrapped her feet in wet cloths that tightened as they dried, and caused day after day, week after week, and even year after year of excruciating pain. The infections her cousin endured led to her death at age nine, but that did not stop White Peony's mother from increasing the binds until her toes broke, one by one. They were wrapped tighter, and she was made to walk on them over and over to complete the process of creating beautiful tiny feet.

Once her feet were bound, Grandmother was confined to the Women's Chambers, never leaving the house again, except to move to her husband's family home upon her marriage and the end of her first pregnancy. It was there, in this women's space, that she was taught the special phonetic characters that comprised the *nu shu*.

Because White Peony's feet were perfect, she was given the honored privilege of being paired with a *laotong*. This honor of being matched to another, "old same," meant that grandmother would be bonded together with another girl, bound by a contract written in *nu shu*. A *laotong* match was as significant as a good marriage, promising the girls lifelong emotional companionship and eternal fidelity.

White Peony and her *laotong*, Waning Moon, visited one another regularly, sharing meals, a bed, an everlasting commitment, and deep love with one another. This rare privilege meant Grandmother had a "sister" for life, to take her through foot binding, marriage, childbirth, and death.

As an old lady my grandmother hobbled on her tiny stumps of feet, barely able to make it from chair to chair. She told my mother of the horrors she endured when she was young. Her greatest challenge was getting along with her mother-in-law, a woman required by tradition to be demanding. White Peony endured her insults, holding herself strong. Her love of her *laotong*, Waning Moon, made all of life's challenges bearable.

My mother grew up with Waning Moon as a second mother. No decisions were made without her, and the children were brought up together. When these *laotongs* married and were required to move from their natal home to that of their husbands, they continued to visit with one another regularly, and to write letters to one another in *nu shu*.

After Grandmother went to live with the "Great Spirit," my mother came to this country. With trepidation, my mother told this story to me. Although forbidden to discuss this when in China, she felt telling her tale was the only way to honor her departed mother.

Mildred Finds a Family

I was thrilled to move back to Denison House after a terrible experience with the family I met when I was on the Orphan Train. Everyone has been kind to me, and no one has made me work to earn my keep. They have fed me, given me clothing, and most importantly, made certain that I have friends.

My best friend is Dorothy, who is nine years old just like me. She lives with her mother and father in a room right down the hall from where I stay. I spend a lot of time with them. Her mother is very sweet, but sickly, so she is always home. Her father is a kind man who finds little jobs to keep him busy and to bring extra money to the family. Recently, he announced that he saved up enough money to buy a small apple orchard and farmhouse north of the city, in a town called Chelmsford. They said they are planning to move at the end of the month.

I started to cry when they told me their good news since I was sad they would be leaving me behind. Dorothy's mother put her arms around me and asked if I would like to move to the farm with them. I could hardly believe my ears. I like being at Denison House, but the idea of living with a family and having Dorothy as a sister was very exciting. I said "yes" right away. I am not sure if her mother was just taking pity on me when she saw me crying, but everyone seemed excited with the idea, especially Dorothy. I have packed my few belongings in anticipation of leaving with them next Tuesday.

Thank you to all the kind folks at Denison House. I will miss you all.

GLOSSARY
HEBREW

afikomen   אֲפִיקוֹמָן
Half-piece of matzoh set aside for a searching game by the children after the
Passover meal

babka   באבקה
An Eastern European sweet cake, traditionally made from a twisted length of yeast
dough and baked in a high loaf pan

challah   חַלָּה
Braided egg bread

chametz   חָמֵץ
Leavened foods that are forbidden during Passover

charoses   חֲרוֹסֶת
A sweet, dark-colored paste made of fruits and nuts eaten at the Passover Seder.
The color and texture is meant to recall mortar

El Maleh Rachamim   אֵל מָלֵא רַחֲמִים
"God full of compassion" is a prayer for the departed, recited with a haunting
chant at funeral services, on visiting the graves of relatives and on the anniversary
of the death of a close relative

erev Rosh Hashanah   עֶרֶב רֹאשׁ הַשָּׁנָה
The evening before the holiday of Rosh Hashanah, the Jewish New Year

ha'makom   הַמָּקוֹם
A way to comfort mourners. "May God console you among the other mourners
of Zion and Jerusalem"

hamantashen   המן־טאשן
A triangular filled-pocket pastry associated with the Jewish holiday of Purim.
The shape represents the hat of Haman, the villain in the Purim story
(literally 'Haman pockets')

havdalah   הַבְדָּלָה
Hebrew for "separation," a Jewish religious ceremony that marks the symbolic end
of Sabbath and ushers in the new week

knaidel   קנײדל
A matzoh dumpling eaten during Passover

Kol Nidre   כָּל נִדְרֵי
Aramaic declaration recited in the synagogue during the evening service on the
holiday of Yom Kippur

kosher   כָּשֵׁר
Foods that conform to the Jewish dietary regulations of kashrut (dietary law)

kosher for Passover   כָּשֵׁר לְפֶסַח
During the holiday of Passover, Jewish law forbids the consumption or possession
by Jews of all fermented grain products (chametz) or related foods

kugel קוּגֶל
A baked pudding or casserole, most commonly made from egg noodles (Lokshen kugel) or potato

Ma Nishtana מה נשתנה
The Four Questions, traditionally asked via song by the youngest child attending the Passover Seder

matzoh מַצָּה
An unleavened flatbread that forms an integral element of the Passover festival. Also made into matzoh farfel or matzoh meal

matzoh farfel מַצָּה פְּלְפֵּל
Matzoh broken into small pieces

matzoh meal אֲרוּחַת מַצָּה
Ground matzoh

mazel tov מַזָּל טוֹב
A Jewish phrase used to express congratulations for a happy and significant occasion or event

Megillah מְגִילָה
The *Book of Esther* is chanted in the synagogue on the eve of Purim and again the next morning

minyan מִנְיָן
The quorum of ten Jewish adults required for certain religious obligations. In traditional streams of Judaism only men may constitute a minyan

mitzvah מִצְוָה
The word means "commandment" and refers to commandments by God. A good deed done from religious duty

(Mourner's) Kaddish הַקַּדִּישׁ שֶׁל הָאָבֵל
Kaddish is a hymn of praises to God, said by mourners. The central theme of the Kaddish is the magnification and sanctification of God's name

Rosh Hashana רֹאשׁ הַשָּׁנָה
The Jewish New Year. Literally meaning the "head of the year"

rugelach רוגלך
A filled pastry originating in the Jewish communities of Poland

seder סֶדֶר
Jewish ritual feast that marks the beginning of the holiday of Passover

Shehechiyanu שהחינו
Common Jewish prayer, said to celebrate special occasions. It is recited to be thankful for new and unusual experiences

"Shema Yisrael" שְׁמַע יִשְׂרָאֵל
("Hear, O Israel"), the first two words of the centerpiece of the morning and evening prayer

shemira שְׁמִירָה
Watching or guarding the body of a deceased person, to protect it as the soul hovers

shiva שִׁבְעָה

After the burial, mourners return home to sit shiva for seven days.
Shiva is simply the Hebrew word for seven

shul שׁול

Temple, derived from a German word meaning "school," and emphasizes the synagogue's role as a place of study

Sukkos סֻכּוֹת

Festival of Tabernacles. Israelites were commanded to perform a pilgrimage to the Temple. Also, this marks the end of the harvest time and thus of the agricultural year

tsimmes צִימֶעס

Traditional Ashkenazi Jewish sweet stew made from dried fruits, carrots, and other root vegetables

Yeshiva יְשִׁיבָה

Hebrew University

Yom Kippur יוֹם כִּיפּוּר

Known as the Day of Atonement, the holiest day of the year in Judaism

YIDDISH
(spoken language transliterated)

ahdank	Thank you
gay ga zinta hate	Go in good health (said in parting)
gefilte fish	A dish made from a poached mixture of ground deboned fish, such as carp, whitefish, or pike
kveling	To be extraordinarily pleased; especially, to be bursting with pride over one's family
Lesbianke	Lesbian
mandel brot	Twice baked cookie popular amongst Eastern European Jews. (Literally means almond bread)
matzoh balls	*Kneydlekh.* Ashkenazi Jewish soup dumplings made from a mixture of matzo meal, eggs, water, and a fat, served in chicken soup
munn	Also translated as *mohn*. Poppy seeds used in a filling, such as for *hamantashen*
shaina meidel	Pretty girl
shpilkes	State of impatience or agitation
tsoris	Trouble, suffering, distress, woe, misery
Zal es zayn azoy	May it be so

Made in the USA
Columbia, SC
16 August 2021

43716096R00157